Also by Kristen Tracy
*Lost It*

# Crimes of the Sarahs

Kristen Tracy

Simon Pulse
New York   London   Toronto   Sydney

SIMON PULSE
An imprint of Simon & Schuster Children's Publishing Division
1230 Avenue of the Americas, New York, NY 10020
Copyright © 2008 by Kristen Tracy
All rights reserved, including the right of reproduction
in whole or in part in any form.
SIMON PULSE and colophon are registered trademarks of
Simon & Schuster, Inc.
Designed by Cara Petrus
The text of this book was set in Adobe Garamond.
Manufactured in the United States of America
First Simon Pulse edition February 2008
2  4  6  8  10  9  7  5  3  1
Library of Congress Control Number 2007934257
ISBN-13: 978-1-4169-5519-1
ISBN-10: 1-4169-5519-4

# ACKNOWLEDGMENTS

I am incredibly thankful that my second book got published. First, I'm grateful to my agent, Sara Crowe, who is truly the best. Big thanks too to Jen Klonsky, who used her incredible smarts to help make this book better. There are many, many kind people at S&S whom I'd like to thank, Michelle Nagler, Bethany Buck, and Michelle Fadlalla among them. Of course, I want to thank my mom. And I'd also like to thank my good friends and readers: Michelle Willis, Ulla Fredericksen, Fred Bueltmann, Linda Young, Scott Dykstra, Jackie Srodes (and family), Adam Schuitema, and Sarah Gessel Rich. Special thanks to Chris Sherlock and Ian Stamp, my Kalamazoo neighbors. And Curtis and Kathy Curtis-Smith, who gave me a delightful tour of their Frank Lloyd Wright home. I'm also grateful to Stu Dybek, my Kzoo mentor. I'm also very grateful to all the nice people at the Kalamazoo Public Library, especially Kevin King and Cory Grimminck. And I'd also like to give double thanks to my dad, the funniest person I know, who has supported me through thick and thin, and never insisted that I drive the big tractor when I come home to visit. Because when it comes to farm equipment, I'm a big chicken. And my dad is kind enough to respect that.

# Chapter 1

Just like mayonnaise, Raisinets, and milk, every criminal has a shelf life. Either you get caught or you evolve. Much like the amoeba, the other Sarahs and I plan on evolving. Of course, since we're in the middle of a job right now, we're obviously not there yet.

"Should I go?" Sarah B asks.

I view this as a rhetorical question. I'm not the leader. That's Sarah A's position, but she's already inside the store. Sometimes, because I'm the driver, when Sarah A is absent, the other two Sarahs defer to me. Though I don't know why. Among the four of us, I'm the least alpha. I'm not headstrong or decisive or anything. As far as the pecking order, I'm the shortest Sarah. Plus, I struggle with anxiety.

"Give her a few more minutes," Sarah C calls from the backseat.

Had I said something, that would've been my answer too. I always favor inaction over action. Sarah B leans back into the passenger seat and smacks her gum. Then she blows a bubble so big that its circumference eclipses her face. *Pop.* She peels off the pink film and pushes the gum wad back inside her mouth. Bubbles never stick to Sarah B's face, because every minute of her life, her T-zone is aglow with oil. It's what I call a Teflon complexion. Except I don't say that to her actual face. *Pop.*

A fact that sucks: Sarah B breaks out more than any other Sarah. Another fact that sucks: Her oily skin will age better than my dry skin. When she's eighty, her skin will be the least wrinkly of all the Sarahs. That is, if we all live long enough to reach that geriatric benchmark.

"Now?" Sarah B asks.

I shake my head. It's not just that I favor inaction; in the beginning, we learned quickly that it was best to enter our targeted stores one at a time. It's blatantly unfair, but salesclerks absolutely stereotype teenagers. Even a group of presumably innocent, Caucasian-looking, female teens browsing the aisles of a bookstore on a Sunday afternoon can send up a red flag. Agism is alive and well, even here in Kalamazoo.

"Now?" Sarah B asks me again. "I feel like it's time."

I nod. I don't know if it's time, but there's so much tension and perfume overload in the car that I'm getting a headache and it would improve the atmosphere immensely if the apple-scented Sarah B left.

"Remember, take the clerk to the board-book display beneath the huge toad cutout. Ask a lot of questions about Sarah Stewart and David Small. Keep the clerk in one area," Sarah C says. She's leaning forward, wedging herself into the rectangle of open space between the driver's and passenger's seat. Her shiny red hair is so close to my mouth that I think I can taste her conditioner.

Sarah B opens the car and slings her purse strap over her neck. For as long as I can remember, Sarah B has feared being mugged. I guess being a thief lowers your threshold for trust.

"I thought it was a cutout of a lizard," Sarah B says.

"He's a toad," Sarah C says.

"How do you know it's a guy? Is it anatomically correct? Did you inspect its crotch?" She blows another bubble and sucks it back inside her mouth.

"First, he's wearing pants. Second, he's a character from *The Wind in the Willows*. It's a guy toad. Trust us."

Sarah C kicks the back of my seat.

"Yeah, *The Wind in the Willows* is about a male toad," I say.

Sarah B tilts her head and squints at us, like she's thinking really hard. Her soft lips turn downward, which usually means that she's confused.

"I bet some cultures consider lizards to be a form of toads," Sarah B says. "They both have reptile brains." Not everything Sarah B says makes perfect sense.

She slams the car door and enthusiastically walks through the strip mall parking lot, her brown hair bouncing around her tan, bare shoulders. Until last week, Sarah B always wore a Detroit Tigers baseball cap. But after she almost got caught shoving a box of Oreos down her pants at a Sunoco station, Sarah A was adamant that the cap had to go. She claimed that the bill shaded Sarah B's eyes, making her look boyish and deceptive.

Sarah A was the only Sarah who saw it this way. Sarah B has very big boobs. There's nothing boyish going on with that rack. But immediately following the Oreo incident, while we sat around Sarah A's bedroom indulging in our looted booty, Sarah A grabbed the cap right off of Sarah B's head and doused it with lighter fluid. I was really surprised that an incoming high school senior kept lighter fluid in her bedroom. Then, Sarah A ran to her bathroom and torched the hat in the tub. At that point, the cap became a moot point.

But we've all moved on from the flaming cap episode. That's clear as I watch Sarah B bounce right through the front doors of the Barnes & Noble. But what else would I expect? She's a resilient Sarah. We're all resilient Sarahs. So while it may be true that we've reached a criminal level of boredom with our city, to the point where we've considered committing much more serious crimes with actual weapons, we're still a very plucky bunch.

"I'll go in ten," Sarah C calls from the backseat.

She's the only Sarah among us who had to legally change her name. It wasn't the easiest thing to do. She and her parents had to petition the family division of the circuit court and pay almost two hundred dollars. Sarah A made Sarah C bring the paperwork to prove she'd done it. Because if you're going to become part of an elite club, there's got to be some standards. Sarah A was very clear about that. So, our freshman year, Lisa Sarah Cody became Sarah Lisa Cody. A bona fide Sarah. For the most part, she doesn't seem to regret it. But who wouldn't want to be one of us? The benefits are stellar. The Sarahs are popular, crafty, goal-oriented, and have loads of unsupervised time. My parents aren't expecting me home for hours. And when I do show up, it's not like they'll pepper me with probing questions about my afternoon. A few years ago, after I joined the school choir, they assumed I was on a good path in life. I look like a good girl, and around them, I act like a good girl. Which is cool. I may be passive, but I do care what people, especially blood relatives, think about me.

"Hey, don't you ever worry that we'll get caught?" Sarah C asks.

She finger flicks the back of my head. I rub the area and keep my hand there to shield myself from a second flick.

"Are you speaking hypothetically?" I ask.

"No, like right now. Don't you worry some hyperaware clerk will spot us?" Sarah C asks.

"That's not what I was thinking about at all," I say.

"Even if we do get caught, I guess it's not a huge deal because we're minors. We'd probably be sentenced to make restitution and pick up roadside trash. But after we turn eighteen, we might want to rethink this lifestyle."

"Lifestyle?" I try to glance at her in the rearview mirror, but her head is tucked down. "This is more than a lifestyle. It's who we are. We're the Sarahs."

"Yeah, I know, but once we're eighteen, once we're in college, we should probably rethink it. I mean, theft is kind of immature. We want. We take. Is it really worth it?"

"Of course it's worth it. Look around. We've got a close circle of friends and a ton of free crap."

Sarah C leans forward again. This time she angles her body so she can face me. I don't look at her.

"But doesn't all the free crap ever weigh on your conscience?" she asks.

"My what?"

Sarah C lowers her voice to a whisper.

"Sometimes, I picture myself handcuffed. Actually, I imagine all four of us in handcuffs, being trotted out to a squad car, the lights flashing, broadcasting our guilt to everybody driving by."

Sarah C mimics a siren by emitting a *wha wha* sound. Then she puts her hand over her mouth to dim the noise.

I'm so shaken up her pessimistic outpouring that my jaw drops open. A light breeze blows into the pocket of my mouth.

She stops the siren sound.

"It's not about the theft," I say. At least that's what Sarah A always says. "It's about the bond. The sisterhood."

"We could get tattoos."

This idea makes me frown. I'm not sure that I want a tattoo. And because Sarah C has the highest GPA out of all the Sarahs and also scored 2300 on the SAT, sometimes her suggestions carry weight.

"Why would we want to put identifying markers on our bodies?" I ask.

"Good point," Sarah C says. "In a lineup we'd be so screwed."

"A lineup?" I ask.

"Yeah, don't you watch cop shows?" Sarah C asks.

"You have time to watch cop shows?" I ask.

I'm surprised to hear this because being a Sarah takes up all my free time.

"This probably isn't the best time to ponder cop shows," Sarah C say. "The criminals usually get locked up."

"Yeah," I say. "Let's ponder something positive."

There's a long silence.

"Can't you think of anything positive?" I ask.

"Stealing stuff all the time is a lot like driving a race car," Sarah C says. "Drivers are warned not to look at the wall when they're losing control, because you tend to steer yourself toward what you're looking at. For criminals that's a very appropriate life metaphor: In order to avoid colliding with the cops, don't think about them."

"I never think about the police," I say. Neither the topic of law enforcement or car crashes strike me as positive pondering.

"Besides the Sarahs, what do you think about?" Sarah C asks. I don't like her tone; it's accusatory. Or her question; it's a little too insightful.

"I think about life," I say.

Sarah C leans into the backseat again, but this time threads her long legs through the center console. Her sandals reach the gearshift. I get the feeling that she doesn't believe me. She crosses her ankles and I watch her toes curl incredulously against the brown suede pad of her shoes. I feel goaded into elaboration.

"I think about life all the time," I say. "It's like a hallway."

"A hallway?"

"Yeah," I say.

"Like at school?" Sarah C asks.

"Okay, but there's no lockers," I say. "It's just a hallway and there's all these doors. But they're closed. So you've got to decide which ones to open and which ones to walk past. But you never know what you're missing or what you're getting until you've already gotten it," I say.

Sarah C doesn't say anything right away.

"That's a very interior metaphor. I spend a lot of time outdoors. That comparison doesn't really work for me," Sarah C says.

"*My life* is like a hallway," I say.

"That's tragic. I really dig trees," Sarah C says.

I turn and look at Sarah C in the backseat. She's twisting a small section of her red hair around her pointer finger.

"Didn't Sarah A tell you to keep your hair pulled back into a ponytail?" I ask.

"She did, but it makes my neck look so long."

"Aren't swan necks considered attractive?" I ask.

"Maybe. But I like my hair down."

"Sarah C, remember the Oreos," I say.

I turn back to face the front and look out the windshield. I'm thirsty. But I never consume any fluid for at least four hours before a hit. Too much anxiety triggers my pee reflex. I can hear the sound of an elastic band snapping itself into place. Sarah A thinks ponytails look wholesome. She thinks it's the right message to send.

"You've got two more minutes," I say.

"I know. I'm going to ask for help in the magazine section.

I'm interested in buying a Spanish copy of *People*."

"But you're not going to *buy* it," I say.

"I know. I'm going to act extremely disappointed by the cover and pretend that I wanted the issue containing *los cincuenta mas bellos*."

"I thought Sarah A said to trill your *R*'s," I say.

"There aren't any *R*'s in the phrase *los cincuenta mas bellos*," she says.

She makes a valid point.

"Maybe you should follow up by saying *muchas gracias* and trill that *R*."

"I'm not trying to sound like I'm an actual Spaniard. I'm supposedly buying it for a summer school report. Overdone inflection might make a clerk suspicious."

"Don't get mad at me. These are Sarah A's instructions," I say.

She doesn't respond. We sit in uncomfortable silence. Sometimes I think Sarah C misses the bigger picture about being a Sarah. It's as if she mixes up the idea that we're good people who sometimes do bad things with the idea that we're deeply flawed people driven to commit deplorable acts on a daily basis. I might have to talk with Sarah A about this again. Last time I brought up Sarah C's negative attitude with Sarah A, I was left with the impression that Sarah A was growing concerned about our group of four.

I got this impression when she ended the conversation by saying, "Sarah T, I'm concerned about our group of four." I don't know exactly what she meant, but it wouldn't surprise me if Sarah A decided to purge one of the remaining three Sarahs from the group. That's the sort of power she totes around. She's a real decider. She even makes decisions for other people. She makes mine all the time. And you never want to cross her.

That's how we lost our fifth Sarah, Sarah Dancer, during the middle of our junior year. But it's not like she was wheelchair-bound forever. Just like three months. And they flew by. And she's totally fine now. Mostly.

Sarah A, our ballsy blonde leader, our thievery guru, our governing Sarah, aka Sarah Aberdeen, has been in the targeted bookstore for roughly ten minutes. It's the job of the remaining Sarahs to keep the clerks away from the Self Help section while Sarah A finds the title she's looking for, *What Color Is Your Parachute?*, and takes it from the store. A typical Sunday afternoon.

Sarah A has the money to pay for the book, even if forced to buy a hardback edition. But if an item she desires is smaller than a toaster, Sarah A prefers utilizing the five-finger discount. It's much more exciting than making a legitimate purchase.

After a few more quiet moments, Sarah C squeaks open her back door and says something haughty under her breath.

I can't hear exactly what it is, but it's probably related to her ponytail. Sometimes, her attitude is the worst. Who brings up the possibility of getting caught in the middle of a job? Talk about a fatalist. And what's so hard about wearing a ponytail? Does she have an overly sensitive scalp?

I watch her long bare legs stride to the store. When Sarah A doesn't wear heels, Sarah C is the tallest Sarah. She also looks the best in shorts. Before us, she played on the volleyball team. She might've been the setter. I can't remember. Now she does Pilates and jogs. Being a Sarah is the only team sport of which she's currently a member. It takes up more time than you'd think.

Being a Sarah is pretty much a sixty-hour work week. We're not running around Kalamazoo willy-nilly, ripping off fashion magazines from Walgreens. Of course, we *do* rip off fashion magazines from Walgreens. Usually the one at the corner of Kilgore and Westnedge. But we're not spontaneous criminals.

"Impulsive thieves are incarcerated thieves," Sarah A likes to say.

We plan our crimes carefully. And we sit around and rehash them a lot too. And we do noncriminal stuff in order to bond. Since it's summer, we drive out to Lake Michigan at least once a week. And we visit Saugatuck. It's an artist community near the lake that's crammed with boutiques. We've stolen a variety of cookie cutters, jars of cheese spread, and Michigan-shaped oven mitts from an understaffed kitchen store there.

And we like to hike around the Kalamazoo Nature Center and watch the injured owls stare powerfully at us from behind their wire mesh cages. And we volunteer at the animal shelter where we mainly focus on the dogs. And we work on our college applications, mostly by discussing the great things we'll say about ourselves in our personal statements. And we bake cookies (using the aforementioned cutters) that we don't eat, because none of us want to be chunky seniors sucking our guts in while back fat ripples beneath our ridiculously priced and somewhat slutty prom dresses. And sometimes we read. We're huge Sue Grafton fans.

Sarah A thinks that the reason criminals get caught has nothing to do with shelf life and everything to do with having a lack of other interests. She insists that criminals need to be well-rounded. It's the only way to stay ahead of the law. She's firm about this. So we've all developed other interests. Except, they're identical and we do them together. Sarah A doesn't think that's a problem.

"So what if we live identical lives?" Sarah A says. "As long as they're balanced."

She makes being criminals sound like a circus act, like we're all traipsing across the high wire, one after the other. Heights make me anxious. I try not to think of our lives this way. That's why I developed my hallway metaphor. Sarah C calls being a thief-at-large a numbers game. She likens our fates to a bad lottery or draft. She's always worried that our number may be coming up. I'm not really sure what Sarah B thinks.

But I doubt the Kalamazoo Police Department wants to lock up college-bound teens who volunteer at their local animal shelter and are willing to clean out the dirtiest dog cages. And I bet none of our Michigan judges want to throw the book at four honor students who also happen to be outstanding altos. We're the backbone of Kalamazoo Central High School's award-winning choir. Why should the law be interested in us? We barely commit any serious crimes at all. At least for the moment.

It's almost time for me to go. I watch the store's glass windows and stare at the people milling around behind them. There are many interesting ways to style a head of hair. Wait, I think I see a familiar head. I do. It's Sarah C. She's pressed up right against the glass. What is she doing? She's jerking her arm up and down. If I can see her, so can other people. She's going to draw a ton of attention.

I open my door. She's still jerking. Is she having a seizure? Did she suddenly develop epilepsy? Are epileptics not supposed to wear ponytails? She's in the café. Why is she in the café? Oh my God. I get it. She's flashing me the peace sign. She does it again. And a third time. That's the distress signal.

Three peace signs in quick succession means that something's gone horribly wrong. But what could have gone horribly wrong? Nobody's stolen anything yet. It's not against the law to consider stealing a book. It's not even against the law to consider killing the president. Of course, you can never voice that consideration, because that *is* against the law.

I climb out of the car. All this stress makes me feel dizzy. But I don't have time to catch my emotional balance. I better get in there. My Sarah sisters need me.

# Chapter 2

I make sure all of my car doors are locked. Even though it's not a crime-ridden town, I do keep a lot of dimes in my ashtray. And my ashtray, like anyone's, is sort of in plain view.

I need to act normal. While I walk toward the store, I bounce the big jingly wad of keys back and forth between my hands.

I open the first wooden door and smile at the mustached man in mustard-yellow pants exiting the store. Wait. I've seen him before. Suddenly, I know why Sarah C flashed me the peace sign three times. We know this guy. It's Mr. Trego, our former boss. Last year, he ran a fudge shop in town. But then we all quit on him. Sarah A, Sarah B, and Sarah C self-terminated their employment with him in person and returned their uniforms. I stopped showing up. I hate confrontation. And I also liked my uniform. I'm wearing it right now. Khaki pants and a light blue T-shirt that says FRESH IS BEST.

After we quit, it didn't take long for his business to tank.

It probably would have happened regardless of our departures. But, in a random act of malice, Sarah A did spread some vicious untruths about his fudge-cooling process. None of us have seen him since his demise. But he's here now. With his distinctive swagger. And smell. And lazy eye. Last fall, he vanished and we thought that was the end of him. But now, just like those Canada geese, Mr. Trego is back.

I try to veer to the other door, but it's locked. Our paths are destined to meet. I try not to look him in the eye. Especially his lazy one. I glance down at my own sandals and my pink-polished toenails. He's holding open the second wooden door for me. I don't know what to do. I try to calm myself by asking, *What's the worst thing that could happen, he demands my pants?* But then I imagine all these awful things he could say to me about dodging responsibility and leaving him high and dry. I don't want to get within earshot of such accurate character assassination.

But the Sarahs are inside and I'm supposed to be inside, too. I wrestle with my options. Then I do the easiest and most polite thing. I walk through the open door. After I pass beneath the arch of his arm, I turn my head to keep on eye on him. I notice two things: First, his armpit smells like barbecued hot wings. Second, he's boldly looking at my butt. I mean, he's staring right at it. *What is Mr. Trego doing? Trying to determine whether or not I'm wearing my fudge-shop pants?*

His motives don't really matter. I feel like I'm being dissected, and that always makes me uncomfortable. I'm several feet inside the store, but I can still feel him looking at me. I turn my whole body to face him, and to take my butt out of his view. Clearly, he can discern that this is his fudge-shop shirt. That's when I notice my nipples. This is too much drama for them. Frightened into rigidity, they're projecting right out of my T-shirt.

"Sarah Trestle?" he asks.

In a defensive move, I look him in the eye and shrug. He frowns at me and shakes his head. Then he reaches his hand toward me, like he's going to touch me. Before I can do anything useful, like leave, I'm clobbered by my own anxiety. I have an uncontrollable urge to pee and there's nothing I can do.

I mean, it's right here. And so is Sarah C. She's shaking her head back and forth. Her red ponytail wags behind her as her mouth forms a perfect O. She mouths the word *no*, trying to encourage me to hold it, but it's too late. I can feel the sea of pee inside of me, and there's no stopping it. Mr. Trego is watching too. The door has fallen closed, but he's still there, behind the panes of glass. I look around for Sarah A. She needs to know that I'm aborting the plan. But I can't see her. The Self Help section is buried too far into the belly of the store. I should run. I have time.

Instead, I let loose a puddle of my own urine on the welcome mat. There's so much liquid that it flows onto the ceramic-tiled floor. There's an actual sound. People turn and look. A wet spot has bloomed on my crotch and down my leg. The cotton absorbs what it can. I throw my hands down to cover the area. But it's too big. Sarah C hands me a copy of *People*. It's the Spanish edition.

"I'll buy it," she tells the clerk standing next to her. "I'm heading to the counter right now."

The clerk nods.

"Take it," she tells me. *"Vamanos!"*

I unfold the magazine and hold the glossy pages over the large pee mark as I run for my car. I have to hurry past Mr. Trego. As we pass in the alcove, our arms brush against each other.

"Why don't you go ahead and keep that outfit," he says.

But I'm not thinking about my pilfered uniform anymore. Or the heavily populated Barnes & Noble where I just wet myself. I'm worried about Sarah A. She's going to kill me. She's been looking forward to reading *What Color Is Your Parachute?* all week. I think she's on the brink of making an important life decision, maybe even choosing her college major. And that choice could really affect the rest of the Sarahs too.

Once in my car, I sit atop the magazine and wait for the

other Sarahs. Sarah C comes out first. Sarah B follows about a minute later. But Sarah A doesn't come until the established meeting time. We wait almost twenty minutes for her.

She saunters out of the store like nothing has happened. Her blonde hair spills around her neck and she's smiling. But it's her fake smile. Her pink lips force themselves to show a crescent of white teeth. She opens the passenger door and climbs inside. She smells like a cross between a blueberry muffin and a vanilla bean. After she closes the door, her whole demeanor shifts. Her mouth turns cold and expressionless.

"That was really stupid," she tells me.

"It was Mr. Trego," Sarah C explains. "Sarah T has been avoiding him ever since we quit."

"Big deal," Sarah A says. "The pay for that job was a joke."

"But I hadn't returned my uniform," I say. I jerk my thumb toward my shirt.

"I doubt he wants it back now," Sarah A says. "And if he does, he's a serious pervert."

"Good point," I say. My throat feels tight. I sound squeaky.

"We all make mistakes," Sarah C says.

"Yeah, but not the kind that involve our own bodily fluids," Sarah A says.

I start the car.

"Sarah C, I have some awful news," Sarah A says.

"What is it?" Sarah C asks.

"Benny Stowe was inside the store. He saw everything," Sarah A says.

"He did *not*," Sarah C says.

"Well, he didn't see it," Sarah A says. "But I told him about it."

"Why?" Sarah C asks. "If he didn't see one of my best friends pee her pants, why tell him that one of my best friends peed her pants?"

Benny Stowe is Sarah C's longtime crush. He's cute and one of the most popular guys in school. She's always trying to look good in front of him.

"One of the clerks brought out a mop and one of those yellow plastic buckets on wheels," Sarah A says. "I had to tell Benny something. It's not like I'm going to lie for no good reason."

I pull the car onto Milham.

"Did Benny seem grossed out?" I ask. I'm mortified to learn that Benny Stowe knows about my pee issues. But there's not much I can do about it now. Except hope that in the near future a minor head injury resulting in short-term memory loss befalls Benny Stowe.

"Totally," Sarah A says. "Even after it got mopped up, he wouldn't step in that area. He took a long stride over the damp spot to get to the magazines."

"Maybe he thought the wet tile would be slippery," I say.

"He was probably more worried about getting pee on his

shoes," Sarah A says. She flips the visor down to shade her face from the sun. "How can we grow as thieves, and move on to the *next phase*, if we can't count on one another to steal a simple book?"

"But we didn't get caught either," Sarah C says.

"You made a purchase. We spent money in there. And that dumb rag wasn't even on sale. The only crime we're guilty of is stupidity."

"Actually, it's against the law to urinate in public," Sarah B says. "I saw a guy get arrested for it at a Tigers game. I think it's a misdemeanor." *Pop.*

I glance at Sarah A's face. It's bright red. What is Sarah B doing? I want this incident to blow over. I roll my window down to increase the ventilation in the car.

"Real crimes have victims," Sarah A says. "Remember what I said when we broke out the windows of Davis Garlobo's Mustang?"

"I remember. After three swings of your baseball bat, you said, 'Davis Garlobo is a pizza-faced asshole who never should have laughed at me because I didn't know how to pronounce Hispaniola,'" Sarah B says. "Then you spat on the hood of his car and called him captain crap-ass."

Sarah A sucks in an angry breath and slowly releases it.

"I meant what I said on the ride home."

None of us answer. If you can't remember Sarah A's words

verbatim, it's best to wait and let her restate them.

"I said that trespassing isn't a true crime. Neither is criminal mischief or vagrancy, because there's no real loss. Nobody suffers. Nobody grieves. But vandalism, that's a crime. Real crimes have victims. Is it that hard to remember?"

I stop us with a jerk at a red light.

"Do you know what helps me remember things?" Sarah C says. "Acronyms. Like scuba for self-contained underwater breathing apparatus or NASA for National Aeronautics and Space Administration."

"Real crimes have victims doesn't make an acronym," Sarah B says. "It's RCHV. It doesn't have a vowel."

"You're right," Sarah C says. "We need an acrostic. Like Kings Play Chess On Fine Grain Sand for the taxonomy of organisms: kingdom, phylum, class, order, family, genus, species."

"I know. Rod Carew Hates Vaseline," Sarah B says.

"Rod Carew?" Sarah A asks.

"He's one of the greatest baseball players of all time. He had over three thousand hits," Sarah B says.

"Vaseline?" Sarah A asks.

"Vaseline or any balm," Sarah B says, "is used by some pitchers to juice the ball. There's all sorts of variations: spitball, scuffball, mudball—"

"Who cares? Am I surrounded by idiots?" Sarah A asks.

She turns around to glare at the backseat Sarahs. "No wonder this town had the largest psychiatric hospital in the state of Michigan. Clearly, mental problems still abound."

Nobody says anything else as I drive us back toward our Winchell neighborhood.

"Drop me off first," Sarah A say. "It's starting to smell."

I shift my weight on top of the magazine and the moist pages rub against each other releasing a noise that sounds like a wet kiss. I'm nearly to Sarah C's house, but I pull into a driveway and turn around. What Sarah A wants, Sarah A gets.

At speeds topping forty miles per hour, I proceed to the Marlborough Building. It's a hoity-toity place where a lot of professional-type people live. It has a slate roof and stained-glass windows and decorative tiles and a swanky recessed entranceway. A lot of really old people live there, too. Mostly the kind who have already started to die.

I think the building is totally overrated. I mean, fix the elevator. Every time we come to visit we've got to ascend five whole flights of stairs. Sarah A thinks it's the best place to live in Kalamazoo. She likes having rich hall neighbors. Sometimes she steals their mail. She takes pride in the fact that she's the only Sarah who's committed a federal offense.

"The air is so balmy," Sarah C says, sticking her arm out the window.

Nobody responds. She pulls her long arm back inside the car.

I speed down Oakland. It used to be a tulip-lined street. Sadly, the tulips lost their heads during a thunderstorm the last week of May. Now, with June in full swing, most of our streets are flanked by rows of decapitated, wilting stems. I turn down South Street and decide not to comment on the condition of our local flora. When I pull up to the Marlborough Building, I slam my car into PARK. I try smiling at Sarah A, but she's already climbing out.

"I'll call you later," Sarah A says. "I'm disappointed in everyone. Especially you," she says, aiming a perfectly manicured index finger at me.

"I understand it wasn't my best moment," I say.

"That's an understatement," Sarah A says. She flips her hair and licks her lips. "You're not going crazy, are you? I think this is about the same time your brother started losing it. The summer before his senior year. Liam read that book about Tonto and became a totally different person."

Liam is my brother. I never knew that Sarah A thought he went crazy. But I do remember him reading a book about Tonto. Our mother is one-half Potawatomi. Liam thinks this is a big deal. In high school, he went on a serious Native American literary jag. But I'm not like him. I'm not interested in myself in a genealogical or political sense. When it comes to my ancestry, it's not something I think about.

"Liam read *The Lone Ranger and Tonto Fistfight in Heaven*," Sarah C says. "It's a movie now called *Smoke Signals*. Sherman Alexie wrote both."

"I didn't know that," Sarah B says. *Pop.*

"Well, Sherman whoever's book made Liam go crazy and become a totally political psycho person. Seriously. Look where he ended up . . . Stanford," Sarah A says with disgust.

"Oh, I didn't wet myself as a political statement," I say. "I probably have some kind of disorder. A treatable one," I add.

Sarah A rolls her eyes.

"I don't think Liam went crazy," Sarah C says. "And even if he did, Liam is way less crazy than your brother."

Sarah A shuts the door with a thud.

"Vance is on very effective medication now," Sarah A says. "And nobody is allowed to call my brother crazy except for me and his therapist. Do not disparage my family."

"Sorry," Sarah C says. "I didn't mean to do that."

Sarah A raises her eyebrows. "Sing group is off tonight," she says. "And tomorrow."

We all watch her practically skip up the carpeted, covered walkway to the building's front doors. This relieves me. Already, she's bouncing back from the day's disappointment.

"We could have sing group at my house," Sarah C offers. "Midway though 'Bridge over Troubled Water' we get a little pitchy."

I'm still stopped in front of the Marlborough. An elderly man waiting behind me in a Cadillac honks.

"I think I'd rather rest my throat," I say.

The man honks again and I swing onto the road. Couldn't he wait one minute? What's with the elderly? Vehicularly speaking, they have no patience and consistently overuse their horns.

I pull into Sarah C's driveway and she climbs out without saying another word about sing group or the balmy air. Sometimes, she acts like she belongs in a musical. Like *The Sound of Music*. She's totally the kind of person who would persist against the Nazis, make outfits out of curtains, and then belt out a song about it. A problem-solving personality can be so nauseating. As a Sarah, she should know that.

Sarah B pops her gum at four-second intervals, but doesn't say anything either. She waits until I pull in front of her house and then she's gone, taking her tart scent with her. Maybe I should muster some sort of good-bye. Or make a joke out of what happened so I can lighten the mood. But I drive away. There's no denying it. Right now, sitting atop this magazine, I feel like a substandard, spineless, pee-stained fool. I accelerate into the dusk. This isn't the first time I've failed somebody. And because life is long, I doubt it'll be the last.

I turn onto Taliesin and drive on automatic pilot toward my driveway. I don't see the possum until it's too late. He scampers in front of me and I'm so disconnected from the present moment, thinking about the Sarahs, that I smack him dead. I slam on the brakes. His white body glows pink in my taillights.

There's no way that he's merely injured. I can see a tread mark running down his center. I pull into the carport and look back at the flattened marsupial. Besides a few ants, and a low-flying sparrow in driver's ed, this is the first animal I've ever killed. My first mammal.

"I'm so sorry," I say.

I walk to it. The possum's eyes are closed, but its mouth is turned up in surprise. Like maybe it was expecting to have a future. But then it encountered my all-weather radials.

"I won't let this happen again," I say, tugging my form-fitting wet pants out of my crotch.

I walk away. I don't enjoy confronting death either. As soon as my dad gets home, I'll tell him about the possum. Sooner or later, he'll dispose of it properly. There's way too many of these ratlike marsupials in the neighborhood anyway. I think one of them murdered my neighbor's puffy Pomeranian, Pom-Pom. It was either eaten or stolen. Because one day, that yapping fuzzball was gone. And I doubt anyone in our neighborhood would steal an elderly blind woman's dog. Even the Sarahs have limits.

Once inside, I head toward my bedroom. My parents are at the movies. They're watching a documentary about global warming. Apparently, there's some startling shots of glaciers melting. I can't even believe that they're showing that in a movie theater. Documentaries aren't movies. Everybody knows that.

I tug at my pants again. They're clinging to me in a way that emphasizes my female anatomy. I need a shower. I feel filthy.

Standing beneath the shower's warm flood, I let out a deep breath. I'm filled with this doomed feeling and I can't shake it. It's not about what happened at the Barnes & Noble. Or the possum. It's about the Sarahs. What if Sarah A is planning to dump one of us and downsize our group to three? Am I a dumpee? Shouldn't there be a vote? Wouldn't it make more sense to dump Sarah C?

*Sarah T, I'm concerned about our group of four.*

I turn off the water and step out of the shower. Looking at myself in my most natural state makes me feel so insignificant. Steam hangs in the air, fogging the mirror's glass. Slowly, it erases my short, naked body: brown hair, small boobs, pudgy stomach, thick thighs, and my ungroomed patch of hair down there. Soon, I'm barely visible at all. It's like I'm looking at my own ghosthood.

I grab a towel and wrap it around me. I can feel myself begin to cry. I lift my damp hands and wipe away the tears. I want to be more than who I am, more than just Sarah Trestle. I want to be a part of something bigger than myself. Without the Sarahs, how would I do that?

I'm teetering on the brink of really losing it, of being swallowed by a wave of absolute sadness. I force myself to stop crying, and make the fragile and soft parts of myself, if only for a moment, turn hard. I look back into the mirror hoping to see some of this new resolve, but the glass doesn't return my reflection. All it gives me is a thick, empty cloud.

# Chapter 3

"It's finally time for the *next thing*. We're entering the guy phase," Sarah A says.

Because it's six o'clock in the morning, everything feels very dreamlike. I know I'm talking on the phone, because my mother just handed me the receiver and said, "You've got a phone call." And I'm aware that the person on the other end is Sarah A, because the first thing out of Sarah A's mouth was, "It's me." And telephonically speaking, that's what Sarah A always says. But, being the crack of dawn, I feel fuzzy and surprised.

"Are we entering the guy phase right now?" I ask. "Because I haven't brushed my teeth yet."

Sarah A sighs dramatically.

"Not right now, right now. But everything is lined up. Come over to my house at four," Sarah A says.

I roll over onto my back and stare up at my ceiling.

"In the morning?" I ask.

"No. That's stupid. Come over at four in the afternoon like a normal person."

"And will guys be at your place?" I ask.

"No," Sarah A says. "I said that we're entering the guy phase. We need to ease into it. Each step we take will be carefully chosen."

"You sound very full of energy," I say, yawning.

"It's been quite a night," Sarah A says.

She doesn't elaborate and I don't press.

"Do I need to bring anything?" I ask.

"An open mind," Sarah A says.

We don't say good-bye. Our conversations end when Sarah A is done talking. I hang up the phone and turn back onto my side. This is the first Sarah contact I've had in four days. I think it's the longest I've ever gone without any Sarah interaction since I became a Sarah. One more day and I might've freaked out. I mean, in addition to being out of the Sarah loop, I also missed my weekly Wednesday volunteer shift at the shelter. Nobody called to give me the all-clear to show up last night, so I didn't. I stayed home and stewed about my problems. Which did nothing to improve my emotional well-being.

But now it looks like I stewed for nothing, because the Sarahs are ready to enter the guy phase and I'm right there with them. The purity vow that I took in eighth grade will finally be reconsidered.

"Male/female relationships have a tendency to torpedo female/female relationships," Sarah A said.

At that point, we didn't have Sarah C or Sarah D. It was just me and Sarah A and Sarah B. I was disheartened to hear that guys were so destructive, because at twelve years old I found the prospect of securing a boyfriend thrilling. But Sarah A put the kibosh on those plans.

"We're going to take a purity vow right now," Sarah A said.

It was the first day of school after our remarkable "sponge cake summer." All during break, the three of us had stolen individually wrapped Twinkies from a variety of grocery and convenience stores in southwest Michigan. We cleared somewhere around seventy-four. We sat outside on the front lawn, waiting for lunch to end, and our eighth-grade education in math, aka advanced algebra, to resume. Sarah A put her hand out, palm down, and Sarah B and I put our hands out, palms down, and then Sarah A smacked the top of our hands really hard. Then we all turned our hands sideways and I shook Sarah A's hand and then Sarah B's. And then they shook hands too. Then we spit on our hands and rubbed our knees and pressed them together to symbolize our chaste intent.

"Our purity vow has begun," Sarah A said.

At the time, I thought a purity vow had something to do with keeping your virginity. But ours went a little bit further than that. Sarah A lifted her arm up high in the air and held it there, like she was trying to attract the attention of a higher being so he or she or it could call on her.

"Repeat after me," Sarah A said. "From this point forward, I refuse to let any guy have access to my heart or my stuff."

"Can we define 'stuff'?" Sarah B asked.

"If you have to ask whether or not something is considered your stuff, I think it's safe to assume that it is," Sarah A said.

So Sarah B and I lifted up our hands and repeated the promise. Every few weeks after this, for the first year, Sarah A would think of things to add to our purity vow.

"I will not call a guy, nor will I allow a guy to call me."

"I will not chat with any guy I sit next to in class."

"I will respond to all male attention by laughing in a polite manner and walking away."

When Sarah C and Sarah D joined our group, they had to take the purity vow too. I'm not going to pretend that I was happy with the purity vow. Even though I have my anxiety problems, I always felt like I was missing out on something. Guys seem so fun and interesting. I think Sarah A could sense that I was weak in this area, because she used to remind me quite frequently about the catastrophic and dangerously horny nature of our male peers.

"They'll tear us apart, Sarah T," Sarah A said. "They'll drag your heart out of your chest and throw it down an elevator shaft just to watch it go boom."

Based on the little I knew about boys, hearts, and the mechanical trappings of elevators, I thought this statement seemed plausible.

"Remember what you promised," Sarah A said.

And I always remembered what I had promised. I kept it in the forefront of my mind, where it was as accessible to me as my locker combination. Sure, the Sarahs would talk amongst ourselves about guys we liked, but it never went further than that. Whether they knew it or not, every guy I came across was a potential Sarah destroyer. And so all through eighth, ninth, tenth, and eleventh grades, when I encountered male attention, I laughed politely and walked away. While this purity vow may have curtailed our male/female relationships, it had a weird side effect. The more distance we put between ourselves and guys, the more they sought after us. Our desirability shot into the stratosphere. Presently, the Sarahs are one of the most popular cliques at Central. Guys always try to capture our attention. And how do we respond? We laugh politely and walk away.

"It makes us mysterious," Sarah A says. "Insecure teenagers eat that act up. The guys know we're different. We're what they can't have. And it makes them go ape."

I have to agree. I get plenty of attention from jocks,

thespians, art freaks, and fellow choral students. And our standoffishness seems to have affected the way our female peers treat us too. Everybody from the cheerleaders to the debate queens are nice to us. I don't know if it's because they think we're mysterious, or because we walk around with this fake confidence. Actually, Sarah A's confidence isn't fake. Sarah C's might not be inauthentic either. Same goes with Sarah B. To be honest, I might be the only Sarah who is completely falsifying my current level of self-esteem. But it doesn't matter. Because we're at the guy phase.

"Are you off the phone?" my mother calls.

"Yes," I say.

I pull my blanket close to my neck. I feel tingly. Just thinking about the guy phase excites me.

"Have you arisen for the day?" she asks.

"Nah. It's summer," I say. "I'll arise around noon."

I park outside the Marlborough and see Sarah A sitting on an enormous stone planter out front. She's so happy that her face is glowing like a planet.

"You're late," Sarah A says.

"But it's not four o'clock yet," I say.

"You're the last Sarah here," Sarah A says.

I look around, but I don't see them.

"I sent them to the Munchie Mart for crackers," Sarah A says.

"Who's working? I think the guy with the freckles who wears the beret suspects that we've been stealing his crackers," I say.

"Relax," Sarah A says. "Sarah C offered to buy them for us. It's a great strategy on her part. Periodically entering the store as a paying costumer will help divert suspicion," Sarah A says.

"That is smart," I say.

"I know she can be saucy, but Sarah C truly has a criminal mind," Sarah A says.

"Hmm," I say, nodding in agreement.

Due to the potential ousting of one of us, I don't want Sarah A to overvalue Sarah C. But I think Sarah A is right. After Sarah A, Sarah C has the most felonious brain among us.

It doesn't take long before Sarah C and her red ponytail come swinging down the sidewalk. Sarah B walks beside her, blowing her trademark bubbles.

"Triscuits," Sarah C says, lifting the box above her head.

Sarah A punches her code into the security keypad and pulls open the front door.

"Do you think you'll ever give one of us the code?" Sarah C asks.

"If I give out the secret code to people, then it's really not a secret code anymore, is it?" Sarah A says.

We follow her up the stairs to her condo.

"Is Vance here?" Sarah B asks.

"No," Sarah A says. "He's at therapy. He's supposed to be on the verge of a breakthrough."

Considering his recent breakdown involving the cantaloupe pyramid at Hardings, it's a relief to hear this. I guess in a vague way I'd always wondered what would happen if some random person toppled a melon display at the grocery store and, with reckless abandon, bowled the sizable fruit down the aisles. Now I know. The store manager calls the cops.

"You guys are going to die," Sarah A says, "when you see what I've done."

"Did you steal something big?" Sarah B asks.

"Is it about the guy phase?" Sarah C asks.

"Did you steal a guy?" I ask.

Sarah A throws open her bedroom door and swings her arm out wide to welcome us. Inside, I see four large pillows. Each pillow is wearing a guy's shirt. The shirts are familiar. They look like shirts that guys from our school wear.

"You stole Benny Stowe's shirt for me?" Sarah C asks.

Sarah C runs to the beige button-down shirt and buries her face in its fluffy torso.

"It smells like him," Sarah C says, sucking down a deep breath. "It smells exactly like Benny."

"I took it last night from his bedroom," Sarah A says.

"You broke into Benny's house?" Sarah C asks.

Sarah A smiles wide. She walks over and picks up a pillow, wearing a light blue polo shirt.

"This is Roman Karbowski's shirt," Sarah A says. "I climbed in through a window. He was asleep on his side. I sat on his dresser and watched him. The shirt was on the floor. It's still wrinkled."

Sarah A runs her finger along the shirt's collar.

"Is that Gerard Truax's?" Sarah B asks. "I can't believe it. I've been crushing on him since sixth grade." Sarah B gathers her pillow in her arms and hugs it to her.

There's one pillow left. I guess it's mine, but I don't recognize the shirt. All last year I talked about my interest in Sal Rodriguez. He's an artist who recycles three-ring binders by making sculptures out of them. Usually, he's able to preserve the binder's original cover, which often features a sweet animal like a panda bear or a pony. But he's subversive. Sal inserts ironic thought bubbles over the animals' heads. His panda bears usually condemn China and its record on human rights. Also, Sal's pandas freely admit to having low libidos. The ponies, cartoonlike and unrealistic, talk about how they're aware and deeply ashamed of their commercial appeal amongst tween girls. Sal is the best. But the shirt on my pillow is a conservative yellow-and-white checkered shirt. It looks like something a stuck-up jock would wear.

"Don't you like your shirt?" Sarah A asks.

"Is it Sal's?" I ask.

"Sal?" Sarah A says. "Why would you want that loser's shirt?"

"Sarah T has had a thing for Sal since ninth grade," Sarah C says. "Ever since he led the unpasteurized milk rally in the lunchroom."

"That was so stupid. What kind of heathen drinks unpasteurized milk?" Sarah A asks.

"It's like a movement," Sarah B says. "Lots of my cousins drink it that way. They claim it has more nutrients."

"You can't be serious?" Sarah A asks. "You wanted Sal's shirt? Sal Rodriguez?"

"Different strokes for different folks, I guess," I say.

"Well, I didn't get you Sal's shirt. I got you Doyle Rickerson's shirt," Sarah A says. "Go on. Try it. He wears fantastic aftershave."

"Doyle is the best pitcher Central has had in years," Sarah B says.

"He's definitely hot," Sarah C says.

"Way hotter than Sal," Sarah A says.

I pick up the pillow and wrap my arms around it. All this cushioned softness feels pleasant, but the shirt smells like a stranger.

"What do you think of his aftershave?" Sarah A asks.

"It smells like leather," I say.

"I know. Yum," Sarah A says.

It's disappointing to arrive at the guy stage and be partnered with Doyle Rickerson. I know I should go forward with enthusiasm, but it's hard.

"Doyle has great arms," Sarah B says. "Especially his right one."

"It's settled. He's a stud. Let's sit," Sarah A says.

We all take our places on her carpeted floor while Sarah A sits a tier above us on her bed.

"The ultimate goal of the guy phase is to secure dates for the homecoming dance that will lead to long-term boyfriends, who we will eventually break up with the summer before college," Sarah A says. "This way we'll be poised to enter our freshman year single, yet somewhat experienced."

"But what if Doyle breaks up with me before that?" I ask. It seems possible. I hardly know Doyle. I'm not sure that we share any common interests.

"If you follow all the strict procedures of the guy phase, there's no way he'll break up with you, because you'll be giving him what he wants," Sarah A says.

Sarah A sets Roman's pillow down beside her and I watch it tumble forward off the bed. She doesn't make any effort to retrieve it/him. I feel a hand on my leg. It's Sarah B. When I look at her, she squeals.

"You're going to have sex with Doyle Rickerson," Sarah B says.

"I am?" I ask.

This feels way too fast. And awkward. Normally, I like being swept along with the flow of things. But sex? With Doyle? I don't even know his middle name. Or favorite food. Or shoe size. Or eye color. Or exact height. Or mother's maiden name. I lack too much "pre-sex compatibility" information. I'm not even sure if he wears boxers or briefs or lets everything hang loose.

"Whoa," I say. "I don't know if I'm ready for the guy phase. The date to homecoming sounds good, but beyond that—"

"I haven't even laid out what's required, Sarah T. Calm down," Sarah A says.

"I'm not sure about letting a guy touch my 'zones' or go around my 'bases.' Especially a pitcher," I say, drawing scare quotes in the air.

"What do you have against athletes?" Sarah B asks.

"I thought you wanted to enter the guy phase," Sarah C says.

I feel myself blushing. This is so much pressure. I pull my Doyle pillow close to me and try to slow my breathing down.

"You're getting ahead of yourself. Nobody will start giving up 'bases' until next spring," Sarah A says. "God, Sarah T. We've got our reputations to protect. The guy phase doesn't mean that we go from laughing politely and walking away to giving hand jobs in homeroom."

"Hand jobs?" I ask.

I look at Sarah B and Sarah C. They seem surprised by that comment too.

"I said we're not going to be giving hand jobs," Sarah A says. "Some stuff we're saving for college."

"That's cool," Sarah B says.

I glance at Sarah C to figure out where she stands on all of this. But she's hard to read. Her face is pressed deep into Benny Stowe's torso. Her mouth looks like it's doing something too. Is she unbuttoning his shirt with her teeth? It's hard to tell, but her grip is frighteningly tight. Sarah C's holding that pillow like in the past five minutes she's been able to forge a committed relationship with it. I guess she's been pining for Benny on a deeper level than I realized.

"Why do you look like that?" Sarah A asks me.

"Like what?" I ask.

"Like you're going to die," Sarah A says. "This will be fun. And we'll move slow. I promise."

I find these words calming and so I loosen the grip on my Doyle.

"What I want us to do now is get used to their smell," Sarah A says. "We need to desensitize ourselves to their pheromones, so that their scent will never influence our behavior."

"Does this mean that we get to take our pillows home with us?" Sarah C asks.

She clutches her makeshift Benny Stowe with such enthusiasm that her pillow's top seam bulges.

"Yes, but nobody's parents can see these, because, let's face it, out-of-touch adults might find this weird," Sarah A says.

"I'm so with you," Sarah B says.

I hadn't realized how eager Sarah C and Sarah B were to enter the guy phase.

"What's the next step?" I ask. "After we overcome their smell?"

Sarah A reaches down and retrieves her cushioned Roman. She punches it in the center region to fluff it.

"Luckily, all the guys we like are friends," Sarah A says. "The next phase will be group dating. Our first group date will be the third week of August. They'll invite us to go hiking in the Kalamazoo Nature Center. Then we'll eat pizza at Bilbo's."

"That sounds like so much fun!" Sarah C says, falling backward with a soft thud.

"I love Bilbo's crust," Sarah B says.

"How do you know this will happen?" I ask. It all seems so random and out of our control.

Sarah A licks her lips and shakes her head.

"Sarah T, have you ever heard the phrase 'stick in the mud'? Because right now you're being a serious stick in our mud," Sarah A says.

I stare down at my sandals. I am sort of bucking the flow.

"We should be excited about this. It's the next step," Sarah A says.

Sarah B reaches over and touches my leg.

"Aren't you excited, Sarah T?" Sarah B asks.

"I am," I say.

"You don't act like it," Sarah A says.

"Plus, after the guy phase, we get to go on to the *next thing*," Sarah C says, popping back up to a sitting position.

"It's going to be so cool," Sarah B says, repeatedly swatting her Gerard Truax pillow on the floor.

"That's right," Sarah A says. "After the guy phase we'll quickly move on to the next thing: fake IDs."

Sarah B and Sarah C are so giddy over this that they're making bird noises. Sarah B will finally be able to buy a beer at a Tigers game, plus she'll be able to go to R-rated movies. Sarah C will be able to attend certain mature-themed art shows that travel through Kalamazoo and are restricted to people eighteen and older. I guess it's cool. We can go to dance clubs that are twenty-one and older. I don't really think I need a fake ID, but I definitely won't turn it down.

"It's all pretty great," I say.

"Let's open the Triscuits," Sarah A says.

I watch Sarah C break into the yellow cardboard box and tear open the plastic bag with her teeth. All the Sarahs start eating crackers. Even me.

"I'm surprised that we're moving forward so quickly," Sarah B says. "I mean, with what happened at Barnes & Noble."

Suddenly, all I can hear is the sound of the Sarahs chewing and not chewing crackers. Nobody says anything. The silence is unbearable.

"Yeah, I'm really glad we can put that behind us," I say, swallowing hard.

"I'm not sure that I'm totally over it," Sarah A says.

"But," I say, lifting up my Doyle pillow, "we've launched into the guy phase."

"Yeah, but I guess I think there's room for improvement," Sarah A says.

"Totally," I say. Then I pull my Doyle to me like the apocalypse is imminent and I'll be needing my pillow to do some much needed repopulating of the earth.

"Why couldn't you have been like this when I first gave you Doyle?" Sarah A asks.

I shake my head.

"Fatigue?" I offer.

"Sarah T, I think it's time that we all either put up or shut up," Sarah A says.

Sarah B and Sarah C don't object to this suggestion. I feel alone and vulnerable, like a wildebeest with a leg injury being left behind by the herd.

"I'm willing to put up," I say.

Sarah A gets off her bed and walks to her dresser. She picks up four spiral notebooks and four pens. My heart is thumping inside of me. Is this going to be like those closing moments in reality TV shows where everybody has to vote a person out? There's no doubt in my mind that every other Sarah would put my name down. Sweat forms at my hairline. I rub my face against my overstuffed Doyle to sweep my forehead clean.

"I think it's high time that we articulate a few things," Sarah A says.

She lifts the pens over her head and clicks them several times. Then she tosses them, stabbing them through the air at us, ink-end first. The notebooks are flung to us like Frisbees, and I catch mine mid-flight. Even obtaining my writing utensils feels like a competitive sport.

"I'm going to ask you one question, and you're going to do your best to answer it," Sarah A says.

"Does spelling count?" Sarah B asks.

"No, spelling will not be held against you," Sarah A says. "We'll each have ten minutes. I'll participate too."

I hold the ballpoint tip to the paper and it trembles, marking the clean page with a string of spittle-like ink.

"One question," Sarah A says. "Ten minutes to answer. Ask not what the Sarahs can do for you, but what you can do for the Sarahs."

Nobody writes anything.

"Isn't that a statement?" I ask. "I missed the question."

"I think she's right. It's a play off President Kennedy's famous speech, but it's not a question," Sarah C says.

"Okay," Sarah A says, rolling her eyes. "Let me spell it out for you: What can you do for the Sarahs? Go!"

We all frantically begin scratching on our tablets. All of that advice my junior English teacher, Ms. Pellet, gave me about taking a minute or two to gather my thoughts before I began a timed essay goes out the window. I'm winging it. We all are. We're spilling our hearts. We're giving birth, who cares what the baby looks like?

Predictably, I begin with an analogy about how I see life. It's not like a hallway. Sarah C was right; that's too interior. Life is like a trail.

*What can I do for the Sarahs? Plenty! Being a Sarah is my life. And life is like a trail in the wilderness. Picture it: We're hiking on the trail and there's cougars and trees. These are symbols for our adversaries. And because I'm a Sarah who loves the Sarahs, I will fight these things for the Sarahs. Except I don't know how to fight a tree. But I'd save a Sarah from a falling tree. And if a Sarah ever became wounded on the path, I would never leave her behind, because a wildebeest that gets left behind gets eaten. And nobody should eat a Sarah. This brings me to guys. I will like Doyle Rickerson for the Sarahs. I'll smell my leathery Doyle pillow every night to overcome his pheromones. I'll suck his stink down into the lowest recesses of my lungs for my fellow Sarahs. . . .*

I take a break and shake my hand. My finger is cramping. Plus, Sarah A's phone keeps ringing and it's beyond distracting.

"Should you get that?" Sarah C asks.

"No," Sarah A says.

"What if it's an emergency?" I ask.

"We're doing a very important freewrite!" Sarah A says.

After several more rings, the answering machine picks up.

"Sarah Trestle, it's your mother. I have an emergency. Are you there?"

My mother's voice sounds loud and panicked.

"I have to answer it," I say.

Sarah A's head is down. Her loopy handwriting has already filled two whole pages in her notebook. I run to the phone and listen to my mother rattle off something about having a flat tire, wearing white linen pants, being late for an important meeting, and being roughly three blocks away.

"Can you get here?" she asks.

"To change the tire?" I ask.

"I need help," she says.

"Don't we have AAA?" I ask.

"They'll take forever. I'll miss my meeting," she says.

"I'll come," I say. "I'm leaving now."

I go back into the room and the other Sarahs have written so much that they're literally sweating from the effort.

"My mom has car trouble," I say. "I need to go."

"I'm not surprised," Sarah A says.

"It's not like I have a choice," I say. "It's my *mother*. Wouldn't any of us go and help our *mothers*?"

I've said the wrong thing. Sarah A looks up at me. Her stare is cold, but underneath it, I can tell by her eyes she seems hurt.

"Well, if my mother called me I guess I'd ask her, 'Hey Mom, why did you put me up for adoption? And, who are you? And, how come we've never met? And, would you mind forwarding me some information about our family's medical history? You know, cancer, heart conditions, liver disorders, strokes, general health of your ovaries . . .'"

I blink and blink, as if by rapidly reopening my eyes I can somehow change the picture in front of me.

"I didn't mean it that way," I say. "I'm sorry."

"Leave what you wrote," Sarah A says.

"How much time do we have left?" Sarah C asks.

"Four minutes," Sarah A says.

I feel like I need to say something to Sarah A.

"Um," I say.

"Just go," Sarah A says. "Obviously, *your* mother needs *you*."

I hand Sarah A my notebook, but she doesn't take it.

"Set it on the floor," Sarah A says. "I'll read through them tonight and call everybody with the results. I have a feeling we'll be downsizing."

"What about my Doyle pillow?" I ask.

"Leave it. We wouldn't want your *mom* to see it."

Sarah A puts her head down and continues to write.

It doesn't feel good to leave, but I don't see any other option. As I walk out to my car, I can see my mother a block away, moving toward me in her crisp white pants. Her long brown hair swings around her shoulders. A lot of people think I look like a smaller, high school version of her. She's smiling. She's so happy to see me.

"Why don't you just drive me to my meeting?" she yells.

"Okay!" I say.

"You're a real lifesaver!" she says, picking up her pace.

Old Victorian homes rise up along South Street on both sides, turning the road and its sidewalks into a long suburban hallway. Doors close. Doors open. With or without me, my life is happening. I glance back at the Marlborough, then back at her. I'm ashamed of myself. I wish I was as happy to see her as she is to see me. But I'm not.

# Chapter 4

Am I still a Sarah? It's been a week and I haven't heard from them. I missed my second volunteer shift at the animal shelter. Now it's Wednesday again, animal adoption night, and I feel like I want to go, but I'm not sure that I should. It'll be my third missed shift. It's like I'm not even a volunteer anymore. It's like I've fallen into a deep, miserable hole, and there's nobody down here but me. And a telephone. That isn't ringing.

If I was less devoted to the sisterhood, I'd venture out and try to develop new interests: bingo, racquetball, pottery, or spelunking. I'd go visit Sal at his part-time job at Ridge and Kramer Auto Parts. I might ask him to inspect my windshield wipers and give me some feedback about the projected lifetime of their rubber parts. But I won't. That's not how I'm built. I'm not flighty. I'm loyal. At least that's how I like to view my blind devotion.

I could simply call Sarah A and find out what she thought about my freewrite. But I'm too scared. Why did I include that part about wildebeests? It's not a good idea to compare your friends to large, hairy land mammals. Sometimes I'm so clueless. And why did I bring up Sarah A's absent mother? I should never mention the word "mother" around the Sarahs again. Sarah B has an absent mother too. Mrs. Babbitt had an affair and took off to one of the Dakotas. I think it was the northern one. But Sarah B doesn't seem as wounded by her mother's absence as Sarah A. I guess it's different because Sarah A has so many unanswered questions.

Back in fourth grade, when we first became friends, Sarah A talked about her biological mom a lot. It was mostly information and details that she imagined about her mom. Things that she wanted to believe. But after we hit junior high, right around the time we became thieves, Sarah A stopped talking about her mother altogether. I still remember the last thing Sarah A said about her. We'd taken a tube of watermelon-flavored lip gloss from a health food store (our first theft ever), and we were walking home, smearing it on our mouths, and out of nowhere Sarah A said, "Maybe my mom was just a wreck. Maybe she left me so I wouldn't have to live in her wreckage."

I didn't say anything. I worried that Sarah A had recently found out that her biological mother had been killed in a car accident. But I don't think that anymore. I think it was easier for Sarah A to turn her mother into an enormous disappointment and to finally move on. To leave her too.

This isn't anything I discuss with my mom or dad, because they don't understand the importance of the Sarah sisterhood. They actually think I need to make other friends. They're so misguided. What they call "branching out" would be a total betrayal of the Sarahs.

The phone rings. I snag it right away. It could be a Sarah. My mother is home and I don't need her conversing with any of them. She's always trying to learn more about them. And there's no reason for that. She can tell them apart and knows their last names. Really, isn't that enough?

"Sarah T?" Sarah A asks me.

"Yes," I say. "Are you calling about the freewrites? Structurally, I know mine could've been stronger. Also, the content. That could've been better, too."

"Freewrites?" Sarah A asks me. "You're still hung up about the freewrites?"

"Well, I haven't heard from you since the freewrites," I say. "It's been a whole week."

"Okay. About that. I'm not saying that you're not a Sarah anymore, but your freewrite totally sucked," Sarah A says.

"I agree," I say.

"But they all sucked in their own ways. I don't think that it's fair to bounce anybody because of their lame paragraphs," Sarah A says.

"Sarah C wrote a lame paragraph, too?" I ask.

I'd assumed hers would be an engrossing read.

"Hers was okay. It was a metaphor about life. About how we're all walking down this hallway and there are all these doors that we have to either walk through or past. It was thought-provoking. Probably the best one."

"Better than yours?" I ask.

"Hers was a really deep analogy. You could tell that she's put a lot of thought into it," Sarah A says. "Plus, it was nice not being compared to a wildebeest."

"I know. That was a complete misstep on my part," I say. "But back to Sarah C's freewrite. How does comparing life to a hallway answer the question, 'What can you do for the Sarahs?'"

"Sarah C talked about always supporting our door choices. And her willingness to go first when any of us felt a door looked too freaky to open," Sarah A says.

"I see," I say.

"Anyway, we're going to do something else," Sarah A says.

"What?" I ask.

"I haven't figured it out," Sarah A says. "But once I do, I'll call you."

"Should I come and drive you guys to the shelter tonight? I can throw some pants on and be there in five minutes," I say.

"You're not wearing pants? It's three o'clock in the afternoon," Sarah A says.

I don't say anything. I really wish I hadn't mentioned my pantless state.

"Sarah C is going to drive us. It's probably best if you don't come. I've explained your absence at the shelter so thoroughly that if you showed up tonight it would look suspicious," Sarah A says.

"Oh," I say.

This is very depressing. First, I don't want anybody to think that I have a serious disease or anything. Second, being Sarah A's ride is part of my niche. I'm the taxi driver. I ferry us around in my lemon-yellow Volkswagen. And we have a good time. Sometimes we sing. It's the way it's always been. I never knew Sarah C was such an traitor. First, she stole my hallway metaphor. And now she's taken my niche. She's a much better thief than I realized.

"Enjoy your evening without pants," Sarah A says. "You won't be missing much. After the shelter, we're calling it an early night."

The dial tone is such a sad sound.

I know I can't call the supervisor at the shelter, because it would mess up Sarah A's lie. But I wish I could. He's nice. "Call me Kevin," he always says. But I don't. I call him Mr. King. I think he's almost as old as my parents. Out of respect, all of the Sarahs call him Mr. King. We're actually hoping that he'll write us glowing letters of recommendation for college. What looks better to an admission's board than teens helping unwanted animals? At least that's why Sarah A does it. As for me, I don't mind helping the animals. They seem to appreciate it.

I better just blow off another shift.

I close my eyes. Sitting here in my own personal darkness, all I can do is think about the Sarahs. I like volunteering with them. We're not old enough to touch the dogs. We're in charge of cleaning cages and weighing food and filling water dishes and processing the donated supplies. We're assigned other low-rung duties too. Sometimes we file. Sometimes we hold on to animals by their leashes when a supervisor is standing right there. On adoption night, we try to lure the kindest-looking people toward the animals that have been there the longest. Sarah A is the best at this. She hates seeing people head straight for the puppies. She's come up with great slogans for the older dogs. Some of them are even partially true.

"Give her some love and she'll give you her life."

"This dog has worked in several situation comedies."

"Her pee is weak and won't kill your lawn."

"This one cured her own foot tumor."

Sarah A usually refers to the dogs as girls, even when they're clearly males. She says that people prefer female pets. I think something deeper might be going on there.

I wonder how many will find homes tonight? I wonder how many new ones arrived throughout the week?

At the shelter, there are cages outside so people can leave animals all through the night. I think it's awful that during the cover of darkness people anonymously dump their pets. But it happens. Maybe after the shift, Sarah A will think of what she wants us to do next and call me and invite me over. After three shifts without me, Sarah A has got to feel the void.

Time ticks by. My mother is digging around in her closet. I can hear her. She sounds like a gerbil running in a wheel. That's actually not a rude comparison. My mother is very active. She's a professional closet organizer. She says that your closet is a reflection of your soul. She says that a lot. She also totally overvalues the shoe rack. It's annoying.

"Sarah, have you seen the extension cord?" she asks.

She enters my bedroom wearing her traditional cleaning outfit: sweatpants, a T-shirt, and sneakers. Her dark hair is pulled back with a red bandanna. This touch makes her look somewhat prepared for either aerobics or combat.

"The orange one?" I ask.

"Yes," she says.

"I haven't," I say.

She exhales loudly and walks to my bedside.

"Do you have a bug?" she asks.

"Like the flu?" I ask.

She nods.

"No," I say.

"For a healthy person, you're spending a lot of time in bed," she says.

"I'm soaking up the summer," I say.

"Without any pants, I see."

I look down at my bare legs. I'm not sure why I haven't put pants on today. It just didn't happen.

"Maybe I should go shopping," I say.

"For pants?"

"And maybe some capris," I say.

"Have you and the Sarahs had a falling out?" she asks.

She sits down beside me and places her hand on my calf. She doesn't realize that "the Sarahs" is the formal name for our clique. It's just easier for her to call them that than to refer to them as Sarah Aberdeen, Sarah Babbitt, and Sarah Cody.

"No. We're good," I say. "Busy. But good."

She raises her eyebrows.

"This is busy?" she asks.

She can tell that I'm lying, but she doesn't press me on it.

"You might think about picking up some dress pants," she says.

She knows better than to suggest that I buy a skirt. I'm not a dressy girl. Amongst the Sarahs, I'm the least fashion-literate. My mother dresses better than I do. And I'm okay with this.

"I want to buy jeans," I say.

"You own a lot of jeans," my mother says. "Maybe you should purge a little."

"Purge?" I ask.

"Throw out some of your old jeans. Look through your closet and ask yourself, 'Have I worn you this year?' If the answer is no, you should donate it."

"You want me to talk to my clothes?" I ask. I reach down to the floor and pick up a pair of crumpled jeans. "Have I worn you this year?" I ask it. I lower the zipper and raise it quickly, like it's a mouth. "Yes, you have, Sarah, I'm your favorite pants."

"There's no need to mock me. I'm giving you good ideas," she says.

She gets up and walks out of my room. When she returns, she's holding an empty box.

"Put your purged items in here," she says. "Doing something for others will probably buoy your spirits. At heart, you're a real giver."

"Thanks," I say.

If my mother understood how ironic that statement was, she would have to laugh at it. I can't think of any bigger "taker" in life than a criminal. I glance at my closet. My disinterest in clothes is a disappointment to her. Recently, she told me that my closet had left the world of "teen casual" and entered a realm of "articles of clothing one might find in smoldering piles after a nuclear war."

After purging eight pairs of jeans that I have not worn in at least two years, and several tops that I can't quite remember buying, (but am certain I didn't steal, because I always remember what I steal), and napping on my pleasantly cool but rock-hard concrete floor, I crawl back to my bed. If Sarah A was telling me the truth about having an early night, then the Sarahs should all be back home now. Or maybe they've decided to move on without me, but Sarah A didn't want to tell me. Maybe I should drive past all the Sarahs' homes and see if I can spot them gathered together. No, they'll recognize my Volkswagen. It's impossible to execute a drive-by in my vehicle. Everybody notices a lemon-yellow car.

What should I do? I pick up Sue Grafton's novel *B Is for Burglar*. Maybe I need to read. No. I'm too stressed-out. My vision is blurred. Can being extremely passive cause a brain aneurysm? Is it time for me to finally start acting a little alpha? I pick up the phone. I've put this off long enough. I need to sort this out. So I dial my brother. I'm not calling Liam for counsel, because that would be a waste of time. Just like my parents, Liam doesn't get the Sarahs either.

I call him in California in the hope that he can be persuaded to call Sarah B for me. I need to find out if the other Sarahs are there. They could be singing. Or smelling their pillows. Or planning future crimes. Wait. They could be launching into the next leg of the guy phase without me. All of the sudden, things feel very life or death. I don't bother easing into the conversation by asking Liam questions about himself or his classes. I get to what matters.

"Liam, I need you to call Sarah Babbitt immediately," I say.

"Why don't you call her?" he asks.

"What do you mean? I don't want to talk to her," I say.

"I don't want to talk to her either," he says.

"Just ask to speak to Sarah Cody."

"I thought you wanted me to call Sarah Babbitt."

"I do. I want to know if Sarah Cody is at Sarah Babbitt's."

There's a pause. I can hear him chewing gum.

"What if Sarah Cody answers Sarah Babbitt's phone?"

"Just hang up. They have caller ID, but they won't recognize your number."

"No."

"Please."

"I'm in college now, Sarah. This is beneath me."

"But you're my brother."

There's a long silence. I worry that he's hung up the phone on me. Then I hear more gum-smacking.

"I'm not going to do this. You're acting like you're in junior high."

"I'll give you something," I say.

"I don't want your money."

"It's way better than money."

"I'm listening," he says.

"I'll read that bingo book you've been harassing me about."

"*The Bingo Palace* by Louise Erdrich?"

"That's the one," I say.

"Don't read it for me. Read it for yourself."

"I could care less about bingo," I say.

"It's not a book about bingo."

"Then it's a very misleading title."

"Sarah, you know Erdrich is one of my favorite Native American writers. You need to get past all your Sarah Aberdeen and Sarah Babbitt and Sarah Cody issues."

"I don't have issues," I say.

"You are an issue," he says.

"Liam, if you don't call Sarah Babbitt and ask to speak to Sarah Cody, I'll tell Mom and Dad about that thing that you don't want me to tell them."

"What thing?" he asks.

This is a tactic that I picked up from Sarah A. I don't really have anything to hold over Liam, but sometimes it's possible, by using underhanded means, to trick an incriminating tidbit out of somebody.

"We both know exactly what thing I'm talking about," I say.

"Weasel-like conduct is so unflattering," he says.

"Squeak, squeak, frrp, frrp," I say, trying to sound as weasel-like as possible.

"You can't blackmail me about smoking pot forever," he says.

I had no idea that my brother smoked pot. This is useful information in more ways than one. It's not like there's an expiration date for blackmailing your brother concerning cannabis use.

"Marijuana should be legal anyway," he says.

"But it's not. Do you need Sarah Babbitt's number?" I ask.

"Let me get a pen."

I tell him to call me back right away. I sit with my hand on the phone. If Sarah B is at Sarah C's, then Sarah A lied to me and they're moving on without me. Maybe Sarah A figured that the guy phase would be easier to accomplish without me. And Doyle. And if that's happening, what will I do about it? How do you shoehorn your way back into your social group?

"Was she there?" I ask.

"No," he says.

"Thank God!"

"They're both at Sarah Aberdeen's."

I almost drop the phone.

"Why would they be there? Are you sure?"

"Her mom said that they were making cookies and singing and working on their applications for Michigan."

"Michigan State?" I ask.

"No, U of M."

"Did Mrs. Babbitt ask you who you were?" I ask. That's a lot of information to give out over the phone.

"I said I was Don from the shelter."

"But there isn't a Don at the shelter," I say.

"Duh," he says. "Sarah, maybe you need to branch out of your current peer group and make friends with people named Bibi or Janice or Pam."

"Yeah. Branch out," I say.

"Don't be bummed. That Aberdeen kid is bad news."

"Sarah Aberdeen is not bad news. She just doesn't deviate from her standards."

"I meant her brother, Vance."

"You shouldn't judge other people. I hear that he's on very effective medication now. He's practically normal."

"I'm just trying to cheer you up. Okay?"

"Liam, I killed a possum."

"On purpose?"

"I accidentally ran it over three Sundays ago with the car. It's still in the driveway."

"Don't worry. Dad'll get to it. Sometimes animals just go splat."

"He didn't go splat. He went smoosh."

"Sarah, that's TMI. Listen, I'm helping out with a rally this week. I'm late for the planning meeting."

"Oh." He doesn't say what kind of rally, but I know it's some sort of antiwar rally.

Liam thinks the world's problems can all by solved by diplomatic measures like trade embargos and economic sanctions. I think that's sort of naive. Because the world has been making tanks for at least a hundred years. Which suggests to me that armored vehicles equipped with artillery must be useful in peace negotiations. Besides, with so many wars raging in so many countries, what does marching down a street in San Francisco really accomplish?

"Go do something," Liam says.

"I'm resting," I say.

"I meant with your life," he says.

He doesn't wait for me to say good-bye. I'm just left with a dial tone again and I have to deal with it.

I can't believe the Sarahs are making all these new strides without me. The summer is slipping by. It just doesn't feel like I've earned permanent banishment. I wrap my arms around myself and close my eyes. I feel delicate. Like a tulip petal. Or a blade of grass. Or a grasshopper leg. Once, our government teacher snapped a twig in two right in front of our class to demonstrate the fragility of the individual. Then he took a group of twigs and bundled them together and tried to break them. But he couldn't. They bent, but he couldn't break them. I think he was lecturing on the Civil Rights movement in the sixties, and the power of civil disobedience.

After class, Sarah A said, "That's just like us. We're as strong as a stick bundle."

I remember feeling so relieved, picturing myself as one of those protected inner twigs. But that's not me anymore. I might never be a protected inner twig again. I'm a lone vulnerable stick. I take a deep breath and open my eyes. There's no denying it, the Sarahs mean a lot more to me than I ever realized. I'll do anything to get back in with them. Anything.

# Chapter 5

After a good night's sleep, I start out my Thursday somewhat determined to rob a bank. Okay. I don't think I can execute such a high-stakes heist by myself. But I can complete a dry run in which I take copious notes, detailing each difficult and deliberate step. Clearly, said notes will be a surefire way to impress the Sarahs. Not only will it speak to my criminal mind, but it will also address my level of commitment. And emphasize my potential. The plan is so fabulous that my skin intermittently goose pimples as I wash my face and brush my teeth.

For this idea to be a complete success, I need the dry run to be as realistic as possible. I've got to move forward as if I'm literally prepared to hold up a bank. This includes arming myself. We are not a gun-equipped household, so my options are limited. My dad keeps a baseball bat near the front door. But I need a weapon that can fit in my pocket. I dig through my sock drawer. I find a golf ball. A pack of gum. A very old wristwatch. Lots of nickels. Socks. A thermometer. A pocketknife! Perfect.

I knew it was in there somewhere. I shove it in my left jeans pocket. Then I grab a pair of my mother's panty hose to stick over my head. I've seen enough movies to know that a mask is essential. Then, I draft a note. I keep it simple: I want one hundred thousand dollars in small bills—immediately. I shove it deep inside my front right jeans pocket, along with my "borrowed" mask, and walk into the kitchen.

"I made French toast," my mother says.

Her brown hair is pulled back into a loose ponytail. With cheeks blushed and eyelashes curled, she's ready to go somewhere. Her coral lips are glossed to glasslike perfection. But she's not the kind of mother who overdoes her makeup and leaves the house looking heavily spackled. Her primp job is usually both lovely and respectable. I'm surprised that she made French toast. Due to our kitchen's galley construction and malfunctioning oven, my mother hasn't been clocking much culinary time. I glance at her version of French toast. It's considerably lacking on the French part. Basically, it's browned bread. It's from a box. And she cooked it in the toaster. Not the toaster oven. Just the toaster.

"All I want is a banana," I say.

She reaches for the banana hook and pulls off a slightly green, medium-ripe one for me.

"What are your plans for the day?" she asks.

I shrug my shoulders. She only asks me that question as a

courtesy. She never presses for a detailed answer. She eagerly surrenders the banana.

"Good thing you drove me to my meeting last week. I got the job! I'll be organizing Dr. Pewter's closets. Her entire condo is a rattrap. I won't be back until dinner."

"Does she have actual rats?" I ask.

My mother squeezes her eyes closed and sticks out her tongue in disgust.

"She might. I don't know what it is about academics. On the one hand, they make excellent *Jeopardy* contestants. On the other hand, they live in bestial filth."

"What's her specialty?"

"*Beowulf*."

"Devoting your whole life to the study of Grendel and his mother, doesn't that say it all?" I ask.

"You're so smart. You're ready for college right now."

"Or culinary school," I say. I'm not totally serious when I say this, but sometimes I think it would be fun to be a pastry chef. I'm a huge fan of icing.

"Sarah, sometimes the universe works in mysterious ways. And when a group of anonymous donors appears out of nowhere and they offer to cover all four years of college for every Kalamazoo high school student, I think it's a sign that the universe wants you to go to college and not culinary school."

I shrug. My mother is talking about the Kalamazoo Promise.

Last year, a group of superrich people who live in the area, but wish to remain unnamed, donated a quarter of a billion dollars to establish the Kalamazoo Promise. So now, if you're enrolled in Kalamazoo Central High School or Loy Norrix, you get four free years of college anywhere in the state of Michigan. The secret rich people will pay your tuition for you. It's automatic. You just get it. For, like, the next thirteen years.

People in Kalamazoo are still sort of shocked about it. When it happened, the Sarahs all decided to apply to the University of Michigan. By far, it's the best school in the state. And it's expensive too. Some people consider it Ivy League.

"I'm not really planning to go to culinary school," I say.

I smile. And bite off the head of my banana. My mother unties her apron and folds it into a square. She pats it and winks at me. That's her way of saying she wants me to take care of the kitchen mess, though the counter is basically spotless. I nod. She must think that she's running behind. She is very type A. I think if she had to show up late to something, she'd spontaneously combust. She grabs her infamous and enormous black shoulder bag and races out the door.

"Dinner at seven. We're barbecuing franks and the Crock-Pot is stuffed with beans."

"Wait. I need to tell you something," I say.

Her hand is on the doorknob. She releases it and flips around. This is sort of surprising. I mean, I never tell her anything.

"What?"

I clear my throat.

"I killed a possum."

"I saw. Your father will take care of it. Eventually."

I watch her perfect perky body walk out the door. It might be true that I am a smaller, high school version of my mother, but I'm also pudgier. How did I get the plump gene? How can she eat barbecued franks and indulge in a mountain of beans and not gain weight? I reach deep into my pocket and rub the note between my thumb and finger. It's such a stupid idea. I really should bag it.

Instead, I finish my banana, clean up the kitchen, and drive to the Educational Community Credit Union four times. Each time takes me anywhere between seven and nine minutes. The traffic light on Stadium is a killer. Not only is it long, but lots of other cars run it. I write this down in my notebook. Then I stuff it underneath the seat.

Sitting inside my car in the bank's parking lot, I start to sweat. Huge drops roll down my back. It's not just the stress; I'm sitting in the sun. I pull out the notebook. I write:

*Consider robbing the bank in spring or fall, as I would not want to put panty hose on my head in bone-crushing heat.*

Then I stow the book away again.

I roll my window down and take a deep breath. I watch

a girl clomp up the sidewalk in a pair of flip-flops. She's holding a blue Popsicle. She licks at the juice between her fingers. I close my eyes. That kid looks way too innocent. Like she belongs in a pudding commercial. I open my eyes and watch her go inside the bank. I'll wait until after she leaves to case the place. I have a heart. It feels creepy to plot a criminal act in front of a Popsicle-sucking child. I close my eyes again. Even inside my car, it smells like summer and cut grass.

When I was five we moved to Kalamazoo. We came here via Livingston, Wyoming. I vaguely remember that place. A bear knocked over our trash can once. Also, I think a deer got trapped in our garage and dented my mother's van. I guess it's true that the West is still wild. After we arrived in the Midwest, my parents assumed Liam and I would make friends with everybody we met. For Liam, that was true. For me, I endured nearly four friendless years. If you arrive on the scene in kindergarten and pee yourself during snack time, it greatly limits your ability to mingle amongst your peer group and build lasting connections. The pants-wetter stigma ascended with me into grade school and beyond.

It was in fourth grade that I met Sarah Aberdeen. I felt like she saved me. I mean, because she literally saved me from being hit by a van. The crossing guard was escorting a group across Broadway. I wanted to cross Winchell. I looked to my left and then went. Then I heard this horn honking. And I felt Sarah A yank me by my collar back onto the sidewalk. Then my life continued. And I became a Sarah. I felt like I couldn't thank her enough. It felt like she'd been sent right to me at that exact intersection. Maybe she'll show up again.

I watch the overly blonde girl leave the bank. The Popsicle is gone. She's sucking on a lollipop. Don't they teach kids about tooth decay in elementary school anymore?

Before I go into the bank, I pop my trunk. This is where the stolen money will go. I've heard about the dye-packed money that bank tellers give to robbers. The dye explodes and stains the bills so that the money becomes marked and worthless. I bet if we rob this bank, we'll get a dye-pack. What a waste. Who'd want to risk robbing a bank only to end up with crappy, unusable cash?

To avoid this fate, the Sarahs should separate the stacks of bills into coolers. My trunk can easily hold four small coolers. We'll divide the money and stuff it in the coolers. We'll have to be quick about it, but we'll have time. One of the backseat Sarahs will make sure that the lids are on tight. Then we'll drive off. Even if one explodes, the other three coolers will be fine.

After we get away, we'll bury the contaminated cooler in the ground somewhere. Holy shit. This idea is so good that I feel like I must be channeling Bonnie and Clyde. In fact, it's so fantastic, I don't even need to take a minute to write it down, because it's not going anywhere. I'm in love with my innovative cooler-strategy. As I walk to the bank, I'm so proud of myself that I can't stop smiling.

I enter the building and stand in the corner by a staged beach scene meant to entice customers into taking out a home equity line of credit in order to travel to tropical places like Bermuda and Hawaii. They've trucked in actual sand and propped up a surfboard. A deflating, lopsided beach ball has rolled off to the side. I kick it toward the corner. It ricochets off a post and comes back to me. I pick it up. As I hold the bright red ball and scope out the bank, it's clear to me that I should have brought my notebook with me.

There's a lot of things to keep track of. First, the number and location of all cameras I've passed to get to this point. Second, the exact distance from the parking lot to the front door, and from the front door to the tellers. Third, the basic layout of the bank. Fourth, the fifty or more other things that require consideration before committing armed robbery that are to me, like most teenagers, unknown.

I back up against a window. I should read a book about bank robbing before executing a dry run. And even though it's tempting, I should not Google this information because the police are totally allowed to search your computer. And I've heard of situations where your computer is used as a character witness against you in court.

I reach into my pocket and feel my mask and the note. I reach into my other pocket and touch the pocketknife. That's when I realize how tight my jeans are. Am I bloated? I can't believe I didn't notice how obvious the bulging outline of the knife was before I left my house. I might as well be wearing a T-shirt that says I AM CARRYING A POTENTIALLY LETHAL BLADE. Is it illegal to enter a bank armed with a weapon and a threatening note?

I look around. Everywhere I look I see the glassy eye of a camera. And really friendly-looking tellers. And toddlers. And a long, snaking line. And a deputy sheriff. I need to get out of here.

I know Sarah A hopes that one day we'll become a band of female bank robbers, crisscrossing the country while stuffing our Escalade with bags of money, and I hope that my cooler-strategy will take us one step closer, but I'm not the kind of person who can single-handedly complete a dry run in preparation to rob a bank. The scenario makes me feel too fragile. And freaked out. In fact, as I stand here like a conspicuous and sweaty hog, I'm surprised anybody has ever been able to successfully rob a bank.

I'm done. But before I leave, I throw the beach ball back into the tropical scene. Sadly, the ball bounces against the surfboard making it slam to the ground. I had no idea surfboards weighed so much. Everybody in the whole bank turns to look at the source of the crash. Then they look at me.

"It got away from me," I say, holding my palms up to let them know that I don't mean any harm. Then I lower my left hand to conceal the pocketknife bulge. Maybe it could be mistaken for a tampon. Or a roll of quarters.

Then I hoof it outside. I wonder, if I weighed less, would I sweat less? Actually, I'm not heavy. My problem is that I lack muscle tone. I try flexing my arms. Except for the bones, they're all mushy. Maybe I should start lifting weights. I wonder if that's something the other Sarahs would enjoy? I glance back at the bank in my rearview mirror. I feel pretty good about my decision not to commit a felony. I don't bother pulling out the notebook to write any of this down. All I want right now is a Big Gulp at the 7-Eleven.

As I drive down 9th Street, taking stock of a group of freshly shorn sheep dotting the roadside pastures, I realize that I know the car in front of me. It's Sarah C and her seafoam-green Corolla. I speed up. All the Sarahs are in her car, bobbing along to the radio. Wait. I can't believe it. There's a fourth person in the car. She's in the backseat and she has a very small head. It almost looks like a dog's head. It is! The Sarahs have adopted a dog.

Sarah A has mentioned wanting one before. She planned to volunteer with it and visit elderly patients in hospitals. The shelter has a program for that. It's called the Pet Visitation Project. Mr. King has mentioned it several times. He and his golden retriever, Copper, visit people in hospitals and residential facilities once a month. All you need to become a volunteer is an easygoing pet.

Sarah A thinks it'll really make her college entrance essay stand out. She thinks that visiting sick children in hospitals with a rescued dog will give her a clear advantage. She says it will make her memorable. I guess I didn't take her canine ambitions all that seriously. I thought the dog was hypothetical. But she really did it. That's such a huge thing to do without me.

I'm so close now that I'm tailgating them. Sarah B is in the backseat and she waves to me. I honk. And flash my lights. I really wish my parents hadn't taken away my cell phone last March, because I could call the Sarahs right now and meet up with them and tell them about how I almost planned a bank robbery. It's not a completely lame story, because I did knock over a surfboard.

But the Sarahs don't slow down. I see Sarah A hit Sarah C's arm and they accelerate. Then they run a yellow light. I stop. I don't want to get a traffic ticket. My heart is racing. I want so badly to be inside that car with them. And their dog. Discussing the guy phase and our futures. I watch as the glare from their bumper fades away into nothing. I wonder where they're headed. I wonder what they named the dog.

# Chapter 6

"I always say that if you see a possum during daylight hours, you're doing the community a service by running it over."

My father scoops up the dead animal with the shovel's blade.

"I've never heard that," I say.

"Possums are nocturnal. If they're out during daylight hours, they're most likely rabid."

"I hit this one at dusk."

"I wouldn't lose any sleep over it. That's a borderline situation."

I nod. It took my dad over three weeks to finally dispose of the thing. My mom actually wrote it down on a "To Do List" that she stuck to the refrigerator. It said RELOCATE DEAD POSSUM. I watch my father walk into the woods and then return with an empty shovel.

"Lake looks nice. And so does the trail. People are really picking up after their dogs this season."

I take for granted the fact that I live in a house overlooking a lake. I glance over at Asylum Lake. I know, it's a very unfortunate name for a body of water.

"Do you think we'll ever get a dog?"

"Sarah, you know how your mother feels about dander."

"But we could get a shorthaired dog. Or a no-haired dog."

My father frowns. He's started growing out his beard again, so his face looks increasingly scruffy.

"You'll be in college in a year. I think your dog days are behind you."

That's a misleading statement, as it suggests that I once had a dog or the possibility of owning a dog, which I've never had.

"I'm going to head down to the lot this afternoon and do some paperwork. You're welcome to come hang out and look at the cars."

I don't know why my father has the impression that I harbor the desire to accompany him to his used car dealership to look at the cars. He asks me about once a month and I always refuse. Liam enjoyed looking at the cars. Sarah prefers to do other things. Like hanging out with the Sarahs.

"I've got plans."

"Really?"

My father looks at me suspiciously.

"I'm going to hang out with the Sarahs," I say.

"I wondered if something might be up with them. I haven't seen them in weeks."

"It's this new thing we're trying," I say.

"I think it's good you're taking a rest."

He puts his hands on his hips and looks at our house. It's one of the four houses in our neighborhood that was built by the architect Frank Lloyd Wright. It's a Usonian home. But I'm not totally sure what that means. The house has really small bathrooms. And a kitchen that resembles a tight alley. And cement floors throughout. But it's got this enormous fireplace and hearth and amazing windows that make the outside and inside totally blend.

"Sometimes things change," he says. "And sometimes that change can be so destructive that it demolishes the very foundation of the thing itself."

I nod, even though I have no idea what he's talking about.

"Sarah," my mother calls, waving the phone over her head. "You've got a phone call."

The hair stands up on the back of my neck. I'm thrilled. My dad was getting way too serious. When people start talking about change, it makes me think of menopause and I don't know why anyone would want to talk to me about that. Especially my father. I race to the house and take the phone.

to my room. I know it's a Sarah. I can feel it in my bones.

"Hello?"

"It's me," Sarah A says.

"How are you? I saw the dog. What kind is it? It looks like a Lab. Did you guys even see me? I thought you saw me, but I wasn't sure."

"Oh, we saw you."

"Oh."

"The dog is a yellow Lab. I named him John Glenn. Everybody likes John Glenn. I mean, he was an astronaut. And a U.S. Senator. And a Marine Corps fighter pilot. And a Presbyterian elder. And the first American to orbit the earth."

"That's a great name."

"I know. It'll really make my essay stand out to say that I visited terminally ill people with my shelter-adopted Lab, John Glenn."

"It's pure genius."

Awkward pause. I think I hear her yawn.

"I've missed you guys."

"I thought of what we need to do," Sarah A says.

"You did?"

"Let's face reality. The guy phase is going to be a huge transition. And then there's college. We've all got to remain completely committed for the Sarahs to survive."

"I believe you," I say.

"Because senior year is when it all happens. The applications. The campus tours. The decisions. I mean, getting into U of M isn't going to be a cakewalk. And we'll each be deep in the throes of a successful relationship, which will be a complete time-suck. We've got to work hard and be on the same page."

"I look forward to the time-suck. And give me the page number and I'm there."

"Yeah. I'm just not sure."

"What can I do to make you sure?"

"Compete in the challenge."

"The challenge?" My mind flashes back to what happened to Sarah Dancer. I'm so screwed. I have weak ankles.

"All the other Sarahs, including myself, are doing something to prove our commitment. We're meeting at my house tonight."

"I'm there." What a relief. The challenge isn't what I thought it was. I'm not going to have to jump off anybody's garage. At least not for the sake of demonstrating team loyalty.

"You have the rest of the day to do something important. Something that demonstrates your commitment to us. The Sarah who completes the least impressive act is going to be voted out."

"Really?"

"Really."

"What is everybody else doing?"

"I'm not going to tell you that. But Sarah T, you need to aim high."

I'm almost ready to hang up because I think our conversation is over when I hear screaming on the other end of the line.

"My brother is being such a jackass. If he touches me again I might have to call the police."

"Are you talking to me?" I ask.

"Of course I'm talking to you. Because I haven't spoken to Vance in over a year. Because he's crazy. And I don't indulge crazy people in conversation."

"Right," I say.

"Because crazy people should learn how to not be crazy anymore, so that I can have a normal life again," Sarah A says.

"I hear you," I say. "Hey, what time tonight?"

"Six. Looks like my psycho brother is going to throw grapes at me. I might have to train John Glenn to eat his rabbit."

"Bye," I say, hanging up the phone. Sarah A's head game with Vance makes me extremely uncomfortable. It's almost as if she's trying to drive him more crazy than he actually is. She won't talk to him. She just won't. Even when he's nice. She pretends to talk to him when their parents are around, but any other time, she won't acknowledge him, and only refers to him in the third person. I think it's a form of manipulation. Or harassment. Or maybe just cruelty.

I wish she knew how to handle things differently. But who am I to sit in judgment of Sarah A? I've got Liam. He's basically normal. And she's been saddled with a tweenage psycho brother who attacks cantaloupes. In public.

Okay. I can do this. I've got to complete a task. I was born to complete tasks to demonstrate my worthiness to be a Sarah. Think big. I either need to vandalize something or steal something. But which? It would be so anticlimactic to vandalize something, because I can't show up with proof of what I did. Unless I take a picture. But I don't have a digital camera. Can I get 35mm film developed before six o'clock?

Maybe I should vandalize something small enough to bring to the meeting. Wait. Vandalism is the wrong choice. Sarah A is the best vandal ever. She's even vandalized moving objects and ill-tempered farm animals. She'd be so underwhelmed with anything I could possibly do. I need to steal something. I need to show up tonight with a trophy. Okay. What would Sarah A want?

Maybe I should steal the rest of Roman Karbowski's shirts for her. Or I could take a couple pairs of his pants. Wouldn't the bottom half of somebody have different pheromones than the top half? Shouldn't we be desensitizing ourselves against those scents too? I think lower-regions smells would be the ones that we'd want to protect ourselves against the most. That's where things get dangerous. Wait. Maybe Sarah A would think I was upstaging her if I stole a good chunk of her future serious boyfriend's wardrobe. Even though I have outstanding intentions, perhaps it's wise to steer clear of her guy and his pants.

Then it hits me. I know. I know what I need to do. I need to steal something that Sarah A will truly admire. Something to which she has very limited access. Something that she finds intriguing. Something that is illegal for sixteen-year-olds to purchase or consume. Clearly, that something has to be booze. Because of Vance, her parents don't keep any liquor in the house. It's so taboo. For her, more than the rest of us, alcohol is truly a banned and precious substance.

I don't mean to suggest that any of the Sarahs drink. We rarely do. We're not good at it. We've only tried it three times. At Sarah C's. Our drink of choice was a mixture of Baileys, Kahlua, vodka, ice, and milk. On all three occasions, we dumped generous amounts of everything into a blender and prepared our concoction by grinding the ingredients on the CRUSH ICE setting. We drank them quickly from tall plastic tumblers. As a result, each Sarah has puked and been hungover three times. Apparently, we have a tendency to overdo it.

I grab a second banana for additional fuel and race out to my car. Finally, I feel so optimistic. Stealing a nice bottle of liquor will really impress everyone. In all of our crimes, rarely have I ever been the actual thief. I'm usually the driver. Or the lookout. Historically speaking, I'm practically a bystander. But this heist will cement my status as a real criminal. As a real Sarah. Everyone knows that stealing alcohol is a much more serious offense than stuffing a box of Oreos down your pants.

I drive to Tiffany's liquor store on West Main, because Sarah A has talked about a nice bottle of cognac there. I walk up and down the long aisles crowded with bottles. Holy crap! Cognac costs an arm and a leg. I stand in the middle of the store staring at the bottle Sarah A has long admired. It's kept behind a locked glass case. I'm shocked by the price tag. It costs $3,500. What's cognac even made out of? Hundred-dollar bills?

"Can I help you?" a clerk asks me.

I must stick out like a rogue lime in a lemon display. I don't know what to do. The only thing running through my mind is one single word: *Abort! Abort! Abort!*

"Nah, I'm just looking."

"Don't even think about stealing that bottle," he says.

My eyes grow wide. Is this guy a mind reader? Do I look like a thief? I can feel myself breaking into a massive, hoglike sweat again. I point to myself.

"Are you talking to me?" I ask.

"It was a joke. That bottle is priceless."

"The price tag says thirty-five hundred dollars."

"I mean it's irreplaceable."

"How is that even possible? Has the world stopped making cognac?"

"No, it's the container, not the contents. That bottle was designed by a Russian-born French painter named Erté. He's known as the Father of Art Deco."

"I don't know much about art. But the bottle is pretty."

"Erté hand painted it."

Then he looks at me hard, like he's studying me. I hate it when people look at me this way. It makes me feel so scrutinized and transparent. When I'm getting ready to rob a store, it's a lousy combination. Because I know that I'm getting ready to do something wrong, and I can't take the ocular judgment. I feel myself blush. Then I feel my own pee tingling inside of me.

"Bye!" I yell.

I run out the door. I don't wet myself. Once I sit down in my car and am by myself, the impulse to pee goes away. I wonder if I need therapy. Maybe acupuncture would help. Or hypnosis. Or drugs. If I have this kind of problem with urine retention now, what will I be like at seventy?

I pull onto the road, feeling like a total loser. If I have any chance of getting back in with the Sarahs, I've got to commit a real crime. And fast. But what? It has to have a victim. Real crimes have victims. *Rod Carew Hates Vaseline.* What would Sarah A like? What would make Sarah A happy?

I turn onto West Main and head out of town. I know something that Sarah Aberdeen would like. She's mentioned wanting one before. They're always catching her eye. Especially around the holidays.

I'm going to steal a donation jar! Robbing from a needy organization will mean lots of victims. Plus, I'll turn over the cash to Sarah A and she'll appreciate that. My crime is rotten and unethical. It's exactly what she loves. In fact, it's so fabulous that I've stopped sweating and my bladder feels absolutely empty. For me, before a job, that's a good place to be.

# Chapter 7

It's so much easier to commit a crime in your head than it is in real life. I stand, like a paralyzed chicken, in the 7-Eleven eyeing the donation jar. But I can't take it. Shoplifting is much more fun when done in groups. It's as if stealing something by yourself makes your conscience grow, as if maybe me and the other Sarahs have been sharing one small conscience together all along. Right now, I just don't feel breathless and alive with excitement. Honestly, I feel a little empty.

I try to run my hands through my hair, but I can't. Before getting out of my car, I pulled it back into a very tight and wholesome-looking ponytail. I glance at the cashier and smile, then feign interest in the magazine rack. I'm relieved that the clerk doesn't look familiar.

I'm not an idiot. I drove to a 7-Eleven several miles outside of Kalamazoo. It's not like I'm ever coming back to this place. I peek at the checkout area again. All I need to do is rip the jar off the counter and run. But the clerk looks like he's in pretty good shape. What if he's a jogger? What if he gives chase? Maybe I should leave.

"Can I help you?" he asks.

Luckily, I remember Sarah A's foolproof method for robbing convenience stores. It's called the go-fetch strategy. First, you come up with a difficult-to-find item. Then, you ask the clerk to fetch it for you. This distracts the cashier away from the register and front door long enough to allow you to take whatever you want and run.

"I want orange juice."

"It's back there," he says, pointing toward a wall of refrigerators.

"Not just regular orange juice," I say. "I want the kind without pulp."

He smiles. He has nice teeth. And kind eyes. I bet he's the type of person who totally follows the Golden Rule, but life keeps screwing him over anyway.

"Yeah, I hate pulp too. I think we have that kind. Let me check."

He walks back to the freezer. Now is my chance. I grab the Plexiglas box. It's shaped like a house and has a big slit in the top of the chimney where people can slide in their money. It's stuffed with change and dollar bills. I mean, it's totally filled. Wow. It's heavier than I thought it would be. And there's a chain. And it's bolted to the counter. Oh my God. Really crappy people must come in here and try to steal the donation jar all the time.

I look back into the freezer area. The clerk has gone all the way into the rear of the store. He's standing behind the rows of refrigerated drinks. He doesn't see what I'm doing. The milk cartons are blocking his view.

I yank hard. It doesn't come loose. I yank again.

"Do you care which brand?" he calls to me. I can barely hear his muffled voice.

"Tropicana!" I yell.

"Can it be from concentrate?" he asks.

"No. One hundred percent pure juice!"

I give it one more tug. Somewhere in the kinked middle, one of the chain's links pops open. It's almost like a metaphor for the Sarahs. It's the weak link that breaks the chain. I hear the back door shut. He's walking toward me with a carton of juice. I race to my car with the money-stuffed house, trailing a couple of feet of chain. I throw everything in the passenger seat and peel out. The clerk runs after me. He's holding something in his hand. Is it a gun? Holy crap! Are clerks allowed to shoot fleeing thieves? They can't. Can they? Over a donation jar?

I'm already pulling out onto the main road before I realize what he's holding. It's his cell phone. Great. He's taking a picture of my car. Why did I pick out a lemon-yellow Volkswagen

Jetta? I push hard on the gas pedal and my tires squeal. I don't want him snapping a photograph of my license plate.

"Drug addict!" he yells.

Drug addict? Is he talking to me? I may commit crimes, but I'm no drug addict. I even try to avoid eating refined sugar and consuming too much caffeine. Do I look like a drug addict? I glance in the rearview mirror. My eyes are bloodshot and the normally deep brown irises look faded. My skin is pasty. I'm sweating again. Maybe I do look like I'm on something. I turn my focus back to the road. Pennies rub against nickels. Quarters jostle into dimes.

As I speed down M43, the vibrating change jingles. It almost sounds like it's singing. I set my hand on the small roof to quiet the noise. It's like that scene in "Jack and the Beanstalk" where the harp keeps crying for her master. But in the end, instead of recapturing her, the giant dies and Jack escapes. Sometimes, the thief gets away.

I arrive at Sarah A's a little early. Of course, I pulled into a nearby K-Mart before showing up, so I could count the money. This little house holds more than you'd think. I've got $118.95. There were a lot of crumpled-up dollar bills. Even some fives. Even a couple of tens. The donation is for a Belgian draft horse named Buttons who impaled himself on a fence post during a bad thunderstorm. I think if you've got enough money to own a big old horse and a fence, then you should be able to afford all the vet bills too. Actually, I'm telling myself whatever I can in order not to feel guilty about stealing this jar.

I carry the house under my arm. Once inside the alcove, I press the intercom button and dial Sarah A's number.

"It's Sarah T."

"You're early," Sarah A says. "Go walk around the block. I'm not ready."

I'm tempted to tell her that I'm carrying a big, transparent box full of money, but I don't want to ruffle her feathers.

"I'll come back in five minutes," I say.

"Give me ten."

Even the little intercom box emits a dial tone. I push the pound key to shut it up and walk back out to my car. As I sit, I can see Sarah B and Sarah C strolling down the sidewalk. Sarah B's face is hidden behind an enormous bubble. *Pop.* They walk past the Kalamazoo Art Institute and they don't even see me. Sarah B doesn't look like she's holding anything. She just has her purse slung over her neck. And Sarah C appears to be in possession of an animal. It looks like a cat. I think I know that cat. Sarah C is such a phony. Sometimes it takes the theft of your own life metaphor before a person wakes up and realizes who her *real* friends are. For the sake of self-preservation, I plan on being phony right back to her.

I beep my horn and they finally see me. They both wave. Before getting out of the car, I stuff the donation jar in an empty grocery bag. I feel so conspicuous toting an unconcealed, stolen box of money around.

"You guys look great!" I say.

"It's nice that you're back," Sarah C says.

I give her a big fake smile.

"Yeah," I say. "Cool cat. Did you steal it from a store?"

Sarah C shakes her head.

"Not exactly," Sarah C says, rubbing the cat under its fluffy chin.

"Is it tranquilized?" I ask.

I don't think I've ever seen a cat look so tired.

"No, it's naturally lethargic," Sarah C says. "Which is convenient, because it doesn't have the energy to scratch me."

I'd never thought of lethargy as a positive attribute before.

"Can you believe that one of us might get the boot?" Sarah B asks. She shifts her weight from her right leg to her left and fidgets with her purse strap. "Pirates used to kick other pirates out of their lives all the time. They would take the ousted pirate to a deserted island and abandon him without any provisions. Usually, all he got was a gun with one bullet."

"I doubt Sarah A will be providing us with firearms," Sarah C says.

"How come you know such much about pirates?" I ask.

This isn't the first time I've listened to Sarah B let loose random pirate trivia.

"Are you serious?" Sarah B asks. "Our culture has been obsessed with pirates for years. Haven't you noticed all the eye patches and puffy shirts floating around?"

"No," I say.

"She's right," Sarah C says. "America has reached a state of pirate saturation."

"I never even think about pirates," I say.

We start walking toward the Marlborough. The cat seems content to sleep in Sarah C's arms.

"Maybe we pulled off such great crimes that Sarah A will end up keeping all of us," I say.

Neither Sarah B or Sarah C respond to that comment.

"All this competition stresses me out," I say. "Once it's decided who the Sarahs are I hope we can get back to that place of just being friends and supporting each other."

"When were we ever at that place?" Sarah C asks.

"Being a Sarah has always been stressful," Sarah B says. "We're robbing stores, like, every week."

"Maybe we could move toward that place," I say.

"Maybe we could go to some ball games," Sarah B says. *Pop.*

"I'd go," I say.

"I don't foresee any changes of that nature looming on

the horizon," Sarah C says. "That's just not what the Sarahs have ever been about."

"I guess," I say. But for the first time, I'm thinking, *Why can't the Sarahs be about something like that?*

"Maybe if you think your life is like a hallway, you expect to see a few new doors appear. But I don't think in our case that's a realistic option. Sarah A picks the doors," Sarah C says. "In fact, she'll be picking another one this evening."

I almost stop walking. I'm shocked that Sarah C would bring up my hallway metaphor right now. First, she disses it. Then, she steals it. And now, she flings its shortcomings right in my face. She must be playing a head game with me.

"That's not really how I see life anymore," I say.

"Is it like a trail now?" Sarah C asks.

"No," I say. I try to think fast. What do I think life is like?

"You think life is like a hallway trail?" Sarah B asks.

"No, I think that life is like those moving sidewalks at airports. You're always going forward. And you've usually got baggage with you. And you've got to get around other people and their baggage. But in the end, you're always making progress. Even when you stop for a break, the sidewalk moves you along without you personally providing your own locomotion."

"A moving sidewalk?" Sarah B says. "What if you're handicapped?"

"Don't those things break down all the time?" Sarah C says.

"That's a lot like life too," I say. "No matter how hard you try to do everything the way it's supposed to be done, sometimes things get screwed up and you wind up having to declare yourself out of order."

I was aiming to pass along a deep message, but I think it came across as a little odd.

"What?" Sarah B asks.

"I think that metaphor is more interior than your last one. Some airports don't even have healthy air," Sarah C says.

"They don't?" Sarah B asks.

"Airborne illnesses are rampant. That's how my aunt thinks she contracted TB," Sarah C says.

"Your aunt has tuberculosis?" I ask, taking a step back.

"Relax. She lives in Colorado. I've only met her once and she was wearing a special mask," Sarah C says.

"That's so eighteen hundreds," Sarah B says.

"Actually, it was a neat-looking mask. It resembled a duck's bill," Sarah C says.

"We're going to be late," Sarah B says.

"Wait, before the gauntlet, I want you guys to know that I've always considered you my best friends. You two can always count on me," Sarah C says.

"Unless one of us gets knocked out," Sarah B says.

"Even if one of you gets bumped, you can still call me," Sarah C says. "I know this is a competition and that we're supposed to be ruthless. I mean, the guy phase is coming. And we all want to be part of it. But whatever happens, you still have my number."

"That's good to know," I say.

It's such a huge disappointment that the only Sarah who seems committed to preserving a friendship with me at this point is the one Sarah I know I can't trust and who may or may not have been exposed to a contagious and fatal disease.

I'm not sure how much Sarah C's offer matters, because as we climb the stairs to the Aberdeen's condo, I'm pretty sure that I'm not going to get voted out. I did my crime. And I've got money and an enormous horse victim to show for it. I just have this feeling that my crime is way better than anyone else's. What could possibly top it?

# Chapter 8

Sarah A swings open the door and the first thing I see is a drooling, tail-wagging, yellow dog.

"John Glenn," Sarah B coos, reaching down to pet his head. "Doesn't he look smart? He must have a high IQ. I bet if he wanted to, he could be an astronaut dog."

I get the feeling that Sarah B's comments are meant to flatter Sarah A. And from the smile on Sarah A's face, I think it's working. But as soon as John Glenn's snout moves toward Sarah B's crotch, she's much less enamored by his stunning IQ.

"No," she says firmly. "That's a very sensitive area."

Finally, Sarah A invites us all inside. I don't think John Glenn looks smart at all. In fact, after sniffing all our butts, I watch him trot to the bathroom and insert his head inside the toilet bowl. That dog is never going to orbit the earth.

"I see we have a cat," Sarah A says.

John Glenn returns to the entranceway with a damp muzzle.

"John Glenn, leave it. Good boy," Sarah A says.

What he lacks in intelligence, he makes up for in obedience. John Glenn freezes, while Sarah A leads us back to her bedroom. The condo feels cool and quiet. Sarah A's parents are rarely home. They're both orthodontists, and apparently, Kalamazoo is the bucktooth capital of the universe. Because it's Saturday and they're off fitting braces and gluing retainers into mouth after mouth. Their profession is reflected in their paint choices. The walls glisten a soft white enamel color. Even the half wall separating the kitchen from the living looks like a pristine incisor. Even though it's lucrative, I could never pursue a career in orthodontics or dentistry. I'm not even that comfortable looking inside my own mouth.

"Can't we hang out in the living room?" Sarah C asks.

There's a TV in there and that room has very comfortable couches.

"Vance is home," Sarah A says.

We all pick up our pace. Luckily, Sarah A's bedroom is an off-limits area. Ever since his brief stint in juvenile hall, that is something that the Aberdeens strictly enforce. Sarah A locks the door. Outside, I can hear John Glenn pacing in the hallway.

"Sit!" Sarah A yells at the door.

Even though she's probably talking to the dog, the other

two Sarahs and I immediately fold down to the floor. Sarah A claims her spot on her bed.

"Let's start with you, Sarah C. Tell us about your crime," Sarah A says.

"Well, my focus was on the crime's victim. I selected Sunny Gwyn. Let's face it, she's a negative-attention whore. She doesn't wear deodorant to choir for the sole reason that she wants people to smell her presence. She's constantly injuring her arms in PE, so she can wear Ace bandage wraps and slings and have people carry her books. And when she's on her period, she purposely bleeds through so that everybody will look at her butt. And I could go on."

"So what did you do?" Sarah A asks. She bites her bottom lip, and leans over her bed's precipice.

"I stole Digits, her precious eight-toed cat."

Sarah C lifts the mostly white cat up beneath its belly and we all applaud. I remember when Digits was just a kitten and Sunny brought him to sixth grade show-and-tell. We were all impressed by his multi-toed, deformed paw. Even the principal came to take a look. Later that year, Digits made the local news. Along with a parrot that could sing "La Bamba."

"How did you do it? I thought Digits was an indoor cat."

Sarah C nods and sets Digits down in her lap.

"Digits spends a lot of time in Sunny's bedroom window."

"You broke into her house?" I gasp.

"No, I slit her screen."

Sarah C pulls out a box cutter from her back pocket and rubs her thumb along its side, extending the sharp blade.

"Nice," Sarah A says. "Let's move on to me."

Sarah A points to three large paper sacks stacked at the foot of her bed.

"I went beyond the call of duty," Sarah A says. She flips her blonde hair over her shoulder and smiles. "I robbed the entire first floor of the Marlborough."

We all start cracking up. Sarah A is a riot.

"How?" Sarah B asks. "You did it by yourself?"

She lifts her eyebrows up into the middle of her forehead.

"Mostly," she says.

"Tell us everything," I say.

"Relax. I'm getting there."

Sarah A gathers the bags closer.

"First, I seduced the building's maintenance man."

She presses her upper arms against the outside of her breasts, squeezing her boobs together, making them look huge.

"After distracting him with my assets, I borrowed his keys."

"Didn't he notice that you took them?" I ask.

Sarah A rolls her eyes at me like I'm a dope for asking that question.

"Right before he left for the night, I popped into his office to ask him a generic question about space heaters. He went to get a pamphlet for me, and I took a spare set of keys," Sarah A says.

"So you didn't really use your boobs," Sarah C says.

"What's the difference? I got the keys," Sarah A says.

Sarah A reaches into the first bag and pulls out a deep red chenille scarf.

"The first floor occupants are mainly elderly people who don't like stairs. On Saturdays, a bunch of them attend a bingo tournament. So I helped myself."

From another bag, she pulls out an alabaster vase. And a small radio. And several boxes of Thin Mint Girl Scout cookies. And eight bars of Godiva chocolate. And a pair of gold hoop earrings. And a stack of DVDs.

"Do old people even have good DVDs?" Sarah C asks.

"I took the first four seasons of *The Rockford Files* and *Gunsmoke: The Director's Collection* and three DVDs of some show called *Emergency!*"

Sarah A sets them in a tidy stack.

"And I can always trade them in," she adds.

We nod. She really thinks things through.

"And I took this steam iron," Sarah A says.

She pulls a heavy silver iron from the last bag.

"Why?" Sarah B asks.

"It just looked really well-made," Sarah A says. "And who doesn't need a well-built iron?"

As I look at Sarah A's haul, it's clear that she's not in danger of being voted out. She stole a lot of interesting crap.

"Where are the keys now?" Sarah C asks.

"Well, the key ring actually had keys to the office. So after I was finished shopping, I put them back."

"You took some weird stuff. Why didn't you take their electronics?" Sarah B asks. "That's worth way more."

Sarah A shakes her head back and forth and puckers her mouth like she's disappointed in that question.

"I took things they wouldn't miss right away. Stuff they might think they just misplaced. Once they realize it's gone, they'll probably accuse people they know of taking it. Nobody thinks a robber is going to break into their swanky condo and walk off with their chocolate. No old person is going to call the police about a missing iron. And if they did, the cops wouldn't do anything about it. They'd think the old coot was senile."

We all start applauding. At first, it's just light and polite, but soon we're really getting into it. Slapping our hands together and hooting for Sarah A in true admiration. She stands up and takes a dramatic bow, her long hair falls to the floor, and Digits comes to life and lunges at it.

"Get it off!" Sarah A yells.

Really, Digits isn't being all that aggressive. He's just pawing at the bottom wisps.

"That furball will totally cause split ends," Sarah A says.

Sarah C scoops him up and sighs.

"He's just a cat."

"We'll dump him at the shelter tonight," Sarah A says.

I'm tempted to tell her not to. It seems like we've had our fun. Maybe we should take Digits back to Sunny. But I just think these things. I don't want to rock the boat.

"Do you hear that?" Sarah C asks.

We're all quiet. There's a whirring sound followed by a dull thud.

"It's Vance. He's probably taking apart the coffee table again," Sarah A says.

"He takes apart your coffee table? That seems destructive," Sarah C says.

"Furniture disassembly is the least of his problems," Sarah A says.

"But we're safe, right?" Sarah C asks.

"Sure. You know how guys are. They always need to be doing something with their hands," Sarah A says.

"I know what you mean. All my uncles smoke," Sarah B says. "And they're pretty chain about it."

The whirring sound stops. Then Sarah A flips on the stolen radio.

"Let's tune him out."

We all nod in agreement, but I'm sort of surprised that the Aberdeens allow their son to use power tools.

"You can't tune me out forever!" Vance yells.

"He has great hearing," Sarah C says.

"I thought you said he had a breakthrough," I say.

"You know how it is with the mentally deranged. Take one step forward. Take two steps back," Sarah A says.

"What do you think he wants to talk about?" Sarah B asks.

"Do I care? With all that's going on in my life, do I have the time to care?" Sarah A asks. "Besides, he's almost thirteen, he's still a *tween*. What could he possibly say that's of any value to me?"

"One day we'll have a meaningful conversation!" Vance yells. "We'll have a sustained dialog. One where we'll both be able to air our brains."

"Vance likes to use a lot of therapy-speak when he's not being kept in a mental health facility," Sarah A says. "He doesn't understand that he's just too crazy for me to love."

"Ouch," Sarah C says.

Sarah A reaches for her Roman Karbowski pillow. She places it in her lap, leans into it, and takes a big sniff. I glance around her room. I can see my Doyle Rickerson pillow plopped on the other side of her bed.

"Hormones make guys so complicated," Sarah A says.

"Women have hormones too," Sarah C says.

"But we're not complicated. We're normal," Sarah A says.

She inhales deeply into her pillow a few more times and then sits up straight. "Okay. Sarah B, what did you steal?"

Sarah B stands up and unzips her pants.

"Mine is kind of show-and-tell. I stole a Brazilian bikini wax."

The other Sarahs and I burst out laughing. Is she kidding?

Sarah B pulls her jeans down and then her underpants. Wow. No she's not. Next thing I know, I'm looking at her bare pubic area. It's very smooth and pink.

"Didn't that hurt?" I ask.

"Yeah."

"I thought they left a strip of hair," Sarah C says.

"No, that's optional."

"So after they waxed you, you ran out of the salon?" I ask.

"No. When I scheduled the wax, I went for the cheapest person. I figured she'd be the least experienced. Why else would she charge the least? So, when she got to the final strip, I started screaming as she pulled it off. I told her she took some skin."

"So you just complained and got the wax for free?" Sarah C asks.

"No, I told them that I was using Retin-A."

None of us say anything. We don't know why that's important.

"You're not supposed to get a bikini wax if you're taking

Accutane or using Retin-A. They increase skin fragility and that can cause tearing when the wax is removed."

"Gross," I say.

Sarah B pulls her underwear and jeans back up and sits down again.

"Yeah, but I'm not taking that stuff. I only said that because it made them liable for any tearing. I could sue them for waxing me without asking me the proper questions."

Sarah B has this proud look on her face and her smile is totally big, but I'm not sure that she actually committed a crime. If you still have to retain a lawyer to fully accomplish your theft, then you didn't even complete it, right? It's like partial robbery. I totally think she might be going home. But I don't say anything.

"I also took these," she says.

She reaches into her purse and pulls out six bottles of nail polish, three lipsticks, a pumpkin-scented candle, and a gift certificate.

"I stole all this stuff, but they gave me the certificate for my next waxing. But anyone can use it."

She hands the certificate to Sarah A, who takes it and smiles politely. It's hard to figure out how Sarah A feels about this.

"It's for an eyebrow wax, too," Sarah B says.

"They use the same wax on your face that they use down there?" I ask.

"Yeah, but it's pretty safe. I mean, I did hear about a woman suing a salon in New York because she got herpes in her eye, but that could've been a fluke. And seriously, isn't there a risk involved with anything that's worth doing?"

I nod like I agree, but really, I'm thinking, *Holy crap, it's possible to get herpes in your eye?*

"Aren't you worried about ingrown hairs?" Sarah C asks.

"No. They gave me special lotion to use."

"That was really interesting," Sarah A says. "I have to hand it to you, for a tomboy, you did a nice job thinking outside the box. Well done."

I'm surprised to hear Sarah A say this. Maybe she's just trying to build suspense. Because it's clear to me who should be voted out. I think it's clear to everyone. Finally, Sarah A turns to me.

"It's so good to have you back," Sarah A says. "And keep in mind, if you need to use the bathroom, just go. You don't even need to ask. We'll understand."

I force a smile.

"Thanks," I say.

I clear my throat and pull the Plexiglas house out of the grocery sack.

"I stole this from a 7-Eleven just out of town. It's got $118.95. Isn't that wild? I mean, that's so much money."

Suddenly, things feel very weird. Nobody is saying anything.

They're just all looking at me like they're stunned. They must be really impressed.

"I can't believe you did that," Sarah A says.

"Well, I know it's pretty bold of me, but I really want to be a Sarah. I felt it was a pretty good crime."

I smile big. But nobody else is smiling back.

"That's a shelter horse. His name is Buttons," Sarah C says. "We made those donation jars last week."

"That's impossible. How can it be this full? Nobody in this town is that generous," I say.

"We poured the old change into the new box. We thought it would encourage people to donate more. Sarah C said it was a fact that people don't like to be the first ones to put money in the jar," Sarah B says.

"I don't know if it's a fact," Sarah C says.

"Sarah B and Sarah C each put in ten-dollar bills," Sarah A says. "I even put in a five!"

"At harvest time, Buttons pulls sleighs for hayrides at orchards," Sarah B says.

"I didn't know about that," I say.

"Yeah, they let terminally ill kids ride the sleighs for free," Sarah A says.

"I just didn't know."

"Basically, you stole from us," Sarah A says.

"No, I stole from Buttons. From the shelter."

Nobody answers me and nobody will look me in the eye. Sarah C focuses on Digits and pets him behind the ears. Sarah B looks at her lap and scratches her crotch. And Sarah A has her eyes closed and is breathing really slowly.

"Real crimes have victims, Sarah T, but *we* should never be your victims. Your fellow Sarahs should never have to pay for your crimes."

"I'll return it," I say. "I'll think of another crime." I'm starting to feel very panicked.

"It's too risky to return it. Somebody could see you. You need to send a cashier's check to the shelter for the amount you stole."

"Okay, I'll take the money to the bank and cash it in."

"No. The donation jar stays with us. Why should we have to pay for your mistake?"

Admittedly, it doesn't seem fair that I have to come up with $118.95 to send to the shelter while Sarah A gets to keep the jar, but I'm willing to do whatever is necessary.

"I'll do it. I just don't want to be voted out."

Neither of the other two Sarahs are looking at me.

"This isn't a small thing, Sarah T."

I can feel tears forming.

"You know, letters of recommendation are pretty important for college. You just put all of that in jeopardy by what you did. Getting into the University of Michigan is tough. You get that, right?"

"I do. I know. We need to be well-rounded. We need school interests and charity interests and the shelter was our charity interest. I get it."

"Do you think Mr. King will write us letters if he finds out we stole from the shelter? That we robbed from a maimed, kindhearted Belgian draft horse? Your fellow Sarahs and I have volunteered—have cleaned up after yapping and shitting dogs—for two years to get a good letter. Do you understand how big this is?"

"I get that now, but I didn't know. When I stole it, I didn't have a clue."

"As a Sarah, you can never be clueless. Ever. You've always got to think of who you're representing. It's completely unacceptable to put us all in jeopardy like that."

"I didn't know." Which is the truth. I'd never really thought too deeply about how anybody would be affected by my crime.

Sarah A is standing now, walking toward the door.

"Well, you know now. I'm sorry to say this, but this is the worst crime."

I wait for one of the other two Sarahs to possibly say something in my defense, but neither do. I stand up.

"Is this it?" I ask. "It is over?"

"I believe it is," Sarah A says.

I'm stunned. I guess I have to leave. It would be weird and desperate if I didn't, right? Sarah A turns the doorknob and I'm ready to walk out and go home, but I can't. Why? I'd like to say it's because a newfound strength is building inside of me and for the first time in my life I don't want to retreat. But that's not it.

Vance is blocking my path. He's standing in the doorway, with his eyes opened so wide that they look a little like golf balls. He's applied a liberal amount of hair gel and teased his coif into a stiff Mohawk. He's also applied thick lines of black shoe polish to his face, presumably to look like some kind of warrior.

At first, I think it's comical. But then he shoves me out of the way and lifts a power screwdriver over his head. He slips it into the door's upper brass hinge and commences unscrewing it.

"My brother really needs to leave," Sarah A says. "This is an off-limits area."

"Vance," I say.

"No, do not talk to him. Do not!" Sarah A says.

Sarah A and I back up. Sarah B and Sarah C climb onto Sarah A's bed.

We all watch the door fall down. He tosses the screws onto the carpet.

"Sarah, we are going to have a dialog," Vance says. "No borders. No boundaries. No walls."

Across the hall, I can see that he's removed the bathroom door from its frame too. I wonder if he's removed every bedroom, closet, and bathroom door in the condo.

"Sarah C, maybe we should put Digits in a drawer," Sarah A says.

Sarah C nods and hands Sarah A the cat. When Sarah A reaches into the drawer, she sets Digits inside with her right hand and pulls out a handful of silverware with her left. She hands it to me. They're butter knives.

"Take one and pass them around," Sarah A says. "If he's being serious, you've got to defend yourself. Don't let him disfigure your face!"

Sarah A keeps a knife, and I take one and hand one each to Sarah B and Sarah C. They eagerly take them. But I still have two knives. I drop the extra one on the carpet and hurry over to the bed to join Sarah B and Sarah C.

"No, no," Sarah C yells.

I watch as Vance runs into the room and scoops up the extra butter knife. Then he starts releasing awful screams and stabbing at the air.

"What were you thinking?" Sarah A asks.

I shrug.

"Maybe you should just have a conversation with him," Sarah C says.

"Yeah," Sarah B says.

"It's something to consider," I add.

"Are you nuts? Are you all high? Do you want something bad to happen to me?" Sarah A asks. "Seriously, how can anyone converse with that?"

Vance punches the knife in the air and screams. The veins in his neck bulge.

"I want a dialog!" he yells. "I will not be ignored!"

# Chapter 9

My first instinct is to reattach the door. Where did Vance set the power screwdriver? I glance around, but then I realize that I don't really know how to operate a power screwdriver. Plus, none of the other Sarahs make any moves toward the fallen door. I decide it's best just to do whatever they do. All four of us huddle on the bed. Then we commence releasing anguished screams.

We aren't screaming words or anything. We're just making high-pitched sounds. Personally, I think we sound like a flock of startled birds. Maybe seagulls or pelicans. At one point, I hear Vance screaming too. But I'm wrong. He's not. It's just the Sarahs. We're freaking out.

"Get over here and talk to me!" Vance says.

"Holy shit!" Sarah A says. "Run!"

We all jump off the bed and start racing around pell-mell. For some reason, none of us leave Sarah A's room. We keep running around inside it, sort of pinballing off the walls.

"You're insane!" Sarah A yells.

For a second I think she's yelling at me, but her comments are directed at her maniac brother, Vance. This is good. She's finally talking to him. Let the dialog begin.

"Don't try to dismiss my feelings by making me look like a psycho," Vance says.

"You think I'm making you look like a psycho?" Sarah A says. "Check out a mirror."

I must not be in very good shape, because all this running and excitement fatigues my thigh muscles and turns them all rubbery. How much more actual running do we have to do? Sarah A hasn't even led us out of her room. How serious is this? Are we really in imminent danger? It's not like we're being threatened with steak knives.

Breathless and red-faced, eventually all the Sarahs stop running around and gather next to Sarah A's closet in the corner. Tragically, it's the kind of closet that doesn't have a door. You just walk into it. It has zero potential for operating as a bunker.

"Talk to me!" Vance yells. "Get over here and talk to me!"

He's standing on top of her bed, holding the knife firmly in his right hand.

"No," Sarah A says.

"But I'm your brother," Vance says.

"He's a giant wad of psychiatric problems," Sarah A says.

"Somebody needs to put him in a box and study him, just like a rat."

Sarah B shakes her head back and forth and smacks her gum.

"I don't think PETA lets people do that anymore. Not even scientists."

"Scientists can absolutely still do that," Sarah C says, her red hair streaming around her shoulders in a wild mess. "They're growing two-headed rats in labs across the country and then conducting experiments, like, only feeding one of the heads. You just have to put the rats in a big enough box."

Soon, Sarahs B and C are so busy talking about the ethical treatment of rats, mainly focusing on the most humane-sized box in which to raise two-headed, mutated rats, that they're completely missing the stabbing. So I point it out.

"Look at Vance!" I yell.

"He's lost it," Sarah A says. "He's on a one-way street toward a straitjacket."

Vance is kneeling on Sarah A's bed. He's thrusting his butter knife blade into my Doyle Rickerson pillow over and over again. I didn't think a butter knife could pierce anything, especially not a cotton shirt *and* a pillow. But Vance strikes my Doyle pillow with such force that he actually punctures the mattress below. Feathers swim through the air.

"Maybe you will end up dating Sal Rodriguez," Sarah C says.

Each time Vance punches the knife down, he releases a grunt. This rhythmic pumping goes on and on. As I stand watching, I'm struck by a weird thought. Maybe Doyle Rickerson's pheromones have triggered some sort of psychotic break. How powerful are pheromones anyway?

After assaulting the pillow, Vance continues his attack on Sarah A's bed. Suddenly, things feel very scary. I mean, this kid is out of control.

"Mom and Dad will institutionalize you," Sarah A yells. "You won't even get sunlight."

Vance stops stabbing her comforter and stares at her. His brown eyes don't look like they belong to a tween in the midst of a psychotic rage. Instead of looking crazy, his eyes just look sad. Standing there in the corner of Sarah A's room, I can totally sympathize with him. He's all alone. Like a twig. And I know exactly what that feels like. It's like everything in the world can hurt you. It's like you're not even sure if you exist, because you barely feel real. He stops knifing the bed and stares at Sarah A.

"Why do you hate me?" he asks.

"I don't hate you," Sarah C says. "I can almost empathize with you."

"No, my sister, Sarah Aberdeen, why do *you* hate me?"

Sarah A bites on her bottom lip. "I think you're a freak. And you embarrass me."

I'm tempted to interject and try to steer the discourse toward a less insulting tone, but I don't really know how to do that. I glance at Sarah B and Sarah C. They're each holding their butter knives, blade out, in Vance's direction.

"I bet if Mom and Dad had never adopted you," Vance says, "that my life would be better."

"Maybe," Sarah A says, tossing her hair over her shoulder. "Your birth hasn't exactly been a boon to my life. I bet if Mom knew how emotionally retarded you'd turn out, she never would have had you."

That's when I notice the change in his eyes. Yes, they're still sad, but they're also enraged. Now he's the one who sounds like a bird, like a giant pterodactyl. Or at least how they sound in movies when they attack their prey. Emitting this weird cry, he lunges toward Sarah A. But since we're all grouped together into a single Sarah clump, he's swinging his knife toward all of us.

"Run! Run! Protect your face!" Sarah A yells.

She reiterates this survival tip like she's had experience. All the Sarahs flee the room, running one right after the other. Of course, I'm the last Sarah. How is it that I'm always the Sarah bringing up the rear?

We race to the big open living room.

"Split up!" Sarah A yells.

All the Sarahs pick a corner. Personally, I hate this idea. I feel very vulnerable in my corner near the fireplace. It would make sense for all the Sarahs to attempt an escape from the condo, but Vance has stacked all the unhinged doors in a large pile, effectively blocking the main entrance. I've never met anyone so intent on having a dialog.

Vance has stopped running. Breathing heavily, he plods down the hallway toward the living room. There's a white foam forming around his mouth. I've never seen a person create mouth froth before. His mohawk has tipped to the left, curling over like a cresting wave. The war markings he drew on his face have smeared. The black smudges make him appear dirty and strange. Vance Aberdeen looks like somebody I don't even know.

"Look at yourself," Sarah A says. "No wonder you don't have any friends."

I jerk my gaze toward Sarah A. She should really stop egging him on. I mean, what's the point?

"You ruined my life," he says.

"Whatever," Sarah A says. "This whole dialog is pretty lame."

"I hate you," Vance says.

He lifts the knife over his head and runs at her. I duck my head down and close my eyes. I also drop my knife and plug my ears. But I don't realize that I've dropped my one piece of cutlery until I hear it clatter onto the ceramic tiles that line the fireplace.

"Stay armed!" Sarah C yells at me.

But it's too late. I'm totally ill-suited for knife battles. I keep my ears plugged and squint at the awful situation unfolding in front of me.

Interestingly, the other Sarahs react much differently. None of them retreat. I watch as Sarah C and Sarah B move toward Vance. While Sarah A throws her arms up to protect her face, Sarah C kicks Vance behind his knees. And as he's falling, Sarah B grabs his legs. Somehow, she does this without letting go of her knife. But her butter knife isn't the one I'm most worried about.

I watch Vance plunge his bright blade toward Sarah A's crossed arms. Then, Sarah A quickly pivots her body, and Vance falls down onto the carpet chin-first. His face paint leaves a big skid mark where he fell. Sarah C sits on his back. Sarah B continues to hold his legs. Sarah A kicks him three times in his side.

"Don't make any sudden moves," Sarah C says. "I've got a box cutter in my pants."

Vance releases a depressed moan. Then I hear this loud crash and I think that an earthquake must have struck Kalamazoo, because it sounds like the Marlborough Building is falling down.

"Mom! He tried to kill us with a knife."

In an attempt to enter her home, Mrs. Aberdeen has

opened her front door and sent the tower of doors tumbling every which way into the foyer. She shoves hard to get the front door to swing fully open.

"I don't believe it," Mrs. Aberdeen gasps.

"I hate her!" Vance screams. "I wish she were dead."

I guess he is sort of stupid, because this is not the time to be airing those particular feelings.

"Girls, stay on him. Mr. Aberdeen is coming up the stairs."

Vance wriggles beneath the other three Sarahs, but I don't think that he's sincere in his escape attempt. I bet he's doing it because he thinks that's what he ought to do. I mean, that's what I'd even do.

"You should see my room, Mom. He's a savage. He stabbed my new bed to shreds. And he's totally stained the living room carpet with shoe polish."

Mrs. Aberdeen looks very pale. She lets her handbag fall to the floor as she approaches her girl-clobbered son.

"Why did you do this?" she asks.

"I hate her!" he says.

He's crying now, squashed by the weight of the Sarahs and probably his own shame. Like a reluctant tube of nearly empty toothpaste, it's as if the pressure of the Sarahs is forcing the grunts and sobs out of him. His mohawk has splintered into several sections. It has no upright integrity left whatsoever.

"I hate her!"

"Stop saying that. She's your sister."

"Not by blood! I'm just unlucky!"

Sarah A makes a pained face, like she's actually been wounded by his comment. "How can you say that?" she asks.

"Vance, stop it!" Mrs. Aberdeen says.

"What's going on?" Mr. Aberdeen yells.

Standing in the doorway, he looks like a character in a sitcom—backlit, bald, and clueless. He hurries inside the condo, his belly bouncing as he runs.

"He attacked the girls with a bowie knife," Mrs. Aberdeen says.

I'm tempted to point out that the attack was executed with a butter knife that Sarah A and I provided. And that we all had butter knives too. But I stay mum. When somebody gets worked up into hysterics, it takes a lot of energy and carefully chosen words to deflate the situation. I just don't have it in me.

"He tried to take out my eyes," Sarah A says. "My fellow Sarahs are the only thing that saved me."

Mr. Aberdeen picks up the four scattered butter knives and hands them to me, like I'm some sort of knife receptacle.

"Thank you," I say, grouping their handles together like a bouquet.

Mr. Aberdeen steps on the back of Vance's hand and pries

the fifth knife out of his grip. Mr. Aberdeen gives me that one too. The metal feels warm. Like it's been lying in the sun. "Sarah, you need to leave," Mr. Aberdeen says.

He's talking to Sarah A and he sounds very sad. Like a man who's finally agreed to surrender.

"But I didn't assault anybody!" Sarah A says.

"We need to sort this out. Get your things. Go stay at Sarah Trestle's for the night."

"Kick him out, not me. I belong here!"

"Sarah Louisa Aberdeen, take some things and spend the night at Sarah Trestle's. Your mother will call the Trestles right now to make the arrangements."

"And Sarah Trestle," Mrs. Aberdeen says to me, "You're going to have to take your dog home. I'm sympathetic to the fact that you want a dog, and to your mother's severe allergies concerning dander, but we just can't keep John Glenn here anymore. You understand, don't you?"

"I told my parents about how your mom wouldn't let you keep John Glenn, about how I'd take care of him for you for a few months," Sarah A says.

"Our condo rules are strict. If we get caught with a dog, we'll be fined," Mrs. Aberdeen says.

This is so bizarre. Why would she lie to her parents about John Glenn being my dog? Why wouldn't she just tell them that she wanted a dog?

"Okay," I say, nodding in agreement. Because really, what am I supposed to say?

"I'll call your mother and explain everything," Mrs. Aberdeen says.

"You don't have to explain about John Glenn. I should probably do that," I say.

Mr. Aberdeen's face is as red as a cherry tomato. He's gotten Vance to his feet and has a tight grip on his arm.

"Get your things, Sarah. Go to the Trestles'. We'll sort this out soon enough," he says.

All the Sarahs escort Sarah A back to her room. I glance over my shoulder and watch Mr. Aberdeen shake Vance's arm. The light tugging makes him wobble. A part of me feels like I should go in there and explain how everything really happened. But not a very big part of me.

"Sarah T, do I need to bring my own towel?" Sarah A asks.

"No," I say.

"How about my flip-flops? Does your shower or tub have fungus?"

"No," I say.

"Can you think of anything I'm forgetting?" she asks.

"John Glenn," I say.

"Yeah, where is he?" Sarah A asks.

Sarah A and I follow a faint panting noise into the bathroom. Vance used John Glenn's own leash to tie him to the toilet's reservoir tank. John Glenn seems unfazed. He's no stranger to toilets.

"Does he have any treats or toys?" I ask.

"No," Sarah A says.

"What about dog food?" I ask.

"There's a big bag of Alpo underneath the kitchen sink."

I almost frown. She feeds my dog Alpo? I don't know how I feel about that. I always figured if I had a dog I'd feed him an all-natural dog food like Breeder's Choice. Sarah A and I walk back to her bedroom and John Glenn merrily trots behind us.

The other Sarahs are cleaning up the remains of our contest. Sarah B puts all her nail polishes and other loot inside a sack for Sarah A. Sarah C has the stolen donation jar concealed in its original grocery bag. Sarah B and Sarah C hand it all over to Sarah A. She doesn't bother to say thanks.

"Am I forgetting anything else?" Sarah A asks.

"Didn't somebody shove Digits inside your sock drawer?" I ask.

"God, I almost forgot," Sarah A laughs, smacking the heel of her hand to her forehead.

"I'll take him to the shelter tonight," Sarah C says.

"Oh, let's hold off," Sarah A says. "Let's see how interesting things can get."

"I guess I can keep him at my house," Sarah C says. "We already have a cat. So I've got the basic feline necessities."

"Whatever," Sarah A says.

"What about your Roman Karbowski pillow?" Sarah B asks.

"Sarah T, can you grab that for me?" Sarah A asks.

"What about my Doyle pillow?" I ask.

"That thing will forever be associated with the time my brother tried to stab me," Sarah A says. "It stays."

So we all walk out of Sarah A's room. Mrs. Aberdeen is kneeling on the floor where Vance fell. She has the phone in one hand and a scrub brush in the other. I don't see Vance or Mr. Aberdeen. Once we're out of the condo, the other two Sarahs wave good-bye and break off, heading in a different direction. Sarah A and I return their waves and climb into my car. John Glenn hops into the backseat like he knows that he belongs there.

"You should probably put Roman Karbowski in your trunk," Sarah A says.

I get back out of the car and set the pillow in my trunk. When I climb back inside, Sarah A appears very calm. She's yawning. It's almost as if what just happened inside her condo was not the freakiest and most dramatic moment ever. I had no idea she was *this* resilient.

"Well, you're one lucky coward," Sarah A says.

I start my car. I guess that's what you call a backhanded compliment.

"I've been displaced. This changes everything," Sarah A says.

I'd assumed that my lackluster performance during the Vance attack had cemented my ousting from the Sarahs. Everyone seemed so upset about the Belgian draft horse situation, especially the part about me stealing from my fellow Sarahs. And then I didn't help subdue Vance in any way when he launched his final assault on our leader. And I was the one who unintentionally provided him with a knife. If I were the head Sarah, I think I'd even kick my own butt out of the group.

"It's not like I can knock you out of the group when I have to shack up at your house with you."

"I guess," I say.

But really, I'm thinking that she totally could.

"Consider it probation. If you can do something to redeem yourself, we'll let the other stuff slide. It'll be like water under the bridge."

I nod. But the phrase "water under the bridge" makes my heartbeat quicken. It reminds me of a scene in a movie in which a killer dumps a body wrapped in a shower curtain into a river from the great height of an overpass and says, "You're just water under the bridge."

I feel real queasy. Like I could throw up. Instead, I swallow hard and force the fear and vomit back down inside of me. John Glenn barks.

"Open up the moonroof," Sarah A says.

I do.

She reaches her left arm up through the open roof, so the night air can blow through her fingers. I thought she wanted me to open it for John Glenn.

"What's wrong? You should be so happy. I'm going to let you worm your way back into your old spot," Sarah A says.

She brings her arm back inside the car and touches the nape of my neck with her cold hand. It feels reptilian and creepy and makes me want to scream. My old spot. It should be exactly what I want right now. But I have mixed feelings about it. Let's face it, I'm the grunt. It's my job to take needless amounts of punishment and grief and shit. Sarah A pulls her hand away from my neck and it begins to turn warm again. She smiles at me. I smile back. Picturing my life without the Sarahs is like picturing myself without legs. How would my life work?

"I *am* so happy," I say, pulling into my possum-free driveway.

I park the car. John Glenn is panting in my right ear. I have this feeling that Sarah A will be staying with us for more than a night. I crack open my door. Sarah A is already striding to my house. I take John Glenn's leash. Ready or not. Let the worming begin.

# Chapter 10

"I don't quite get it. How again does having a dog help you get into college?" my mother asks. She's placed a wet washcloth over her nose and mouth in an attempt to filter out any possible dander that might be floating through the air.

"This is John Glenn," I say. "It will look great on my entrance essay to talk about all the important work I do with him."

"Important work?" she asks. "What kind of work does a dog do in Kalamazoo?"

"We'll visit sick people," I say.

"And that requires a dog?" she asks.

I was planning on introducing John Glenn to my mother after breakfast. But when a dog sees his first deer, leaping around outside your bedroom window, apparently he likes to vocalize his enthusiasm.

My father seemed somewhat okay with the idea of introducing a canine to our household.

"He looks like a champ," he said, as John Glenn barreled

down the hallway, barking at the long-gone deer on the other side of our living room windows. "He doesn't have any medical problems, does he? Hip dysplasia? Tumors?"

"Oh, he's in terrific shape," Sarah A said.

"I'm willing to have a dialog about this," my father said as he left for work.

"A dialog?" my mother said. "What do you mean a dialog?"

But my father didn't elaborate. He winked and left the four of us—me, my mother, Sarah A, and John Glenn—to further hash this out. At which time, my mother drenched a washcloth and attached it to her face. Just like open-winged, gold-plated eagles symbolizing glory perched atop flagpoles across America, or the Liberty Bell hanging in its showcase in Philadelphia, representing, well, liberty, I think my mother placed the cloth on her face to create a visible emblem of her dog protest. She stands for doglessness. Also, wearing the washcloth makes her look sympathetic.

"In a year you'll be in college. This is no time to bring a dog into your life," my mother says.

I'm so tired that I release a yawn. My mother takes this the wrong way and wags a finger at me.

"This is serious!" she says. "I have allergies!"

"I'm partly to blame," Sarah A says. "I told her I thought that volunteer work would be a good fit for her. She has such a big heart."

My mother pulls the washcloth away from her face. "I can't believe you'd just bring a dog home," she says.

"It felt like my only option," I say. "Please, Mom. Let's give it a week and see."

"See what?" my mother asks.

"See if your allergies act up," I say.

My mother's eyes don't look red. She hasn't wheezed at all. I think her problems with animals might be rooted in psychological rather than physiological issues.

"What do you plan on feeding it?" she asks.

"Breeder's Choice," I say.

"And how do you plan on purchasing it?" she asks.

"Dad seems on board with the whole dog operation," I say. "He said he'd pick up provisions after work."

"Not only do I feel double-teamed," she says. "I feel manipulated."

John Glenn pads into the living room and looks out the window on to the lake. He makes a whining noise.

"I think he wants out," Sarah A says.

"Then get him out! Don't let him pee on the rug!" my mother yells. "Out! Out!"

I take John Glenn by the collar and lead him outside. Sarah A follows me.

"That went really well," she says. "Your mom went from pissed to disillusioned to acceptance in less than five minutes."

John Glenn inspects the perimeter of our property, lifting his leg up whenever he encounters a tree.

"I don't want to manipulate her," I say.

"That's all part of life," Sarah A says. "You'll get used to it."

"I don't know if I want to get used to it," I say.

Sarah A walks toward my bedroom window and with the toe of her sneaker clears leaves from a stepping stone.

"Nice rock," she says.

"We took it last summer from Lowe's," I say.

"We did? It looks so heavy," she says.

"It weighs sixteen pounds. We loaded it in the bottom of a cart and wheeled it right out of the store. We were going for a record. The heaviest thing we'd stolen before that was a flashlight. Don't you remember?" I ask.

"Did we only take one?" Sarah A asks.

"No, we stole two. Sarah C took one home and I took the other," I say.

"Why didn't I take one?" she asks.

"Because you don't have a yard," I say. "You live in a condo."

"Yeah, I like what's carved into it," Sarah A says, bending down and tracing her finger along the thick blocky letters etched into the stone.

*"Life is not measured by the breaths we take, but by the moments that take our breath away."* She stands, sighs, and

in a gesture of mock-swooning clutches her heart.

"I'm thinking about giving it away," I say.

"I see your point. As far as rocks go, it's sort of lame and Hallmarky," Sarah A says.

"That's not why," I say. "It makes me feel weird."

"Because it's lame?"

"No, because I stole it. Every other thing I've stolen I keep in my room. I hide them away. This is so public. I guess I feel like it's too public."

"Are you being serious?" Sarah A asks.

"Yeah."

Using her shoe, she drags some cut grass and leaves back over the stone's gray surface. "You need to get over it. For the guy phase to work, we've got a lot more stuff to steal. If you hang on to all of it and stick it in your room, not only will you end up weighed down by a gigantic load of meaningless crap, but your bedroom area might turn Doyle skittish. You need a place with ambience, like mine."

I ignore the guy angle altogether. My room is big. It can hold a lot more stolen goods. But *meaningless crap*? Every time we steal something, I feel like I'm taking a huge risk. I don't want Sarah A to characterize our hauls in a way that diminishes their importance.

"Meaningless? I've still got the first thing we ever stole," I say.

"What's that?"

"The lip gloss. Seventh grade. It's watermelon flavored. Don't you remember?" I ask.

"No. You've still got lip gloss from seventh grade? Doesn't that stuff go bad?"

"It's empty. I keep the container," I say.

"For what?"

"For the memory."

Sarah A leans her body against my house and rests her head against my bedroom window. "Sarah T, you're freaking me out. You're like this woman I saw on a daytime TV show who couldn't throw anything away. Not even her tampons. *After* she used them. With the sort of problems you have, I'm afraid to put you anywhere within a thousand feet of Doyle Rickerson."

"I'm not anything like that," I say. "I totally throw my used tampons away. But the stuff we've taken, that's different. It matters." Doyle Rickerson isn't what's at stake for me right now. I'm concerned about what Sarah A thinks of me and my tendency to hold on to our loot.

"By now, most of what we've stolen is trash," Sarah A says. "A used lipstick container should be thrown in the garbage."

"Lip *gloss*," I say. "It's the first thing we ever stole."

"It's not the first thing *I* ever stole." Sarah A pushes herself away from my house and walks toward a small oak. She grabs its trunk with one hand, like it's a pole, and begins walking around it in circles.

"It's not?" I ask.

She circles and circles. Her grip on the tree rubs off the dry bark. It sounds like rain as it falls into the grass.

"You think I waited until the seventh grade before I started ripping stuff off?"

"I guess I did," I say.

"Yeah. That's not how it happened," Sarah A says.

"So, how did it happen?" I ask.

Sarah A stops her circular plodding. "Wait. Where's John Glenn?"

I look around. He's gone.

"Would he try to run back to your condo?" I ask.

"How would I know? I don't have a dog brain," Sarah A says. She lets go of the tree and brushes her hand against her shirt.

"John Glenn! John Glenn!" I yell.

I run down the hill toward Asylum Lake. Sarah A doesn't follow me. When I get to the main trail I can see John Glenn several yards ahead of me on the dirt path sniffing a painted turtle, Michigan's state reptile.

"John Glenn! Come here!" I yell.

John Glenn walks toward me with his golden head lowered.

"Bad dog," I say. "You can't run away from home."

"You should probably put him on a leash before you take him outside!" Sarah A calls from the top of the hill.

"Yeah," I say.

"He doesn't seem to respect limits with you," Sarah A says.

I don't say anything. I don't know if that's true. John Glenn and I take a shortcut, weaving through maples, oaks, and tall grass to reach the top of the hill.

"Having a dog is turning out to be a big responsibility," I say.

"You'll adapt," Sarah A says. "That's one of your best qualities. You're an adapter."

I reach the top of the hill and my thighs burn. I'm breathing heavy. I let go of John Glenn's collar and he races toward the back door.

"Look at him. He seems right at home," I say.

"What's that supposed to mean?" Sarah A says. "He was happy when he lived at my place too. He's just a dog, Sarah T. He'll love whoever feeds him and be happy anywhere he lives."

We're standing side by side and, with her shoulder, she gives me a rough nudge, almost knocking me down.

"Ouch," I say.

"I'm sorry. I didn't mean to hurt you," Sarah A says.

I watch her walk to the back door and open it. John Glenn rushes inside. A breeze stirs the holly bushes beside my house.

I rub my shoulder. She didn't nudge me that hard. It's just that I wasn't expecting it. I take a deep breath. It must be weird for Sarah A to be booted out of her own house. I bet being displaced like this makes her think about when her mother left. It's probably harder for her than I realize. Last night, she wasn't even given a choice. Her parents told her—demanded—that she pack her things and leave. I bet it made her feel helpless. I imagine it made her feel a lot like a twig.

# Chapter 11

Dawn has cracked open another blue day. And after sharing my bedroom, my bathrobe, my toothpaste, and my parents with Sarah Aberdeen for a whole week, it's become clear to me that this arrangement will continue for a second week. At least, that's the time line I overheard Mrs. Aberdeen giving my parents. Apparently, that's the soonest Vance could be placed in a wilderness camp for troubled teens located in the Utah desert. I guess there was a waiting list. America must be overflowing with screwed-up teenagers. It sort of makes me afraid to ever camp in the western wilderness. That place sounds like it's crawling with nutso delinquents.

Sarah A hopes Vance gets mortally wounded by a Gila monster. Actually, her exact words were, "I hope that shithead gets set upon by a Gila monster. They're poisonous, you know. And totally found in Utah."

But I told her that outcome was pretty unlikely, because

I'm a faithful viewer of Animal Planet, and I've never heard of a Gila monster killing anyone.

"Considering the rugged terrain, Vance could possibly be attacked by a cougar," I said. *"Possibly."*

Sarah A didn't like hearing my dissenting point of view.

"It's more than possible," she shot back.

"You're right," I said, smiling. I'm not an idiot. I know when to shift gears.

I have to admit that all this conversation is the best part about having Sarah A as a temporary roommate. We're bonding. Before we go to bed at night, we talk a lot. Usually, we discuss what Sarah A thinks of the world. This requires a lot of active listening on my part. I don't know why, but I think I'm more interested in what Sarah A thinks about local and global issues than what I think about them. I know she's flawed. I know she's far from perfect. But I admire her. She's so strong. She doesn't let anybody mess with her. And when she believes something, she's unwavering in her commitment to her own ideas. She's solid. And it's awesome.

For instance, she's not afraid to hold a minority opinion. Last night, I found out that she likes baby harp seals, but despises whales.

"I could care less if Japan harpoons every last one of those blubbery beasts," she said.

So I said, "Seals make way better stuffed animals."

And she said, "Seals rock."

And I said, "Absolutely. If there's two things the world can live without, it's whales and terrorists."

And she said, "I hope they both go extinct."

And I said, "Maybe the terrorists will start killing off the whales. Or vice versa."

And Sarah A made a noise like she was swallowing, which I think meant she agreed.

It's clear Sarah A and I are getting closer. She's sharing more and more of her criminal ideas with me. It's like she was born with the perfect crooked brain to commit crimes. She's figured out ways to override the credit card function in vending machines so that in addition to getting free cans of soda and bags of chips, change will actually shoot out at her.

And she knows where the city has recently planted expensive ornamental plum trees. She's created an elaborate plan to uproot and sell them. Though, she hasn't quite ironed out who the customer base will be or how we'll transport the delicate and leafy contraband. She's hoping to use the Internet and a Ryder truck. I really admire her. She thinks big. She isn't afraid of her own ambition or imagination.

John Glenn comes to my bedside and whimpers to be let out.

"I'll take him out," Sarah A says.

"Cool," I say. "Don't forget his leash."

When she comes back she sits down next to me and presses her cold hands against my neck.

"You're lazy," Sarah A says.

"It's summer," I say. "I enjoy sleeping in."

"Do you know what I like most about staying with you?" Sarah A asks.

I roll onto my back and stare up at her. Even without makeup, she's the prettiest Sarah.

"Our talks?" I ask.

"No. You have basically no supervision whatsoever. This will be the perfect launchpad for the guy phase. I couldn't have planned it any better," Sarah A says. "I didn't realize that people still offered their kids such huge pockets of dangerous freedom. Were your parents hippies or something?"

I blink several times. I'm the kind of person who has to transition from sleep to wake.

"My parents aren't *that* old," I say.

"Yeah, having old parents would be such a burden. Poor Sarah C."

"How old are her parents?" I ask. I didn't realize they were elderly.

"They're in their *fifties*. And it totally affects her. That's why she's always thinking so much. Because her parents are mature and decrepit and close to death. That makes a person more meditative."

I don't say anything. I stretch instead. And ponder that whole fifty-being-close-to-death remark. Maybe that's true in poor countries where they have to wear tire treads for shoes and kids aren't vaccinated against the mumps. But in America that can't be the case. Because our senior citizens are freaked about Social Security going bust. And why worry if you'll already be dead? I yawn.

"I think that's part of the reason why my parents had me stay with you and not Sarah C."

"Because her parents are in their fifties and close to death?"

"No, because they used to be hippies."

"They did?"

"They own a health food store. Nobody but hippies manage those things. And I bet my parents didn't want me to stay with Sarah B because she comes from a broken home. I mean, she's being raised by a single parent."

"But her dad is so great." I sit up. But this quick vertical maneuver makes me feel dizzy and I lower myself back to my pillow.

"He's a mechanic!"

"But he's really involved in her life. They go to sporting events together."

Sarah A rolls her eyes. "Yeah, well, she's barely middle class."

I try to keep my eyes from widening. I wonder if Sarah A talks about me like this when I'm not around. Probably. I smile through this observation. I guess we all gossip at some point in our lives. Nobody is perfect.

"So the reason you're staying with me is because my parents weren't hippies, are still married, and are middle class?"

"Don't sell yourself short. Your brother goes to Stanford, and your father owns a car lot. You're upper-middle class. And my parents are orthodontists. They're responsible people. They're not going to ship me off to live in a questionable environment."

"Do you really feel that way?" I ask.

"Of course," Sarah A says.

I don't know if I totally believe her. I think it must ruffle her somewhat that her parents shipped her off. I yawn again and stretch my arms over my head.

"I don't care about the reasons why you're here," I say. "I'm just glad you came to stay with me. My home is definitely a healthy environment."

I should have knocked on wood. My last comment is like a cue for dysfunction and mayhem to start raining down on my happy, healthy home. Out of nowhere, my father screams, "That man is a shithead!" This never happens. Why is this happening? My father is a procrastinator, not a screamer. But it's like he's trying to openly demonstrate that our house might actually be a questionable environment.

"He's got a big, antagonistic head stuffed with certifiable shit!" my father yells.

"Calm down. It's just an inflatable monkey," my mother says.

"Big Don knew I'd bought the duck. He knew I'd paid big dollars for that inflatable. He purposely bought King Kong to dwarf me," he says.

"It's not that bad," my mother says.

"That ape's head casts an afternoon shadow right over the row of Passats. They're huge sellers! They can't be in some big ape's head shade."

"Maybe you can talk to him," my mother says.

I can hear my father slam the refrigerator door. This is not like my dad at all. He's not a fighter. He's like me, an adapter. From my room, Sarah A and I listen to the lively discussion unfold.

"Who's Big Don?" Sarah A asks me.

She seems thrilled by this familial discord.

"My dad's competition. He owns the lot across the street from him."

"What's an inflatable?"

"Those huge balloonlike things that businesses put in front of their buildings to draw in customers."

"Your dad bought a duck?"

"It's a cool duck. It has black sunglasses and is as big as a school bus."

"And his competition bought King Kong?"

"It sounds like it," I say.

Sarah A slides on my slippers and races to my bedroom door. She opens it and pokes her head out.

"I'm sorry to jump into your conversation," she says, "but why not buy Godzilla? That would even the playing field. It would be an epic battle played out with inflatables, Godzilla versus King Kong. Everyone knows Godzilla would win."

I'm tempted to tell Sarah A to get back inside my bedroom. This isn't any of her business. I'm the one who picked out the cool duck inflatable. But I don't. I hear my father's footsteps rushing toward my room. Sarah A squeals and runs back to her bed.

"Are you decent in there, girls?" my father asks.

"Yes," I say.

He opens the door and his increasingly scruffy face emerges before us.

"You really think Godzilla could beat King Kong?"

"They made a movie about it. I'm pretty sure Godzilla won. He's way bigger than Kong and Godzilla can breathe fire."

My father walks all the way inside my room. A dot of skim milk glistens like an iridescent pearl in his chin hair.

"Sarah?" he asks me. "Have you seen that movie?"

"No." I don't know much about King Kong. And everything I learned about Godzilla I gleaned from watching Liam play with his Godzilla action figure. When he was ten, Liam went through a Godzilla phase, which occurred very much before his "pre-social-conscience phase." In addition to his bright green Godzilla action figure, Liam also had that monster on a plastic lunch box. "I bet Liam has. He spent an entire year worshipping that beast. I'll call him. But that sounds right. A lizard that can breathe fire should be able to defeat a big ape."

"He's not a lizard; he's a dinosaur," Sarah A says.

My father grins and rubs the milk dribble from his chin.

"This is a great idea," he says. "I'll shelve the duck until next year."

"But the duck is cool," I say. This is frustrating. I'm no expert, but doesn't Godzilla kill people by stepping on them with his big lizard feet? And doesn't he also crush cars, even police cruisers and ambulances? And wasn't he created in Japan? Why would you stick him in an American car lot, especially in Michigan? How will that boost sales? Plus, he's got gargantuan teeth. It's a total mistake. Ducks make people feel comfortable. Dinosaurs remind people that petroleum is a finite and dwindling natural resource.

"I need more than a duck, Sarah. Waterfowl is no match for King Kong. Your friend is right. I need Godzilla. Big

Don won't be getting the upper hand on me in sales this summer."

My father pretends to take off an imaginary hat as he bows in Sarah A's direction. This makes me feel very blah inside. I don't want my father to fall under her spell. It's one thing for me to suck up to her, but it's a totally different story to involve the rest of my family.

My father zips back out to the kitchen. A minute later, I hear him slam the front door. He's gone. Sarah A looks at me all twinkly eyed and sticks her tongue out at me.

"Were you the one who picked out the inflatable duck?" she asks.

"No," I lie.

"Whatever. Let's get ready. We've got a big day. I need to stop by my condo. Plus, I've got some shopping to do. And we'll be meeting up with the other Sarahs. Tonight, we're getting rid of Digits. And then I'm calling Roman Karbowski. Finally!"

"Getting rid of Digits?" She makes it sound like we're going to toss him out of a speeding car or drop him into a lake.

"Relax. It's just a cat. And didn't you hear what I said? I'm going to call Roman Karbowski tonight." She grabs her Roman pillow and takes such a deep breath that the corner of Roman's shirt collar is pulled into one of her nostrils. When she exhales, it falls away.

"I'm so happy," she says.

Sarah A puts on my slippers and shuffles to the shower.

"Remind me to bring a pillowcase," she says.

"One of my pillowcases?" I ask.

"Yeah. And pick one you're not going to miss."

# Chapter 12

As long as Sarah A is housed under my roof, I doubt I'll be taking a hot shower. Which is not only uncomfortable, but might be unhygienic, because I'm pretty sure that lukewarm water doesn't clean a body as well as hot water. My sixth-grade science teacher talked incessantly about molecules and speed and lots of other stuff that we had to totally trust him about because Winchell Elementary School didn't have microscopes. My teacher said that as water warms, its molecules bounce around and increase its cleansing properties.

The kind of water Sarah A leaves me is filled with very laggard molecules. Most likely, I'm showering in liquid that's barely washing me. It's probably just making me damp. Sarah A squeaks the faucet off. I think she's singing. Her voice sounds chipper. Our chorus teacher says I have a solemn voice. I think that means I sound honest. The Sarahs haven't met for a sing group in weeks and surprisingly, I don't even miss it.

Sarah A didn't close the bathroom door all the way. I can see her naked profile as she sweeps a towel across her wet, perfect skin. She slips into her clothes and wraps a second towel around her head. John Glenn noses the bathroom door open and sticks his head right inside the toilet bowl.

"That doesn't seem sanitary," I say.

"He's just a dog."

I don't enjoy hearing Sarah A say that.

John Glenn pads back into the room and lays down at the foot of my bed. I like that instead of seeking Sarah A out for affection, my dog gravitates toward me and my living zone. I thought it took longer for dogs to transfer loyalty, that steadfast allegiance was bred into them at a cellular level.

It's my turn to shower. I grab my towel.

"Sarah T, I think you shower funny," Sarah A says.

"You watch me shower?" I ask.

"No. When I go into the bathroom after you're done, there's water everywhere. Do you freak out and have panic attacks while you're in there? Are you claustrophobic? Is it related to your pee-issues? Do you suffer from some sort of rare liquid dysfunction?" she asks.

"No. When the water gets cold I jump out," I say.

"Yeah, your water could be hotter," Sarah A says.

I go inside the bathroom and close the door. I never had a water-temperature issue before she got here. Standing within the cramped four walls of my bathroom, I look at myself in the mirror and take a deep breath. The air smells like blueberries and vanilla. It's Sarah A's unmistakable body fragrance. I would have thought that my scent would override hers, it being my bathroom. But that's not how it works. She's seeping into the walls of my house at the level of personal stink. I reach under the sink for the bottle of Lysol. I release a long, zigzagging spray of it until the small chamber is overwhelmed by the smell of baby powder. I cough a few times and turn on the shower. This feels better.

After my shower, I reenter my bedroom and find a breathless Sarah A holding a shovel. Its steel blade is dirt-caked and John Glenn sniffs it intensely several times.

"What are you doing?" I ask.

She leans the shovel against a wall and smiles.

"You said you felt bad about stealing all that stuff. I figured I'd help you bury it, if you want," Sarah A says.

"Oh," I say. This seems odd, as I was thinking I'd give it away, not entomb it in the earth.

"I dug a hole for you in your backyard."

"I was only in the shower for ten minutes," I say.

"It wasn't a deep hole."

I feel appreciative that Sarah A would carve into the earth for me first thing on a Tuesday, though I doubt the space will be big enough to hold everything I've ever stolen.

"Did my mother see you?" I ask.

"No, I did the deed on the shady side of your house with all those bushes. Nobody saw me."

"And why is the shovel in my room?" I ask.

"I borrowed it from your neighbor. They weren't there when I took it, but they're there now."

"Sarah A, you can't rob my neighbors."

"Why, is there a cop in the family?"

"No, I like them!"

"Okay. I'll return it tonight. But let's not lose sight of the fact that I just dug you an awesome hole."

"Thanks," I say. "I guess I needed a hole."

"Oh, it gets better," Sarah C says, running over to me and grabbing my hands. "Guess what I found buried out there?" She points to my bedroom wall that borders the shady side of my house.

"I don't know," I say. Against my moist hands, Sarah A's feel cold and dry. I pull mine out of hers and notice that both of our hands are streaked with mud.

"I found a body," Sarah A says.

"Holy shit!" I yell.

Sarah A grabs her stomach and starts laughing. "I'm just kidding. I didn't really find a body."

"Ha-ha," I say. I wipe my hands on my jeans.

"But I think that I unearthed a time capsule."

Sarah A walks to my dresser and lifts up a mud-encrusted metal lunch box and a completely wrecked book. She hands them both to me. The lunch box was Liam's. It has a faded green Godzilla on the front with a badly chipped paint job. And the book is about the Potawatomi Indians in Kalamazoo. I flip it open and glance inside. It's many years overdue.

"Who do you think put them there?" Sarah A asks me.

"Liam," I say. She holds her hands out, like she wants to take the items back, and I give them to her.

"Hey, there's something in here," Sarah A says, shaking the lunch box.

"There is?"

What would Liam hide in a lunch box and bury in the earth? Oh, no. What if it's his pot? I try to swipe the box from Sarah A.

"No, I want to open it," Sarah A says.

She unlatches the clasp with her thumb and the lid falls open. A small Godzilla action figure falls to the floor. Sarah A bends over and picks it up. I'm so relieved that we didn't uncover my brother's drug stash that I literally wipe my brow and release a *whew* sound.

"This is in good condition. I bet it's worth something," Sarah A says, holding the toy to the light.

"But it's Liam's," I say.

"I'm the one who found it," Sarah A says.

"On my property."

"Possession is nine tenths of the law. Also, I think if you find something buried in the earth it's community property."

I've never heard that.

"Please give it back," I say.

And to my great surprise she does. I take the action figure and shut it back up in the dilapidated lunch box.

"That's so weird. Liam really is totally crazy, isn't he? I wonder what else he's hidden in your yard. We should locate a metal detector."

Sarah A doesn't wait for my reaction. She goes into the bathroom and washes her hands. Then she starts down the hallway toward the kitchen, flicking them dry as she walks.

"I hope your mom makes us Pop-Tarts again. I didn't realize how much I much I liked Pop-Tarts until I started eating them every morning. Your mom must have a real thing for them," Sarah A says.

"I think it's an anti-stove phase. For lunch we've been eating a lot of Hot Pockets. She's only cooking with the toaster and the microwave these days," I say.

"I don't think that's what it is. I bet she's just really craving Pop-Tarts. I mean, don't you ever get an intense craving?"

"For Pop-Tarts?" I ask.

"For anything," Sarah A says.

"All I usually want in the morning is a banana," I say.

"That's not what I mean. I'm talking about deep down. What do you really crave, like at your soul level?"

"My soul level?" I ask.

"Yeah," Sarah A says. "What does your soul crave?"

"Bananas."

"Well, maybe you have a monkey soul," Sarah A says.

"Morning, girls," my mother says. "Hello, John Glenn."

She drops two Pop-Tarts into the toaster. Our one week test with John Glenn went swimmingly. My mother hasn't had any allergy issues. Her biggest issue with my dog seems to be his constant slobbering when we dine on anything that gives off a meaty aroma.

"What flavor are the Pop-Tarts this time?" Sarah A asks.

"Raspberry," my mother says.

"I love raspberry," Sarah A says. She grins her super-fake smile, but it's nearly impossible for adults to detect its insincerity. She's perfected that thing.

"How about you, Sarah?"

"I just want a banana."

"Those Pop-Tarts smell so good. Do they come with frosting?" Sarah A asks.

My mother turns to face us and flashes a very proud smile.

"No, but I whipped up my own from scratch."

Sarah A releases a *coo* that makes her sound like a pigeon. I thought I was supposed to be worming my way back into my old spot. But it feels like Sarah A is trying to worm her way into my family spot. And I'm not totally okay with this, because it's the only spot where I comfortably fit.

My mother drizzles her homemade frosting over Sarah A's Pop-Tarts and she releases more coos. I take such an enormous bite of banana that I almost gag. Nobody seems to notice. If my mother knew the truth about Sarah A, she wouldn't even want her inside our home, let alone feasting on junk food toaster pastries in our breakfast nook.

But my mother is so far removed from the truth. Mrs. Aberdeen didn't even come clean about the true nature of the Vance attack. My parents are both under the assumption that it was just a spat over which toppings to put on a deep-dish pizza that spiraled into a shoving match that ended with an inappropriate punch in the arm. My parents think the Aberdeens are totally overreacting. I bet they wouldn't if I filled them in on the butter knife angle.

But I won't do that.

"I'd like to apologize for all the exclamatory 'shithead' references this morning. The King Kong inflatable was quite a blow," my mother says.

"I didn't mind at all," Sarah A says, snapping off the corner of her breakfast before setting it in her mouth.

"What do you girls have planned for the day?" my mother asks.

Sarah A always has these answers covered. She thinks that it's very important to vigilantly reassure parents as often as possible that you're goal-oriented, responsible, and chaste.

"That's all they care about," Sarah A has said. "Plus, they don't want you to take drugs. That includes huffing glue, keyboard cleaner, and diesel fuel."

From what I've seen, I think she's mostly right about that.

"I'm going to get a book," Sarah A says.

I'm struck by the word "get" versus the word "buy." My mother doesn't notice the diction dance.

"What's the book called?" my mother asks. She stirs her bowl of frosting, cracking the sugar glaze on top, and ladles a thick stream of it onto another Pop-Tart. She doesn't set this one in front of Sarah A. My mother takes a bite. Crumbs the color of sand tumble onto the countertop. I watch her chew and wonder if she ever plans to use our stove again, for breakfast, lunch, dinner, or warm, yet untoasted, snacks.

"I want to get the *Purple Cow*. It's about how to be successful by standing out from the rest of the crowd. Because a purple cow is way more noticeable than a brown one."

"That's true," my mother says.

"We're working on college stuff too," Sarah A says.

"Like what?"

"Sarah T and I want to draft our personal statement. I think that essay is more important than our grades. It's the only chance we have to tell the admissions committee who we are in our own words."

"Sounds like a project to start now," my mother says. "And revise and revise again."

"That's definitely our strategy for U of M," Sarah A says.

My mother grins. "That's a great school," she says.

"Yeah, Madonna went there," I say. I pull the rest of my banana from its soft peel.

My mother polishes off her Pop-Tart and licks her fingertips. "I still think it's a great school."

"What will you be doing today?" Sarah A asks.

"I'll be at Dr. Pewter's house. I'm stabilizing her pantry today."

"Stabilizing?" Sarah A asks.

"That means clean out and organize," I say. "I thought you stabilized her pantry last week."

"No, that was her laundry room. Next, we'll stabilize the garage." My mother's forehead wrinkles with concern.

"How big is her garage?" Sarah A asks.

"Currently, it contains one broken spa, two crashed bikes, three kayaks, and a disabled Winnebago."

"And four calling birds?" I ask.

My mother stares blankly at me. "I don't know if there are any birds in the garage," she says. "I guess it wouldn't surprise me."

She pats the counter and smiles. That means I'm supposed to clean it up.

"Okay," I say.

She grabs her big bag and is off.

"Four calling birds. It was from the song, 'The Twelve Days of Christmas,'" I say.

"Okay," Sarah A says.

"Get it?" I ask.

"Sure."

"Do you think my mom got it?" I ask.

"It wasn't that funny," Sarah A says. "What you said about Madonna was way funnier."

"All I said was that she went to the U of M," I say.

"Yeah, but you sounded impressed about it. Come on. It's not like going to Michigan made her famous. She had to take most of her clothes off and perform dance routines that involved a ton of floor-humping before that all happened."

"That's true," I say.

Sarah A pulls her hair into a ponytail and snaps the rubber band in place.

"Ready to help me get the *Purple Cow*?"

"Barnes & Noble?" I ask

She shakes her head.

"The library," she says.

I let out a sigh. That's a relief. Other than the planned

cat dump and eventual Roman Karbowski phone call, maybe today will be uneventful. Maybe there won't be any shoplifting. Sarah A clucks her tongue.

"I think I know how to rip the sensor right out of the book. We can do it in the bathroom."

# Chapter 13

Sarah A did know exactly how to rip the sensor right out of a library book. And she did this while locked inside the handicap stall in the first-floor bathroom. I stood on guard in the sink area. The library has a pretty decent sink area. First, it was clean. Second, it was very well stocked. There were enough paper towels and hand soap to weather a national disaster. If I'm ever downtown during a tornado warning, I totally know where to go.

And the crime went off without a hitch. Grab book from shelf. Take book to bathroom. Strip book of sensor. Shove book in purse. Tell security guard to have a nice day. Leave library. Drive at normal rate of speed to Marlborough Building.

Sarah A really loves that cow book. And it came with a free plastic book cover to protect it against the elements. I mean, all library books do. You just usually don't get to keep them. Sarah is reading through the table of contents and first chapter while I circle back around to her condo.

"I'm not sure if it's going to help me pick out a major, but it's great information about marketing. Seriously. In this day and age, it's so important to market yourself."

"To who?" I ask.

"Your target audience."

This is surprising, because I personally don't even know who that would be. Guys? Teachers? Parents? My same-sex peers? I thought corporations marketed stuff to try to manipulate people into buying it. I had no idea high school seniors were supposed to be marketing themselves to some sort of target audience.

"Where's the pillowcase?" Sarah A asks.

I pull to a stop in front of her condo. I reach into my backseat and hand her my least favorite pillowcase. The one that I had a nosebleed on last summer and now it's permanently dotted with brown spots.

"I thought the pillowcase was for Digits," I say.

"No, why would we need to put Digits in a pillowcase? We've already stolen him. He's living with Sarah C."

I shrug. I don't mention how I thought the pillowcase was going to be used in the poor cat's nefarious demise. It freaks me out to think that I might have a more criminal mind than Sarah A. I mean, is that possible?

"Wait here. I'll be right back."

Sarah runs down the covered walkway and goes inside. I guess she forgot to pack some stuff. That's understandable. We got out of that place in a hurry. As she runs, I notice her outstanding posture and the effortless way she enters the building. There's so few people who have that kind of raw and amazing beauty. It's magnetic. It pulls you in. Just standing next to her makes me feel important. Better than that, it makes me feel chosen.

Sarah A isn't in the Marlborough Building long. She races back to the car dangling the pillowcase at her side. Something the size of a loaf of bread is stuffed inside it. I'm actually hoping that it's a loaf of bread.

"Pop the trunk," she says.

Instead of popping the trunk, I accidentally open my gas tank. I decide to get out of the car to open the trunk for her. That way I can shut my tank. With the skyrocketing price of gas these days, you can't afford to leave your tank popped open. Anybody could siphon it right out. Seriously. The Sarahs and I have talked about doing that. Except all of us are skittish about getting gasoline in our mouths. When ingested, petroleum is totally poisonous.

I open the trunk. Sarah A has tied a knot around the top of the pillowcase. She drops the bundle inside next to my spare tire. The bulge inside the pillowcase moves. It sort of hops.

"What's in there?" I ask.

"A rabbit."

"Vance's rabbit? Frenchy?"

"Yeah. You sound like you have a problem with that."

"Well, it's alive," I say.

"It's a rabbit. We're going to dump it at the shelter."

"Are you sure?"

"Totally. I can't stand Frenchy." She shoves her hands, knuckle deep, into the shallow pockets of her capris.

"I don't know."

"You don't have to do anything. I'll do it."

"I have to drive around with it in my trunk."

"What's the big deal?"

My mind flashes to the flattened possum that my father dumped in the woods surrounding our home. I know it sounds stupid, but I made a promise to myself to avoid hurting another animal. This is obviously a violation of that vow. I feel conflicted.

I'm holding the top of my trunk's lid, ready to pull it down, but I can't. "It's a living animal."

"So, people eat rabbits every day."

"Not when they're alive! Not after they've driven around town with them in their trunks. It's almost eighty degrees. The shelter drop isn't until tonight. Frenchy could suffocate."

"Why are you acting like this?" Sarah A asks. "I want to put a rabbit in your trunk. Adapt."

I let go of my car. My arms fall to my sides. "I don't think I can. I think I'd be so worried about Frenchy that I might crash the car," I say.

"You can't be serious. Don't go all environmental all me. Next, you'll want to drive to Binder Park Zoo and open all the cages and release those animals."

Frenchy, still enclosed in the pillowcase, has leaped into the center of my spare tire. I fold my arms.

Sarah A reaches up and slams my trunk so hard that the back end of my car bounces.

"No," I say, grabbing for her hands.

"Yes," she says, keeping her palms firmly planted on my trunk.

I push the 'open trunk' button on my key chain over and over. "I won't do this," I say. My voice wavers, not with its normal indecision, but with determination.

Sarah A looks at me. She's leaning into my car like she's doing a modified push-up off the trunk. Finally, her locked elbows soften and she shoves herself away from my Jetta.

My trunk pops open. Sarah A watches me. I reach forward and raise the lid. My heart is thumping fast inside of me. I'm breaking ranks. But it feels like the right thing to do—for me, for Frenchy, and even for Sarah A.

"Have it your way. We're wasting time. But keep it in the backseat. That thing totally smells."

I don't really want a stinky rabbit in my backseat either, but I feel way better about that than driving around with him withering away in my trunk space all afternoon.

When we get to Sarah B's, she's sitting on the curb, waiting for us.

"I'm so ready to go to a movie," Sarah B says.

"We're going to a movie?" I ask.

"Yeah. We're going to see that new film with the cars in it," Sarah A says.

"What about Frenchy?" I ask.

"You want to bring the rabbit inside the theater?" Sarah A asks. "That's, like, even beyond PETA."

"Is Frenchy in this pillowcase?" Sarah B asks.

"How did you know?" I ask.

"This corner is twitching. It looks like a bunny nose," Sarah B says.

I try to ignore that fact that I have a live rabbit in my car and drive to pick up Sarah C.

"I'm so excited to see that movie," Sarah C says when we pull up to her house.

"About cars?" Sarah B asks.

"No, the one where the guy and girl break up because they have a fight about lemons," Sarah C says.

"We're not seeing that. We're seeing a movie with cars in it," Sarah A says. "We just took a vote and that's the one everybody else wants to see."

"I didn't get to vote," Sarah C says.

Sarah A unfastens her seat belt and flips around to face Sarah C.

"I'm calling Roman Karbowski tonight. I don't want to depress my great vibes by watching a movie about people falling out of love. It's a no-brainer," Sarah A says, pointing to her head and mouthing the words "no-brainer."

I try to break the tension. "Hey, where's Digits?" I ask.

"In my house," Sarah C says. "Probably napping."

"What is it with you and animals? Do you want to take the cat to the movies too?" Sarah A asks.

"No, I was thinking we could put Frenchy with Digits. We could pick them both up after the show."

"Is Frenchy in this pillowcase?" Sarah C asks. "It smells like poop."

"I tried to put him in the trunk, but Ms. Greenpeace over here insisted that he needed to ride with us."

"It is kind of hot in here," Sarah B says.

"It's just a rabbit," Sarah A says. "It's not like we're sticking a baby in the car. Think of Frenchy as an overgrown rat."

Sarah C clears her throat.

"Actually, rabbits are lagomorphs, and are more closely

related to horses than they are to rats or mice," Sarah C says.

"Who cares?" Sarah A says. "There's nothing special about this rabbit. Trust me. Let's get going."

"Actually, the rabbit is one of the only two animals that can see behind itself without turning its head. The other is the parrot," Sarah C says.

"I didn't know that about parrots," Sarah B says.

My car idles in Sarah C's driveway. She hasn't gotten inside the car yet.

"Fine, I don't care. Stick the rabbit in Sarah C's bedroom with Digits," Sarah A says.

Sarah C takes the pillowcase by its knotted top. "This is a smart move, because rabbits can get heatstroke."

"I didn't know that either," Sarah B says.

Sarah A doesn't respond. She opens up the *Purple Cow* and starts reading the second chapter. After a few minutes, I turn off my car.

"Should I go get her?" Sarah B asks.

"Here she comes," I say.

She bounds down her walkway and opens up our door.

"Sorry, Frenchy felt really hot. To lower his temperature, I applied cold water to his earflaps."

"Thank the Lord," Sarah A says. "Because what would the world come to if a rabbit overheated?"

"They were kind of cute together. Left alone, I think they'd develop a symbiotic relationship. Like sharks and sucker fish."

"What are you talking about?" Sarah A asks. She turns her body around so she can directly glower into the backseat at Sarah C.

"What time will we make the drop-off?" Sarah B asks.

Sarah A turns back around and settles into the passenger seat. "After dark," she says.

"Won't your parents notice that the rabbit is gone?" I ask.

"Whose side are you on anyway? Don't you realize that you're on probation? Quit with the commentary."

I don't say anything else. I can hear Sarah C telling Sarah B about an ongoing campaign in Australia to eliminate its non-native rabbit population. The government is spreading a bunny-killing virus, and it sounds very effective.

"Maybe it's too effective," Sarah C says. "The public has been warned to be on the lookout for hungry eagles. On some highways they've actually attacked motorists."

"Wow," Sarah B says. "I wouldn't want to ride a bicycle there."

Sarah A has tried very hard to keep her focus on her book, but she can't take it anymore. She flips around again, partway, this time entangled in her seat belt.

"Do you want to marry a goddamned rabbit or something? Do you want to become a stupid, over-copulating rabbit? Let it go."

Nobody says anything else. I keep my eyes locked on the road.

"I don't want to hear another word about rabbits. Or any other animals. Life is short. Let's focus on what's important. Now we're going to see a movie and we're going to have a good time."

I can hear everybody breathing. Each Sarah has a different pattern of inhalation and exhalation. Mine is the quickest. We usually don't fight like this. Traditionally, we fall in line behind our leader. But something is out of whack. An awkward anger is trapped in the car with us. We keep breathing.

"I didn't mean to yell that loud," Sarah A says. "I think I'm stressed-out about calling Roman tonight. Don't hate me."

She sounds sincere. And somewhat sympathetic.

"We don't hate you," I say. "Do we?"

"No," Sarah B says.

"I don't *hate* anybody," Sarah C says.

Unlike the rabbit odor that has managed to saturate every particle of air within our scent range, the weird tension that existed seconds ago has somehow managed to leak its way out of the car. After several series of breaths, Sarah B offers up a compliment.

"Your hair smells really good."

Of course, she's talking to Sarah A. It goes without saying that nearly all our compliments are aimed at her. Especially when she's in a foul mood.

"Thanks. It's Sarah T's kiwi shampoo."

My what? I don't have kiwi shampoo. I'm tempted to tell her that the kiwi product in my shower is shaving gel and isn't intended to cleanse hair, but I don't. I mean, if she's able to work that stuff into a lather that produces satisfying head-hair volume, then more power to her.

I pull into the Kalamazoo 10 and begin sharking around the lot for a parking spot. I'm glad that we're going to see a movie. I'm tired of talking and thinking. I'm not built for debate.

"Drop me off," Sarah A says.

I pull up to the handicap ramp and let out all the other Sarahs. Then I continue to shark. I don't know if Sarah B and Sarah C have noticed, but sometimes when we go see a movie, Sarah A doesn't always watch the screen. Sometimes, I turn and look at her and she has her eyes closed and her face is perfectly relaxed. It almost looks like she's sleeping, except I know she's not.

When I go to the movies, I like to watch the big screen and be pulled into a totally different place. A foreign perspective. A new world. I guess Sarah A goes someplace inside of herself. I'm just surprised that she's willing to pay almost seven bucks for that experience. Couldn't she just turn out the light in the bathroom and sit on the toilet?

I walk alone past row after row of parked cars. Michigan drivers park crooked. Even I do. I walk inside and buy my ticket and join the other Sarahs. I squeak down in my chair right as the lights dim.

"What's this movie even about?" I ask.

"Cars," Sarah C says flatly.

I sigh. I hope there isn't a ton of honking.

# Chapter 14

After the movie, I drive to Sarah C's to retrieve the cat and rabbit. Sarah C bites her thumb and looks out the car window at the passing houses. She seems gloomy. I think she's become attached to Digits. She has been his sole caretaker.

"It's not like they're going to be put down," Sarah A says as I turn down Westnedge.

She's right. Our shelter does an excellent job adopting out animals. And it's a no-kill shelter too, even for really ugly animals. Luckily, both Digits and Frenchy are pretty attractive. Plus, Digits's bonus toes will probably help him secure a home more quickly. It sounds crazy, but when you're an abandoned animal, anything that makes you stand out from the crowd makes you remarkable. I've seen dogs with burned-off ears end up in very classy and loving homes.

I flip my headlights off and let the car roll to a stop in front of the shelter. The full moon gives us plenty of light to do the deed. I look at the cages where we'll be dumping our animal cargo. This is going to be harder than I thought. I'm not a psychic, but I can sense that this whole situation is about to become mired in drama. It could have been easy enough. It *should* have been easy enough. But when you throw a charcoal gray pit bull into the mix, it's never easy. The big dog is hunched inside one of the larger cages, its snout pressed right up against the bars. Nobody gets out of the car. I've turned my engine off, but there's still a rumbling sound. It's the pit bull. He's growling.

"Some jerk dumped a pit bull," I say.

"It's so loud," Sarah B says.

"It wants to eat us," Sarah C adds. "And I have no desire to die before I kiss Benny Stowe."

"He couldn't eat all of you," Sarah A says. "You're too tall."

"He could eat enough of me," Sarah C says.

I don't think she's wrong either. He's snarling now, like he wants to drag us from the car and chew through our throats.

"Wait till we get close to him," I say.

"We've just caught him off guard," Sarah A says. "Give him a minute."

"What for? Let's just put Digits and Frenchy in that other corner cage," I say.

"Actually, we should probably put Frenchy in his own cage," Sarah C says. "Rabbits can't vomit."

"So?" Sarah A says.

"Digits is a shedder. If Frenchy sucks in all the fuzz and develops a furball he'll die," Sarah C says. "It'll get blocked in his intestines."

Sarah A turns around and swats Sarah C hard on the leg.

"I said no more rabbit crap. What's wrong with you?"

"Okay, let's calm down. There's plenty of spaces. We can stick Digits and Frenchy in separate cages," I say.

"That's not what I'm concerned about," Sarah A says.

I look at her blankly. What else is there to be concerned about? We need to dump these animals and move on.

"I want that dog," Sarah A says.

"What do you mean?" Sarah C says.

"What do you mean what do I mean? I want him," Sarah A says.

"After he's processed, if he passes his socialization tests, you can adopt him," I say.

But I think that's a bad idea. Because if her parents don't want to break the rules and risk getting fined for concealing a friendly yellow Lab like John Glenn in their condo, I seriously doubt they'd change their minds and take in a vicious beast.

"I don't want to adopt him. I want to sell him. I know somebody who'd buy him," Sarah A says.

"That's crazy," Sarah C says.

Sarah A cracks open her door. "I want him," she says.

Sarah C tries to grab Sarah A's arm, but Sarah A pulls away. She gets out of the car and slowly approaches the caged pit bull.

"He'll kill us. He looks like a total bite-off-your-face kind of dog," Sarah C says.

Sarah B and I both nod in agreement.

The pit bull rests his rump down in the cage as Sarah A stands in front of it. I think the dog looks like he's getting ready to strike.

"Can killer dogs chew through cages?" Sarah B asks.

"I don't know," I say.

"What is she thinking?" Sarah C asks. "I'm holding a cat."

"I've got a rabbit," Sarah B says.

"It's in a pillowcase," Sarah C says.

"Yeah, like that's going to protect anyone," Sarah B says.

"At least Frenchy is hidden and can't see what's going on," Sarah C says. "Digits is freaking out. His claws are firmly planted in my thigh. It's going to leave a mark."

I'm not sure what I'm supposed to do. Maybe I should honk the horn. But Sarah A is so determined. By challenging her earlier and refusing to put Frenchy in my trunk, I think I provoked her stubborn and reckless side. She's acting like the taking of the pit bull is essential. I have no idea why she feels this way.

"Go talk her out of it," Sarah B says.

I shake my head no.

"Do you want that thing in your car?" Sarah C asks. "How else are we going to transport it?"

Okay. I don't want the pit bull in my car. Sarah C makes a very good point. I get out and slowly walk over to Sarah A and the cages.

"See, he's nice," Sarah A says.

The pit bull has forced a milky-colored front paw out of the cage and hooked it around a bar. Sarah A is petting it.

"I don't think you can really determine his temperament while he's still in the cage," I say.

The pit bull takes his big, wet tongue and begins sweeping it across the cage's front.

"He's trying to give kisses," Sarah A says.

At this point, I'm not sure if she's lost touch with reality, or if she's completely locked in high-level manipulation mode to the point where in addition to manipulating me, she's also manipulating herself.

"We've got a rabbit and a cat in the car. This dog is going to freak out," I say. "Maybe we should just leave him."

Sarah A turns to face me and puts her hand on my shoulder. It feels heavier than it should. Maybe she's doing that on purpose.

"Listen, if we pulled up here and saw a hundred-dollar bill sitting in this cage, would you just leave it?"

I look back at the pit bull. He's still licking away.

"It's not the same thing," I say. "I wouldn't be afraid to put a hundred-dollar bill in my car."

"Is this what this is all about?" she asks. She pulls her hand off my shoulder and points her index finger at me. She needs to get a manicure. Her nails are looking a little chipped.

"Yes," I say. "I don't want that dog in my car."

"No, that's not what you said. You said that you were *afraid*. Is that what's going on? You're letting fear stop you? You can't ever let fear stop you. Fear is something weak people feel that keeps them locked in crappy jobs and living worthless lives. Fear is for losers."

Sarah C opens up her car door. "Fear is also part of human instinct. Historically speaking, it's saved a lot of lives."

Sarah A looks furious. She walks over to my car and swings open Sarah C's door.

"If you've got something to say, then say it to my face."

"If this isn't part of the guy phase, which really is where all of our heads should be, I think we should pass on the dog," Sarah C says.

"Sometimes I think the only reason you're a Sarah is so you can get your hooks into Benny Stowe," Sarah A says.

"You're just saying that because you're mad," Sarah C says.

"No, I'm saying it because I think it's true," Sarah A says.

"Come on. Stealing a pit bull is a bad idea. I mean, I've got a cat," Sarah C says.

Digits' back is fully arched and he's releasing an aggressive murmur, sort of like a controlled yowl.

"Give me the freaking cat," Sarah A says.

She grabs Digits by the scruff of his neck and carries the dangling cat toward the cages. I don't tell her to be more gentle. Considering her state of mind, I think she's being reasonably gentle.

By now the dog has sensed the presence of the cat. He's mashing his face against the cage, barking and spewing slobber.

Sarah C has gotten out of the car. I think her thigh is actually bleeding. The pit bull jerks around inside the cage, making an awful rattling noise. He's barking too. And grunting. And banging against the metal walls with his head.

"We better get out of here," Sarah C says.

"Not without the dog," Sarah A says.

Sarah B has not gotten out of the car. That means Frenchy is still inside too.

"Bring the rabbit here," Sarah A says.

Sarah B climbs out of Sarah C's already open door. The pit bull is still going crazy. When I look at him, all I see is an enraged pink mouth filled with jagged white teeth.

"Just toss the rabbit in a cage," Sarah A says.

"Shouldn't we take off his collar and stuff? I mean, won't your mom figure out what we did if some shelter employee finds Frenchy in this cage in the morning and calls your home phone number?"

Sarah A looks totally pissed. And not at any of us. She's pissed at herself.

"Of course, take all the tags off," Sarah A says. "And do the same thing for Digits."

"I already did," Sarah C says.

"You should have done it already too," Sarah A shouts.

"Wait. It's not like I've been living with Frenchy in my bedroom. He was barely given to me," Sarah B says. "And officially, I wasn't even assigned the rabbit."

"Just take off the tags!" Sarah A yells.

Suddenly, there's no time to do anything. It's the end of the world. After working himself into a frenzy, the pit bull has broken out of the cage.

"Jesus," Sarah B screams. "He's out."

"Don't run!" Sarah C warns. "You'll trigger his chase instinct."

That's easier said than done. Sarah A has no problem freezing, neither does Sarah C. But Sarah B takes off running, with the pillowcase swinging at her side.

"Get rid of the rabbit!" Sarah C yells.

But Sarah B has too big of a heart to just drop the pillowcase and let that dog maul Frenchy to death. She turns to me and flings the pillowcase through the air. It sails toward me like a football. The charging dog pivots and changes direction. I watch him kick up dirt as he turns. When I catch the pillowcase, I know that I need to act fast. I untie the knot and dump the rabbit onto the ground. Frenchy doesn't waste a second. He leaps furiously into the trees behind the shelter, and the dog follows. Down the street, a porch light pops on.

"We better get out of here," Sarah C says.

We all race to the car and slam our doors shut.

"Nice throw," I say to Sarah B.

"Actually, you should never throw a rabbit. They have very delicate spines," Sarah C says.

"Shut up," Sarah A says.

I start the car and speed off.

"There's no reason to be ticked off," Sarah C says. "Things went well."

"We just lost a hundred bucks," Sarah A says. "And the freaking rabbit totally got away."

"At least it'll probably live," Sarah B says.

"There's no way we could've transported a pit bull," Sarah C says.

"Yeah," I say.

"That's just media hype. Pit bulls aren't that bad," Sarah A says. "More people are killed by hippo attacks each year."

"Where did you hear that statistic?" Sarah C asks.

Sarah A doesn't respond. I'm sweating. I roll my window

down. I can hear the dog barking a couple of blocks away. It sounds like he's still chasing Frenchy.

"You let a stinky rabbit ride in your car and a mangy cat, what difference is a pit bull?" Sarah A asks. "He wasn't even full grown."

Nobody answers her.

"Do you think Frenchy can outrun that dog?" Sarah B asks.

"I do," Sarah C says. "He's still wearing his tags. I bet somebody finds him and turns him in to the pound within the next day or two."

"What about the dog?" Sarah B asks.

"I doubt it will stay at large for long," Sarah C says.

"And Digits is in the cage, right?" Sarah B asks.

"Yeah," I say. "He's locked up safe."

"You guys are so soft. Life's cruel. Terrible things happens every day. Kids get cancer. People jump off bridges. Space shuttles blow up," Sarah A says.

"I know you're trying to build a convincing analogy, but space shuttles do not blow up every day," Sarah C says.

"You know what I mean," Sarah A says. "Animals die. It just happens."

"Yeah, but I'd like to think that I'm not personally responsible for their deaths," Sarah C says.

"Me too," I say.

"It's so sad to think that people jump off bridges every day," Sarah B says.

"You're all soft," Sarah A says. "We could've gotten big bucks for that dog. I sold a Pomeranian to a guy last month who was looking for a pit bull."

"Why would somebody want a Pomeranian and a pit bull?" Sarah C asks. "That's like buying a chicken and an alligator."

"I guess if you love dogs, you love all dogs," Sarah A says.

As I drive toward Sarah B's house, I can't help but think of my blind neighbor's missing Pomeranian, Pom-Pom. Would Sarah A have done that?

I drop off the other Sarahs and drive Sarah A and myself home.

"What a night," I say.

Sarah A doesn't answer me. I park the car.

"I'm really sick of living with you," she says.

I pull my key out of the ignition. This is horrible news.

How does she expect me to respond?

"You think you're so perfect. You think you're so smart."

"I do not," I say. When Sarah A is ticked off, she must really suck at mind reading, because I'm not even close to feeling that way.

"You pee your pants. You're not that perfect."

I sit motionless. I wish Sarah A was better at coping with disappointment.

"Turn your lights off."

I do, but I'm sort of haughty about it. I flick the switch really quickly and cluck my tongue.

"What's wrong with you?" Sarah A asks. "I'm the one who should be upset."

"I thought this living arrangement would be fun," I say. "I thought it would be like we were sisters."

Sarah A sighs. I'm so disappointed that things are turning out like this. The night feels like a disaster. And my relationship with Sarah A doesn't feel much better.

"Will you still call Roman tonight?" I ask.

"No. Not when I'm feeling like this," Sarah A says.

"How are you feeling?" I ask.

"I'm frustrated. You didn't support me tonight. Not with the rabbit or the pit bull. In fact, you completely undermined me."

"I didn't want the rabbit to die and stealing the pit bull wasn't the best idea," I say.

"I'm not stupid. I know. But at the shelter nobody even considered it with me. I was all alone. I was arguing against all three of you."

She slaps the dashboard in frustration and firmly pushes her body back into the seat.

"But we didn't agree with you," I say.

I can see tears slipping down Sarah A's cheeks. I bite the

inside of my cheek. Sarah A never cries. Sarah A is always in control. I'm surprised to see her this devastated over a dog.

"I know you didn't agree with me," Sarah A says.

"Isn't that part of being sisters?" I ask.

"No. Sisterhood is about love and support. It's about trying to understand each other. Nobody even tried to understand me tonight. You all rallied around one another like I didn't even matter."

"Do you need a Kleenex?" I ask.

"Do you have a Kleenex?" she asks.

"Inside the house."

She wipes beneath her eyes using the back of her hand.

"I felt abandoned," she says. "I felt all alone."

This is sort of weird and dramatic to hear, because the whole dog incident lasted less than ten minutes. Yet, Sarah A makes it sound like her whole worth was tied up in that one moment. This isn't just about the dog. There are bigger issues here. But I'm not sure how to talk to Sarah A. I feel like anything I say will be the wrong thing.

"I'll never abandon you," I say. "I just won't."

"God, Sarah, you make this sound all romantic and sexual and stuff."

"No, I don't mean it that way. I mean it like friends."

She's not crying anymore. She turns to look at me and takes hold of my hands. Her face is damp with tears.

"As Sarahs, we should strive to take risks. We should be braver. We could have at least tried."

"I don't know. It was a big dog," I say.

She squeezes my hands tighter.

"You need to support me. I'll never put us in danger. Not *real* danger. You know that, right?"

I rub my thumbs against her hands hoping that she'll loosen her hold on me.

"Some days we act like we're not anything special at all. We act like everyone else. That's a huge mistake. Because if you're not trying hard to be special, then you just fade into the background. You become wallpaper. If you're not the center, then you're just the periphery. I'm not going to settle with being the periphery. I wasn't brought into this world to be the wallpaper."

I lick my lips. She's crying again. Sarah A really believes everything she's saying. Her grip has loosened. I lift my hands and, using just my fingertips, wipe the tears away above her cheekbones.

"I don't want to be wallpaper either," I say.

"Then we need to go after what we want."

I'm tempted to tell her that while I do consider myself part of the "we" equation, I never wanted that dog. But I decide it's more important to end the night on a good note.

"You're right," I say. "We need to stay tough."

She lifts her hands to mine and threads her fingers through my fingers, pulling our hands into perfect alignment.

"We should always support each other."

"Okay."

"Even through our doubts."

"I will."

"You've got to promise," she says.

"I promise."

She disentangles her hands from mine and presents me with her pinky finger. I offer up mine too. We hook them together and then pull them apart. The quick release makes a snapping sound. The air between us crackles with static electricity. The hair on the back on my neck stands up, as an unexpected feeling of fear snakes through me.

"We're sisters," she says. "Forever."

We turn to get out of the car, but Sarah A pulls on my arm.

"Wait. Remember how you talked about feeling bad about taking stuff, about how you want to get rid of the garden rock?" Sarah A says.

"Yeah," I say.

"And remember how you talked about feeling bad about killing that possum and how you made that promise to yourself not to hurt another animal?" Sarah A asks.

"Yeah," I say. I'm happy that she's been listening so closely to what I tell her. I always figured she was barely paying much attention to anything I had to say.

"You shouldn't feel bad about stuff like that," Sarah A says.

"I don't feel bad all the time," I say.

"But you don't have to feel bad at all. You don't have to feel anything you don't want to feel," Sarah A says.

"What do you mean?" I ask.

"You turn it off," Sarah A says.

Sarah A is smiling again. Her face doesn't look like she's been crying. Her smile is perfect. Her mascara and liner remain unsmudged. When I stare into her eyes they are clear, but empty. Whatever it is that's behind them seems flat. I can't tell what she's thinking. Her eyes glow softly and pleasantly, like two faraway moons.

# Chapter 15

We're at the mall. Mall culture is not my favorite. It's loud here. There's too many people. And I can never find anything I want to buy, let alone steal.

Sarah B is on the hunt for new tops. Sarah A is looking to acquire some bottoms. Sarah C has mentioned the desire to try on shoes. Maybe I should purchase something basic like socks. Sarah A, Sarah C, and I stand outside the dressing room waiting for Sarah B to come out and show us her most recent find. Sarah B walks out and rotates for us.

"No way," Sarah C says. "It makes your boobs look dangerous."

"Dangerous?" I ask.

"A distraction to drivers," Sarah C says.

Sarah C smiles at me and I smile back. But I don't mean it. If I had my choice, I wouldn't be connecting with Sarah C at all, even at the level of civility. How can I trust somebody who would mock my metaphor and then steal it? Every time I walk down a hallway I think of that. And feel this small sting of betrayal. It sucks.

"I think my boobs look under control," Sarah B says, leaning forward a bit.

"No," Sarah C says. "You're imagining that."

I guess I agree. Sarah B is too busty to pull off that tube top.

"You could work at Hooters," Sarah A says.

"Gross," Sarah B says.

But deep down, I think Sarah B took that as a compliment. Sarah B walks to the three-way mirror to look at the offending top at multiple angles.

"Where should we go next?" I ask.

Before our tube-top stop, we looped aimlessly around the mall. When we run out of things to do, one of the other Sarahs usually suggests going to the mall in Portage. Though I don't know why. Nothing exciting ever happens here. And when I wear shoes with heels, like today, my feet get so sore.

I slip out of my wedge sandals, and press my feet flat on the store's dusty wood floor.

"Without shoes you become a completely different size," Sarah A says.

"Yeah," I say.

"Don't you ever wish you were taller?" Sarah A asks me.

I shrug. Of course I wish that. Certain sixth graders tower over me.

"Do you think you'll grow more?" Sarah B asks.

"I don't know," I say.

"I don't think you will," Sarah A says. "I think you've reached your maximum height."

"You're not that short," Sarah C says. "Besides, your body matches who you are."

"It does?" I ask. It bothers me that Sarah C pretends to be nice to me when I know she doesn't mean it.

"Totally," Sarah C says. "You're solid."

Sarah A starts laughing. "What an awful thing to say. You just called her squatty."

"No, I didn't," Sarah C says. "I called her solid."

I look back and forth between Sarah A and Sarah C, like I'm following a volleyball being lobbed and returned over the net.

"Basically, 'solid' means 'squatty,'" Sarah A says. "Don't you think so, Sarah T?"

*Why is she asking me? She wants me to confirm an insult?*

"I don't know," I say.

"Come on, what else could it mean?" Sarah A asks.

"I don't know," Sarah B says. "Bionic?"

"How could 'solid' mean 'bionic'?" Sarah A asks. "That makes no sense."

Sarah B reenters the dressing room to change into her original top.

"I'd take it. Just stuff it somewhere," Sarah A whispers over the dressing room door.

"It made me look like Dolly Parton," Sarah B says. "Minus the rhinestones and vertical height of her wig."

"It was cute," Sarah A says. "You could wear it *somewhere*."

"You girls need help?" A short salesclerk, shorter than even me, walks out of an adjacent dressing room stall. Holy crap! Did she hear what we said?

"We're fine," Sarah A says.

"Good," the salesclerk answers. Her arms are draped with a wide array of cotton pants.

"Thanks, though," Sarah C says.

"It's my job," the clerk says, walking away. "And solid can mean a lot of things. Like 'tough' or 'strong' or 'thew'."

All of our eyes widen.

"Thew?" Sarah A asks.

"It means having well-developed muscles. You know, Mr. Universe is always thewy," Sarah C says.

We all look at her like she's speaking a foreign language. No wonder she rocked the SAT verbal section.

"Let's get out of here," Sarah A says.

My heart is beating very fast. I can't believe Sarah A openly talked about robbing the Banana Republic store within earshot of an employee. That's not like her at all. Sarah B swings open the door and sloppily folds the tube top on a table filled with other castoffs. I feel a little dizzy, so I reach for Sarah A to steady myself. She pulls away.

"What's wrong?" Sarah A asks.

"Are you okay?" Sarah C asks, grabbing my arm as I start to teeter.

"We should probably eat something," Sarah B says.

Sarah A rolls her eyes. I can tell that she's mad at herself for slipping up with that clerk. We're probably all going to be put on a list and be banned from this store and maybe some adjoining or even sister stores like the Gap. Sarah C holds my elbow and we all walk out into the mall's main corridor.

"Do you normally pass out if you don't eat for three hours?" Sarah A asks me.

I feel like pointing out that it's four o'clock in the afternoon and the only thing I've eaten today was a banana for breakfast. But I also feel like not confronting Sarah A.

"I guess it's part of being solid and squatty," Sarah A says.

I look down at my shoes. Why am I at the mall? Why do I do this to myself? I wish I'd stayed home with John Glenn.

"Don't let it sink in," Sarah C says. "She's just mad. Probably at herself."

It's impossible for Sarah C to improve my mood when I know that she's completely fake.

"Did you say something?" Sarah A asks.

I want there to be peace. I try to cover.

"I did. I said I feel like I could eat a whole pizza by myself."

"That's probably part of your problem," Sarah A says.

"Probably," I say.

Sometimes I know I'm too forgiving. I think my easygoing nature ends up making me look like a doormat. But I don't feel like I let everybody walk all over me. Just Sarah A. But that's because I truly admire her. And because deep down I feel sorry for her and everything she's gone through in life. She's been handed so many trials. And she's taken them head-on and wound up fierce. I'm nothing like that. I adapt or retreat, where Sarah A is willing to attack. How can I not admire her?

Sarah C is very sympathetic to my hunger issues and insists that we proceed immediately to the Big Burrito.

"Maybe Roman will be working," Sarah A says.

"Roman Karbowski works at the Big Burrito?" I ask.

"Yeah. He started last week," Sarah A says.

"How did you find that out?" I ask.

"I've been keeping close tabs on all of the guys," Sarah A says. "By the way, I'm sorry to report that Doyle Rickerson pulled a muscle in his groin."

"He did?" Sarah B says. "That's so awful."

"Why are you so concerned about Sarah T's guy?" Sarah A asks. "There's no crossover here. You wanted Gerard Truax and you're getting Gerard Truax."

"I know," Sarah B says. "I'm just worried about the team."

"You act like baseball is the great American pastime," Sarah A says.

"That's exactly what it is," Sarah C says.

"Hey guys, I can see Roman Karbowski working the register through the window," I say. He's tall. And tan. And has brown wavy hair that dangles attractively off his head like he spent all day grooming it to frame his face. Plus, for a guy, Roman Karbowski has unusually pink lips. And they pout. I can see why Sarah A is so drawn to him. Those two could make fantastic-looking babies.

"Okay. We can't screw this up. Follow my lead," Sarah A says. "Got it?"

"Got it," the rest of us say in unison.

The Big Burrito smells like spicy taco meat. Sarah A orders a burrito and some nachos for us to share.

"Mild or hot sauce?" Roman Karbowski asks.

"The green," Sarah A says.

"That's mild," Roman says.

"Hot burns my lips," Sarah A says.

"That's weird," Roman says. "How do you eat your burrito? Tongue-burning I could understand."

Sarah A tilts her head to the side and laughs. We all laugh too, I guess because we're following her lead.

"I'll bring your food over when it's ready," he says.

Sarah takes an orange tray with four water glasses to a far corner table.

"Why did you guys all laugh like that? That was so weird," Sarah A says. "Even Roman thought it was weird. It made his eye twitch."

"His eye always twitches," Sarah C says.

"It does not," Sarah A says. "Don't tear down my guy."

"I thought we were supposed to follow your lead," Sarah B says.

"Use some common sense," Sarah A says. "We want our carefully planned strategy to look totally natural. Group laughter looks orchestrated. It just does."

"I think she's right," I say.

"Duh," Sarah A says.

"Here you go," Roman says, setting down two plates of food. His arms are draped in a thin coat of dark hair.

"It smells great," Sarah A says. "Do you cook like this when you're at home?"

"Isabelle does all the cooking. I just schlep it out to the customers," Roman says.

"Are we supposed to tip the schleppers?" Sarah A asks.

"Tips are always appreciated, but never expected," he says. "Let me know if you need anything. And come say good-bye before you leave."

Sarah A smiles. After Roman makes it back to the counter, Sarah C breaks into a wide grin.

"He's after you," Sarah C says. "He so doesn't act like he has a girlfriend."

"He has a girlfriend?" I ask.

"He and Meena are practically not even speaking to each other anymore," Sarah A says. "She's history."

"Ancient," Sarah C says.

"I think you're right," Sarah B says. "Roman can't stop looking at you."

We all turn and look at Roman looking at Sarah A.

"Don't all look," Sarah A says. "We're being so obvious."

"What's the hurt?" Sarah C asks. "Guys find attention flattering."

Sarah A picks up her fork and waves it over the burrito. "Who's running this? You or me?" Sarah A aims the prong-end of the fork at Sarah C. "I said we looked obvious. Did I stutter?"

Sarah C doesn't answer her.

"I'd like to see you get Benny Stowe without me," Sarah A says. "You couldn't. You know that? You couldn't."

The bells jingle on the door as Meena Cooper walks into the Big Burrito and gives Roman a big hug followed by a kiss.

"I can't believe this," Sarah A says.

"It probably doesn't mean anything," I say. "They'll probably have a big fight later on tonight."

Sarah A divvies up the food and we pick at it. We don't say much of anything beyond polite chatter. Meena stays for ten minutes, and when she leaves, Roman swats her lovingly on the butt.

"There's more than one way to interpret an ass pat," Sarah C says.

"I don't need your sympathy," Sarah A says. "He's still mine. This doesn't alter my plans. Roman Karbowski will be my boyfriend for my senior year."

"I believe you," Sarah B says.

"Me too," I say.

"Don't patronize me," Sarah A says. "I'm going to go over there and talk to him. If I pick up a stack of napkins, that means I want Sarah C to come over and extricate me from the conversation. Got it?"

"Got it," we reply.

But before Sarah A can make her move, Meena reenters the Big Burrito. She's carrying a giant cookie. It's enclosed in plastic wrap and it has a small purple bow stuck on it. I watch the bow tumble to the floor.

"Thanks, Meena," Roman says, peeling the cookie out of the wrapper and taking a big bite.

Sarah A stares at her water cup.

"Are you still going to go?" Sarah C asks.

"I don't think I'd go now," Sarah B says.

"They could still have that fight," I say.

Sarah A softly shakes her head back and forth in disagreement. "In the big picture, this doesn't change anything," she says. "Either those two will break up due to natural causes, or something else will happen."

"Something else?" Sarah C asks.

"The world is a crazy place. Unfortunate occurrences happen all the time," Sarah A says. She places a corn chip on her napkin and smashes it with her thumb. Then she slowly eats all the pieces.

"I should probably head back home," I say. "I need to take John Glenn for a walk."

We gather our trash and throw it away. Sarah A waves politely to Roman.

"Come back and visit me again," he says.

"What a tease," Sarah C says.

"That's how I like them," Sarah A says.

We climb into my car and Sarah A sits down beside me. She looks tired, like she's really been through something.

"I think things are going well," I say.

"Yeah, yeah," Sarah A says.

I pull out of the lot and drive down Drake.

"So what's it like being a first-time dog owner?" Sarah C asks me.

I try to think of something funny that will lighten the mood.

"It's very turdy," I say.

It works. Everybody laughs. Even Sarah A.

When we pull up to my driveway it's crowded with a long line of cars.

"It looks like my parents are here," Sarah C says.

"It looks like my parents are here too," Sarah A says.

"That's my father's Toyota," Sarah B says.

"Isn't that Mr. King's Civic?" I ask.

None of us have time to figure out what's going on, but it feels utterly abominable.

"Should we all go inside?" Sarah B asks.

"What other choice do we have?" I ask.

We climb out of my car and file into my house. Seated in the family room I see everybody's parents, minus Sarah B's mom, and Mr. King. A lot of the mothers look weepy, especially mine.

"Girls, this is so serious," Mr. King says. "We want to talk to you one at a time."

Mr. King has never stood in my living room before. I hold my breath. This must be about what happened at the shelter last night. Somebody must have seen us. What an unholy mess.

"Sarah Aberdeen, let's start with you. The rest of you, go wait in Sarah Trestle's bedroom."

John Glenn speeds over to me at a very fast clip.

"Can I take my dog?" I ask.

"*Your* dog?" Mr. King asks. "I thought that was Sarah Aberdeen's Labrador, John Glenn."

"I can explain everything," Sarah A says.

I take John Glenn by his collar and lead him back to my bedroom. All the charades are about to end. No more games. No more hiding stuff. I wonder what the Sarahs will do now? How are things going to be after our families find out what the Sarahs are really all about? I take a deep breath and hold it. I don't understand my own reaction. I thought I'd be devastated if the Sarahs were caught. But I'm not. As I walk into my bedroom and exhale, an inexplicable calmness sweeps over me. Maybe something good will come out of this.

Once Sarah B and Sarah C sit down, I firmly shut my bedroom door.

"It's over," I say.

John Glenn folds down on the floor on top of a pair of Sarah A's jeans.

"Over?" Sarah C asks. "You've got to be kidding! You think Sarah A is going to come clean about anything?"

"Doesn't she have to?" I ask, jerking my thumb at the door.

Sarah C rolls her eyes at me.

"She doesn't *have* to do anything. Let's listen. I bet it's the beginning of a whole new set of lies."

"No way," I say.

"I think she's right," Sarah B says.

I press my ear to my door.

"Can you hear anything?" I ask.

But neither Sarah answers me. We stand silent, our cheeks flattened against the door's cool surface. Yes, we can hear everything, even one another's beating hearts. Sarah C and Sarah B were right. Even though I shouldn't be, I'm surprised. I lean deeper into the door. Maybe Sarah A simply prefers dishonesty. Maybe it's all she knows.

# Chapter 16

"Is that the truth?" Mr. King asks. "You're telling me Sarah Trestle was the only person involved?"

"Yes," Sarah A says. "I had no idea that she was planning that."

"I don't believe it," my mother says.

"Are you calling my daughter a liar?" Mrs. Aberdeen asks. "My daughter never lies. I trust what she's saying."

"I trust her too," Mr. Aberdeen says.

"I can't believe my daughter is involved in any of this," Mrs. Cody says. "She's an excellent citizen."

"If my daughter were a thief, I'd know about it," my mother says.

Sarah C backs away from the door.

"She's throwing you to the wolves," Sarah C says. "You're going to take the fall for everything."

"But we didn't even steal that pit bull. Really, we didn't break any laws. Did we?" I ask.

Sarah B pulls back from the door and shrugs. Suddenly, there's a ton of yelling. We quickly resume our eavesdropping stance.

"The picture proves everything. My Sarah wasn't involved," Mr. Babbitt yells. "Pictures don't lie!"

"It's very grainy," my father says. "It won't stand up in court."

"I wasn't planning on taking anyone to court," Mr. King says. "I was hoping we could sort it out amongst ourselves."

I push away from the door.

"How can they have a picture?" I ask.

The other two Sarahs stay pressed to the door.

"They must have a security camera," Sarah C says. "It must have only captured you."

"Isn't that impossible?" I ask.

"Anything is possible," Sarah C says. "It all depends on the angle."

"Sarah A is sending you up the creek," Sarah B says.

I put my hands on my hips. I don't want to hear any more. But now Sarah A is speaking again. It's too tempting not to listen.

"Nobody's perfect," Sarah A says. "Sarah Trestle isn't a criminal so much as an average girl who made a mistake. It's probably the only time she's done something like this."

"I think we should bring her out here," Mr. King says.

I gasp. It hurts to hear Sarah A rolling over on me, but an even worse pain awaits me. I don't want to face everybody.

"What should I say?" I ask.

"I'd go with the truth," Sarah C says.

"No, leave me out of it," Sarah B says. "My dad will be so disappointed in me. It'll kill him."

"Literally?" Sarah C asks. "Does he have a heart condition?"

"No, but it wouldn't be fair. I mean, besides a pack of Oreos, I've never stolen anything. I lied about the contest. I paid for my bikini wax. I paid for all that other stuff. Even the certificate for the additional wax," Sarah B says.

"You're kidding," I say. "That's cheating. You should have been the Sarah who got tossed from the group."

"I don't think it matters now," Sarah C says. "Anyway, I cheated too."

I'm so shocked that I lightly punch her in the arm.

"If you didn't steal Digits then how did you end up with him?" I ask.

"I'm cat-sitting for Sunny Gwyn while her family is out of town. I went in and picked up Digits at the shelter this morning. I figured, no harm no foul."

I can't believe that Sarah A and I were the only ones who legitimately competed in the challenge. And Sarah B and

Sarah C were going to let me get kicked out of the Sarahs for committing the worst crime when they never committed any crime.

There isn't time for me to formulate a response. I can hear somebody walking toward my bedroom door. Sarah B and Sarah C scamper toward the center of the room. I don't follow them. I know what I have to do. The door swings open. It's my father.

"You need to explain some things," he says.

He reaches toward my arm and grabs me by my wrist. I let him pull me, offering no resistance. The living room and the inquisition of a lifetime await me. I never thought this day would come. Not this way. Not in my own house. Maybe I should confess my part in everything. Maybe I should take the fall for everyone. Isn't that what a real friend is supposed to do? I'm standing before an audience of parents and Mr. King and Sarah A. This must be exactly how those virgins in South American countries felt right before they were shoved into the steaming volcanoes.

"Hello, Sarah," Mr. King says.

I wave.

He's holding a photo. Sarah C was right. They must have security cameras situated around the shelter. That is so unfortunate. When did they put them up and why didn't they mention it to the volunteers?

"I just want to know what happened," Mr. King says. "I want to hear it in your own words."

I clear my throat. It comes down to this: Do I choose the truth? Or my friends? Before I speak, I don't really know which way I'll go. I look around at all the eager faces. Sarah A keeps her head down. She's playing with the small silver buckle on her sandal.

"Sarah?" my father asks. "Tell us what happened."

I take a deep breath. The truth is going to hurt a lot of people.

"I thought I was doing the right thing," I say.

Really, I'll just tell them I was trying to liberate a trapped dog and helped relocate an underappreciated rabbit and exploited cat.

"We didn't teach you that," my mother says. "I can't believe this."

"You did it alone?" Mr. King asks. He's worked his hands into indignant fists and propped them on his sides. I've never seen Mr. King make a fist before. He must be so disappointed in me.

"Animals should be free," I say. "Even pit bulls."

There's an odd silence. Mr. King tilts his head like he's trying to get water out of his ear. My parents both look surprised. Sarah A appears mortified.

"How does stealing a donation jar help liberate pit bulls?" my father asks.

My knees shake. This is about the donation jar. The clerk took a picture of my car. When Mr. King came to collect the jar, the clerk must've given him the picture. Mr. King recognized me. Now here we all are. This isn't about the shelter situation at all. Okay, I've started my lie and I've got to continue with it. Being dishonest sucks, because you have to keep coming up with new crap to say. Plus, you've got to remember all the old crap in the correct order. I'm thinking as fast as I can.

"I was going to give the horse money to help out pit bulls. They're so misunderstood," I say.

"Like Robin Hood?" my mother asks. "Except with vicious dogs?"

She's on her feet now, walking toward me. She probably wants to look me in the eye to confirm that I'm telling the truth.

"You acted alone?" she asks. "None of the other Sarahs were involved or influenced you in any way?"

I stare into her brown eyes. I don't know what to say to make them happy. I turn away.

"I'm the only one in the picture, right?" I ask.

My mother puts her hands on my shoulders. She wants me to look at her. So I do.

"There will be consequences for your actions," my mother says.

She squints and strengthens her hold on me. I can feel her weight. It's heavier than my own guilt.

"I think she's cleared it up," Sarah A says. "She was trying to redistribute the money. She acted solo. She thought she was doing a noble thing. It makes sense to me."

My mother turns and stares hard at Sarah A.

"I don't feel like I've gotten the whole story," she says.

Sarah A shrugs. "I know. It's very surprising," she says.

"The truth is sometimes hard to hear," Mr. Aberdeen says.

"I find that the whole truth is rarely told," my mother says.

"Sarah, do you still have the jar?" my father asks.

I look at Sarah A. Her bottom lip is thrust out, making her face appear dramatically sympathetic. If I didn't know better, I'd think she was oblivious to my crime. She looks that convincing.

"The jar is in my room," I say.

"I think you know what you need to do," my father says.

"Sarah, I can't believe you did this." My mom lets go of me and moves toward the edge of the room.

I walk down the hallway, wishing that my house had a back door and that I could throw it open and escape into the night and run and run and run. But I open my bedroom door and go to my closet instead. I can feel Sarah B and Sarah C watching me, but I don't look at them. I fear eye contact with them could reduce me to a quivering mass of humiliation.

As I take the donation jar and return to the living room, I feel like I'm holding my own soul. It grows heavier with each step. When Mr. King sees me, he closes his eyes and shakes his head. And I stand there, holding the plastic box. Mr. King reaches out his arms. I give him the box and it feels like I'm handing over so much more.

"This is hard for me, too," Mr. King says. "You've been an outstanding volunteer."

I fold my arms across my chest and focus on not bawling in front of everyone. Right now, a mild flow of tears are all that I allow to escape.

Mr. Aberdeen and his wife both stand.

"I think it's best if we take our daughter with us," Mrs. Aberdeen says.

"Am I going home?" Sarah A asks.

"No. Vance is still there. We'll put you up in a hotel," Mr. Aberdeen says. "It's just for a couple of nights."

My mother releases me.

"Sarah, go to your room," my mother says.

Her tone is flat and bitter.

"I'm sorry," I say.

But it's way too late for that. I glance at Mr. King. I can see the photo. Without a doubt, it's my car. Clearly, I'm the driver. Nobody else is with me. I'm the only person in the frame.

I walk into my room. Sarah B's face looks relaxed and relieved. She's blowing a large bubble. It pops.

"Stress relief," she says.

I nod.

"You didn't have to do that," Sarah C says.

"It's okay," I say.

"We're still your friends," Sarah C says.

I almost smile.

Why is it that it's the backstabbing Sarah who's always there to offer me the most public support?

Sarah B pops of series of bubbles that are so loud they sound like gunfire.

"We're still friends too? Right?" I ask.

"Yeah, but it kind of depends on what happens next," Sarah B says. "My dad probably won't want me hanging out with you. Not after your confession."

"You don't seem upset about this at all," I say.

"Well, the Tigers are having a great season. They're the number one team. This never happens. Now I'll be able to catch some games."

"Baseball is more important than the Sarahs?" I ask.

Sarah B looks down at the ground. "I don't know what to say. I mean, I'm totally in love with Pudge."

"Who's Pudge?" I ask. I have no idea what she's talking about. "What about Gerard Truax?"

"Oh, I still like Gerard, but I love Ivan Rodriguez. His nickname is Pudge. He plays for the Tigers. He's probably the best defensive catcher that ever lived."

"How long have you loved him?" I ask.

She looks up at me, her face soft and dreamy. "All my life."

"Did you know about this?" I ask, pointing at Sarah C.

"She didn't exactly hide it," Sarah C says.

"I've never even heard of this guy, and suddenly he's more important than the Sarahs?" I ask.

"He's the greatest," Sarah B says.

"He's a catcher?" I ask.

"He's a very civic-minded player. He's donated a lot of money and he started the Ivan Rodriguez Foundation. It helps kids with cancer and other diseases," Sarah C says.

"He's the best," Sarah B says.

Things just aren't quite making sense for me.

"So you're out of here?" I ask.

Sarah B nods and gives me a quick hug and is gone.

"This will blow over," Sarah C says.

"I don't know. She seems really hung up on this catcher," I say.

"No, the Pudge thing is a permanent fixation. I'm talking about the bigger picture, about getting caught for your crime."

When she says the word "crime," I feel stung.

She walks out of my room and I watch the back of her

head until she turns the corner and is gone. I feel weak. The Sarahs are finished. Sarah B has already moved on to new interests. My parents think I'm a criminal who commits unnecessary crimes to protect mean dogs. I lie on my bed and roll onto my stomach. I breathe into my pillow, warming it until the fabric around my face feels uncomfortably hot.

"You get to keep John Glenn."

I look up.

Sarah A gathers her things from around the room.

"What?" I ask.

"Everyone thinks he's yours now. Even Mr. King. So he is." Sarah A's face looks blank. I can't tell what she's feeling about all this. "You can put it on your college entrance essay. It's my gift to you."

"But my life is ruined," I say.

"You'll adapt," she says. "That's what you do, remember?"

"Adapt? My parents' opinion of me has been destroyed," I say.

"Okay. Let's not overreact. Sooner or later, one of us was bound to get caught. Be honest with yourself. Are you really so surprised that it was you?" Sarah A asks.

"What?" I ask. "You think I deserved to get caught?"

I want to tell Sarah A that I am surprised. I never thought things could end this badly. My life feels wrecked.

"Your parents are going to keep you under lock and key

for a while. I mean, you got caught robbing a convenience store," Sarah A says.

"But I did it for you," I say.

My voice is trembling. Sarah stoops to pick up a pair of socks and lets out a frustrated sigh.

"You don't believe that, do you? It's like you're disconnected from understanding your own personhood or something."

She sympathetically shakes her head back and forth, looking at me like I'm a lost cause.

"Listen, you didn't rob that store for me. You did it for yourself," she says.

I wince. But I don't deny it. I watch as Sarah A picks up three of my tank tops, wadding them into the giant ball of her own clothes.

"Don't be like this," she says.

I can barely see her face over the large bundle in her arms.

"Thanks for keeping the game under wraps. That's really cool of you. That is something you did for us. But *I'm* not the reason why you took that jar. You drove to that 7-Eleven and ripped that jar off the counter because you wanted to be a Sarah. You did it for yourself."

John Glenn follows her to the door, but she turns him away with her foot. And when he tries to inch toward her and the exit a second time, she forcefully uses her sandal to re-aim his head toward me.

"I don't even like the way stealing makes me feel," I say.

Sarah A tilts her head back and looks at my ceiling. She bites on her lower lip like she's annoyed. "That's something you probably should have addressed with yourself a long time ago."

She opens the door.

"What about the guy phase? The future? Don't you have anything else to say to me?"

"I think John Glenn peed on your carpet," Sarah A says.

I turn and look. There's a puddle near where he was laying, staining my throw rug a deep green. Considering my own bladder anxiety, this seems oddly appropriate. Not only do I have bathroom issues, I trigger them in dogs. Due to the drama, I forgot to walk him.

Sarah A flutters her fingers, drumming them against her wad of garments, halfheartedly waving good-bye. I push my face back into my own pillow. Why did I let her take my tank tops? I feel tears melting into my pillowcase. Why didn't I disagree with anything she said? Suddenly, I can't breathe. The pocket of air that I've been drawing on has run out. I turn my head and take a deep breath.

When I let it go, I'm surprised to feel sobs escaping from somewhere deep inside of me. Feelings that I've been holding down for a long time are finally finding their way out. I try to calm myself, to take a series of breaths. I choke, sputter, gasp. All I can think about is what Sarah A said. Is that why I'm crying? Do I think she's right about why I stole that stupid jar? Yes. I do. And knowing this—believing this—makes me, makes everything, feel so much worse.

# Chapter 17

The inquisition is two weeks behind me, and to cheer myself up I've started sleeping with Roman Karbowski. Not the person. But the pillow. Since Sarah A left him behind, curling up with Roman allows me to feel less alone.

I haven't spoken to the Sarahs. Somewhere around day four, I grew numb to the pain. Actually, I grew numb to everything. I don't know if this is what Sarah A had in mind when she told me to just stop feeling things, but it works much better than the alternative, which is to feel awful about myself all the time.

In addition to my newly implemented curfew, I was forced to give up my volunteer work at the shelter. It was explained to me that due to my impulsiveness concerning animal equality and liberation, I would be a liability. But my life has bloomed with new kinds of activity. I've become essential to my parents' lives. They even take me to work with them. Like I'm a lunch box.

When school starts in three weeks, I imagine I'm either

miraculously going to reattach myself to the Sarahs or finally strike out and make new friends. Except, I'm not really sure how to do that. I have no idea what I'll do. When I picture myself at school, Sarahless, I'm wending through the hallways, burdened by my heavy backpack, all alone.

Sometimes I hope that the school year kicks off with a major Sarah reconciliation. They'll all race to my locker to tell me how much they missed me. It shouldn't matter. I know it shouldn't. But I want my absence to have made them ache. For them to have felt incomplete. I want to hear them say that they were unable to launch full bore into the guy phase without me.

My mother can sense that there's more to the "donation jar" story. So does my father. I'm certain they suspect other crimes. And even though they don't voice this concern, it's clear they each think that I'm protecting the other Sarahs. Thankfully, in the days that followed, neither pushed me toward additional confessions. I admire this about them. They're prepared to let me keep some secrets.

My mother and I are driving to Dr. Pewter's condominium.

"Stabilizing the master bedroom will be a feat," she says. She pulls to a stop in front an old, two-story brown condominium. *A college professor lives in this dump?* I unbuckle my seat belt. For the first time, I realize that my mother's car smells oddly medicinal, like fruit and ointment.

"Your car smells like grapefruit and something else. Something bitter," I say.

"When cleaning defiled pigpens, bitter grapefruit is one of the more pleasant fragrances to encounter."

Dr. Pewter's master bedroom in one of the last rooms my mother has left to clean in this *Beowulf*-obsessed professor's cluttered life. It's my first time coming to her condo. For the past two weeks, we've been working on cleaning her office at Western Michigan University. It's on the ninth floor of Sprau Tower and overlooks a fountain that strongly resembles the YMCA's swimming pool. Except the fountain contains several quack-happy ducks.

Dr. Pewter's office wasn't the receptacle of filth that I'd been expecting. Sure, there were towers of graded essays stacked in leaning piles across her desk. (I skimmed quite a few of them. The majority had earned C's and were dripping with BS.) And she had a ton of Bible-thick books about Old English prosody and *Beowulf*. But I was sort of expecting that. Minus the dust, her work space appeared reasonably sanitary. I wouldn't have wanted to eat a meal or have any surgical procedures done in there or anything. But it wasn't on the verge of being condemned.

"You make it sound like her place is something out of a horror film," I say.

My mother hasn't released her grip on the steering wheel.

"Horror is a good word." My mother frowns, creating a deep crease next to her left eye along her nose. She finally turns off her car and pulls the keys out of the ignition. "She has an abominable home life."

"Can you sum it up in one word?" I ask.

My mother slowly turns to face me.

"Parrots," she says. She drops the keys in her purse and re-grips the steering wheel.

"Parrots?"

"Parrots," she repeats, nervously wringing the steering wheel with both hands.

"You mean she's let parrots overtake her house?" I ask.

My mother shakes her head no.

"Not the house. Just the master bedroom."

She reaches into the backseat and pulls out two pairs of thick leather work gloves.

"They bite," she says.

"I know, we've had a couple at the shelter," I say. "The parrot is one of only two animals that can see behind itself without turning its head. The other is the rabbit."

"Good. You'll be an asset. I had no idea you had parrot experience. I've been reading up on parrots in preparation for today. They have a flock mentality, you know."

"Is that a bad thing?" I ask.

"Never let them gain the upper hand on you, Sarah. Make sure the parrots never go higher than your chest. You need to remain dominant," she says.

"You make it sound like they're going to kill us."

"Birds are dreadfully smart and devious. I wouldn't put anything past a parrot."

Wow, I knew my mother wasn't an animal lover, but I had no idea her distrust for wildlife had reached such a paranoid level.

"Mom, they're not going to kill us," I say.

She bites her lower lip and gets out of the car. I see her pull out a gun from beneath her seat and place it in her cleaning bucket.

"Mother! You can't carry a weapon in your car. Let alone your client's house."

"It's just a squirt gun," she says.

"What good will that do?" I ask.

"I thought you said you've worked with parrots."

"I have, but we never utilized water weaponry at the shelter."

"When birds get wet, they'll generally stop whatever they're doing in order to preen."

"Good to know," I said.

She reaches underneath the seat again and pulls out another pistol.

"That's fake too, right?" I ask.

"Yes, Sarah, it's yours. Now let's go clean."

"Won't cleaning chemicals kill them?" I ask. "Birds are so sensitive about fumes. That's why they get sent into mine shafts."

My mother shakes her head. She bends down to arrange some of her spray bottles.

"I told you. I've been reading up on parrots. I've brought grapefruit seed–based cleansers. The birds will be fine."

"You can clean filth with a grapefruit?" I ask.

"Grapefruit seeds contain an extremely potent compound that can kill staph, strep, E. coli, salmonella, candida, herpes, influenza, parasites, and fungi. You name it. Some say it can even clear up yeast infections."

"Are all those things in her condo?" I ask. "Should we wear rubber gloves underneath our leather ones? Do I need a mask? Am I going to get herpes? Or a yeast infection?" I ask.

I'm struck by nostalgia. Hanging out with the Sarahs was so much more fun than this.

"We're not going to get herpes or yeast infections. And I don't know what ills are lurking in her condo. I'm sure we're properly suited to handle what we have to."

She straightens herself up and gathers her two plastic buckets that are brimming with supplies.

"Do you need help?" I ask.

She surrenders the smaller one and I find it to be much heavier than your average bucket. I follow my mother up Dr. Pewter's cracked cement walkway. Grass and weeds pop up through the fissures, widening the original cracks.

"She should pull these," I say.

"We'll be pulling them after the master bedroom," she says.

I almost object. How is lawn maintenance our job? My mother jiggles the key until it turns and we walk inside.

"It's ridiculous," my mother says. "If you're given the chance at a good life, you should seize it. Stay organized and productive. Match your socks. Fold your underwear. And don't let your parrots run the show."

"Do you hate Dr. Pewter?" I ask.

"I don't hate anybody, Sarah. But people shouldn't let their domiciles run amok."

My mother seems on the verge of tears, which strikes me as odd. My mother is never on the verge of tears. We walk down Dr. Pewter's entrance hall and through her living room.

"It looks and smells clean to me," I say.

"I toiled for weeks in here," she says.

I consider asking my mother why she likes organizing and cleaning in the first place. I always assumed it was her life's love, but her attitude thus far isn't bearing that out. She seems pushed to the limit by Dr. Pewter's messy lifestyle. It's like my mother is taking it personally, when she should be treating it like just another day on the job.

We arrive at the master bedroom and it's clear that there's some sort of bird action going on behind the door. There's muffled squawking.

"Sarah, I want you to remember that when a parrot screams at you, it's important not to yell back."

"Why? Will that scare it?" I ask.

"No, because when you yell back at a parrot, you're just giving it exactly what it wants."

My mother makes it sound like we're going to go to war. It's so easy not to think about the Sarahs at a moment like this, because so much other stuff is at stake. *Wait a minute, by consciously not thinking about the Sarahs, I'm totally thinking about them.* It's crazy how that works.

My mother opens the door. This is more than a master bedroom. It's an aviary with a bed in the middle of it. There are ten tall perches set up around the room's perimeter. They must be at least six feet tall.

"They just crap anywhere?" I ask.

"They're animals," my mother says. "Of course they do."

I count a total of six parrots. They all look like macaws. Three are blue. We had one like them at the shelter. They're called hyacinth macaws and their color is so deep that they're almost purple.

"They're pretty," I say.

My mother doesn't agree.

The other three parrots are scarlets. They're mainly red, especially their chests, but they have bursts of bright blue and yellow on their wings.

"They're big," I say.

"We need to clean," my mother says.

I look around. Other than white bird droppings that litter the beige carpet, I don't see much to clean.

"Clean what?" I ask.

Two of the hyacinth macaws flap their way to one of the slats of Dr. Pewter's four-poster bed. They cock their heads and look at us using just one eye.

"They're creepy," my mom says. "They're evaluating us, deciding who's superior, us or them."

"Maybe this isn't the job for you," I say. "Maybe Dr. Pewter should hire a parrot person."

"I can do this. I'm not going to be thwarted by birds."

She reaches into a bucket and pulls out a yellow sponge.

"I'm going to wet this down," she says, walking to the bathroom.

One of the scarlet macaws, the largest, glides like a kite toward the perch nearest the bathroom door. I watch its feathered belly pass over me.

"Sarah, hand me my gun," she says.

"Mom, it hasn't done anything yet."

"It's above chest level. You're not supposed to let them get above chest level. The book was firm about that."

I pick up the squirt gun and hold it. It's pure black and looks so much like a real gun. I turn it over in my hand.

"Sarah," my mother says.

I look at the gun. It doesn't feel right to water down a bird in its own home while it's minding its own business.

"Sarah Trestle, hand it to me."

"Sarah Trestle," the macaw above my mother squawks. "Sarah Trestle."

My mother throws her arms over her head and runs to me. I look at the parrot. It doesn't have to open its beak to talk. The words just come out.

"It's not doing anything. It's parroting what you said because it's a parrot and that's what they do."

"Sarah Trestle," it repeats. The words sound watery.

It's an odd feeling hearing a bird say your name.

"I bet Dr. Pewter has taught them to say all sorts of things," I say.

"I guess," my mom says.

She's taken the gun from the other bucket.

"This is going to be a long day," she says.

I'm tempted to see what these birds can do. I wonder if they know Old English. I wonder if they can recite *Beowulf.*

"Beowulf. Beowulf," I say, trying to steer them into action.

"Don't encourage them, Sarah."

"Come on, Mom. This is so cool. It's like parrot theater."

"What's so cool about parrot theater?" she asks.

"Beowulf. Beowulf," I say.

Two of the smaller hyacinths fly over me and join the scarlet macaw near the bathroom.

"The Geats. The Geats," one calls.

"They're doing it," I say.

"Shh," my mother says. She looks interested.

"Grendel's in the beer-hall," squawks a scarlet from across the room.

"Deathbed. Deathbed," bugles another red parrot. It drops its head down, and then lifts it back up, like it's trying to play peekaboo.

"Hello, Mother," cries another in a dry voice. It's hard to keep track of which bird is saying what.

"Dragon was a foe. Dragon was a foe," screeches another. Its voice is piercing.

"Deathbed. Deathbed," calls the bed-stationed parrot, its red head moving so fast now it's almost a blur.

"Good-bye," blurts the scarlet near the bathroom.

I watch a white turd drop from beneath its tail feathers and land in the bathroom's entranceway. I'm relieved that it fell on the linoleum and not the carpet. It'll be easier to clean.

After the parrots stop talking, the room falls silent. It's almost like the parrots have flown away.

"And the body parts from the heart, from the soul, to seek glory," I say.

"What?" my mother asks.

"That's how the story of *Beowulf* ends. After he kills Grendel, Grendel's mother, and the dragon, Beowulf dies. 'And the body parts from the heart, from the soul, to seek glory.' I mean, I don't know if those are the exact words. But it's the gist of it." I let her think I'm a genius and don't mention that I just read the lines a couple of days ago at Dr. Pewter's office.

"It sounds tragic," my mother says.

"It's *Beowulf*. He's the hero and he dies. These parrots are better than SparkNotes." The Sarahs would love hearing about them, I think. Especially Sarah B.

For no obvious reason, the parrots erupt in squawking.

"It's the flock mentality!" my mother says.

They begin flying from perch to perch, circling above us. The sound their feathers make when they flap their wings hard reminds me of a flag at full mast cracking in the wind. It makes the hairs on the back on my neck stand up. I look at my mother. Her skin is extremely goose pimpled and she looks like she might start crying.

"Can't somebody else do this? You seem pretty freaked out," I say.

"I am. It's your great-grandmother."

"What?" I ask. This makes no sense. It's the parrots, not my great-grandmother. She's been dead for years.

"Her cats did the same thing to me. All nine of them. I can't take animals en masse."

"What do you mean they did the same thing to you?"

"Their animal presence overwhelmed me," she says.

"You can't take animals, period," I say.

"I know."

My mother slides her squirt gun inside the back of her pants much the way I've seen cops do on television. The birds are screaming. They're through with their performance. Now, they're just making earsplitting noise. I help her gather her supplies.

"So you're done?" I ask. "We're not going to clean?"

"This is the first job I've ever quit," she says.

"Because of the parrots?" I ask.

"Exactly," my mother says.

We hurry out of the bedroom and shut the door. The birds don't settle down.

"We're not going to pull weeds?" I ask. I regret having brought it up, because I don't really feel like doing any bending over.

"I'm done," my mother says. "Those cats, Sarah. They ruined her. Your great-grandmother didn't have to live that way. Nobody does."

My mother rarely talks about her side of the family. Her own mother died several years ago in a car accident in Detroit. Her father lives in Florida. I've only met him twice. My great-grandfather died young. I think he had a lot of problems. My mother has explained her family history this way: "I come from people who experienced a long run of bad luck."

But Liam has a different explanation, a political one. "It's the effects of postcolonialism," he has said and said again. The first time he ever told me this, we were driving to the grocery store. I don't think I'd ever heard the word "postcolonialism" before. "The whole idea was to fracture the family unit. To isolate and wreck and ruin and destroy. Where do you think Hitler got the idea for concentration camps?"

"I don't know," I said.

"American Indian reservations!" Liam yelled, pulling into a parking stall at Meijer.

I still remember the look on his face. It was a combination of furor and unbelievable sadness. I gripped my mother's shopping list and asked the one question that seemed important.

"Mom wrote down cheese, but she didn't say which kind. What do you think, mozzarella or cheddar?"

And Liam turned to face me and raised his hand, not like he was going to hit me, but like he had all this energy and it needed somewhere to go. He made a jazz hand and then turned it into a fist.

"I'm talking about shit that matters, the important ways we're connected to this country, to this planet, and your only reaction is to ask me about cheese? Don't you care how you got here? Doesn't it matter to you that others suffered so you could exist?"

And then I broke his heart.

"Not really," I said. "Maybe one day it will, but it doesn't right now." And I took out a pen and added the word cheddar next to cheese.

My mother has started the car and is driving at a high rate of speed away from the parrot debacle. She still looks pale and her mind seems distant.

"Maybe we should rent a movie," I suggest.

"I don't want to watch anything that will rip my heart out," my mother says.

"Me neither."

She drives us to Hollywood Video, but instead of getting out of the car, we both sit and people watch. There are a lot of couples headed to the Oakwood Bistro. Most of them look like they're wearing uncomfortable shoes. And there are a lot of singles making their way into Sawall's Health Foods. The majority of them are decked out in brown sandals. It seems like information a social anthropologist might find telling.

"Your grandmother was a good person," my mother says.

Tears roll easily off her cheeks and she doesn't try to wipe them away. I don't know much about my grandma Caldwell.

"Your great-grandmother was a good person too. A better person than a lot of people," my mother says.

She takes a few deeps breaths and squints at something. I follow her gaze, but all I see is dark asphalt.

I look at my own hands. Even though I don't completely understand the reason behind it, my mother is crying. I should say something to make her feel better. No good daughter should let her mother be this sad.

"It doesn't surprise me that you come from good people," I say. "You're great." And I mean this.

I hope that didn't sound corny. I didn't mean it that way. My mother licks her lips and unbuckles her seat belt.

"You come from those people too," she says.

I feel a lump form in my throat. Having a criminal daughter must be an enormous disappointment. Maybe that's why she's crying. I crack open my car door.

"You're a good person too," my mother tells me. "I know it."

I don't feel like a good person, and if we weren't related, I wonder if my mother would really feel so positively about me. We walk side by side into the video store. She immediately heads for the new releases, but I tell her to stop.

"Maybe we should rent *Godzilla*," I say.

"Why?" my mother asks.

"Because of Dad, Godzilla has been on my mind lately," I say. "I should learn something about him."

"Don't let Liam hear you say that."

"Why?" I ask. "What does Liam have against Godzilla?"

My mother's answer might explain the buried lunch box and action figure.

She shakes her head. "It's not like that. You called the monster a 'him' and Liam is convinced that Godzilla is female."

"Why would Liam think that?" I ask.

"Quite a few hard-core fans believe that. In one of the films, Godzilla has a child."

I nod. But really, I'm thinking that our family spends way too much time thinking about Godzilla.

"Liam was so disappointed that people didn't understand Godzilla's backstory. The beast was more than just a monster. It symbolized the dangers and anxieties of a postatomic world."

I don't ask her to elaborate on any of that, because the word "atomic" freaks me out.

"Look, they've got *King Kong*," my mother says.

"But he's not even Dad's inflatable," I say.

"But it's a pretty good movie," my mother says. She picks up a box and studies it. "This one starred Fay Wray. And did you know that the original ape was only eighteen inches tall?"

I did not know that and I am surprised that my mother did.

"Does it say that on the box?" I ask.

"No. I read her autobiography. In it, she talks a lot about the fake monkey and her Kong period."

"Her Kong period?"

"It was basically her whole life. It's all anybody wanted to hear about. Her entire existence defined by one film," my mother says.

"At least people remember her," I say.

"I guess," she says. "I've always liked living anonymously."

For some reason, my mind leaps to Sarah A and all her advice about how to live life to its fullest.

"That doesn't work for everyone," I say. "Some people don't want to live on the periphery and be the wallpaper. Some people want to be noticed and do important things."

"For me, cleaning *is* important," my mother says. "I help keep people's lives in alignment."

She doesn't ask me what I think is important and that's a relief. Because I don't know. I may be going to college in a year, but I have no idea what I want to do with my life. When it comes to having a unique purpose or identity, I don't think that I'm much better than one of Dr. Pewter's parrots.

We rent two movies. And when we get home, my mother decides not to unload her cleaning supplies. I notice a red feather clinging to her shoulder and I pluck it off.

"For you," I say.

She takes it and tosses it into the yard.

"I just don't understand animals," she says.

"I think they're a lot like us," I say.

She shakes her head.

"Right. Do *you* freely relieve yourself, regardless of your surroundings?" she asks.

She has no idea of the significance of what she just said. She's not aware of my pants-wetting history, the four slip-ups in nine years: the Barnes & Noble incident, the CD fiasco at Circuit City, the bungled hair-accessories theft at Sears, or the failed pineapple heist at D&W. She does know about my peeing accident in kindergarten. But she's clearly not thinking about it now.

I pretend like what she said didn't bother me, but really I feel a dull pain form in my chest. If I stay on this course, there's no denying that adult diapers might be in my future, and that, socially speaking, I may never fit in.

"I'm glad you want to support your father's inflatable," she says.

I don't say anything. This isn't all about him. I mean, it is and it isn't. I'm deeply curious to find out what trumped my cool duck.

# Chapter 18

In two weeks school starts. The governor changed the official start date, so now all the districts in the state have to wait until after Labor Day before they can ring the back-to-school bell. This means a few extra days with my parents. Our dinners last forever. There's a reason teenagers spend obscene amounts of time with their friends.

Sometimes, I'll be doing the most mundane thing, like washing the dishes, and I swear that I see a Sarah outside my front window. Or I'll be driving with my mom, and I'll spot a Sarah staring at me from behind a tree. I guess it's a form of irony. Since they're nowhere in my life right now, everywhere I go they're turning up.

"He's furious about the lizard," my father says, cutting into his baked potato with the side of his fork. "Big Don figured all he had to compete against was the duck. I may never bring the quacker back out."

"But have your car sales increased?" my mother asks.

My father waves his hand over his plate like he's shooing away a fly. Really, he's shooing away her question.

"Gas prices are shooting up like a rocket. There're problems with the Alaskan pipeline. And could things be any worse in the Middle East?"

"So the Godzilla inflatable isn't driving up sales as much as it's driving Big Don bananas?" my mother asks.

My father scoops up a large spoonful of apple sauce and slides it into his mouth. He smiles big and nods.

"You should see the look on his face," my father says. "My lizard shivers his timbers."

My father reaches over and squeezes her hand. When I watched *Godzilla* and *King Kong*, I wasn't that impressed. I kept thinking, *My duck got shelved over this?*

My father's hand rub turns into a long caress. I hate it when my parents show intense affection in front of me. I look out the living room window. The sun is setting, turning the world pink. I watch a deer follow another deer across the lawn. John Glenn comes and sits down next to me. I pat his head. He's watching the deer too. Maybe they're a couple. Then I watch a phantom Sarah poke her head up over the holly bush. It looks like Sarah A. That figures. It's the third time I've hallucinated seeing her this week.

She waves at me. She's flashing me the peace signal. Wait! I think it's really her.

"I'm going to take John Glenn for a walk," I say.

"But we're eating dinner," my father says.

"I'll be right back," I say.

I lead John Glenn outside and let him go.

"Sarah A," I call out. "It's me. What's going on?"

I circle my house, but I can't find her. I circle again.

"Sarah A!" I call. "Sarah A!"

John Glenn pads up to me and brushes against my leg. Am I going crazy? A cool wind cuts across my face and I walk back to my house.

"Pee time is over," I say.

He obediently trots back in the house.

"Did you see the sunset?" my mother asks.

She and my father have finished eating and are holding hands.

"I saw it," I say.

Believing that I may be delusional makes my stomach ache. I decide to go to my room. Maybe I should read.

"Where are you going?" my father asks.

"To my room," I say.

"I thought you might want to go for a walk down to the lake," he says.

"There're mosquitoes down there," I say.

"We'd wear repellent," he says.

"What do you want to tell me?" I ask.

"I just want to talk," he says.

"I'm going to wash the dishes," my mother says.

Then we're alone. It's me and my father, sitting opposite each other. Our knees are practically touching.

"I know my daughter," he says.

"Okay."

"What really happened?" he asks.

"With what?" I ask

"Why did you take that jar and why do you own a dog named John Glenn?"

"I just love dogs, I guess."

"Sarah, wouldn't you rather tell the truth? Wouldn't that feel better?"

I look down at the tablecloth. I'm not sure that coming clean about my years of petty theft would improve my current situation, let alone make me feel *better*.

"I've told you the truth," I say.

"The whole truth," he says. He doesn't phrase it as a question. "I think there's more to the story. School will be starting. Don't you want to start with a clean slate? With new friends?"

I'm still looking at the tablecloth. It's got a vine pattern that keeps falling over itself.

"I don't have any *old* friends."

"I'm sure, unless you take action, the Sarahs will realign and you'll be part of the mix again."

I frown. My dad doesn't understand how girls work at all.

Getting back into the group will probably take a ton of effort on my part.

"The company you keep says a lot about you. Your friends will determine your future."

"That's why the other Sarahs aren't hanging out with me. I'm a criminal."

"You are not a criminal," he says. "Not exactly."

"You don't get it," I say.

"Help me get it."

I look at him. His eyes have grown soft with concern. I don't want this kind of attention. I don't like disappointing him. Why am I even having this conversation? How can I make it end?

"I think it's obvious," I say.

He reaches to take hold of my hand, but I pull it back, and cross my arms over my chest.

"Sarah," he says.

I feel tears welling up in my eyes. I feel like I could tell my dad about the Sarahs. I feel like the truth is really close to flying out of me. I close my eyes and take a deep breath.

"You never should have shelved the duck. The duck was my idea. The inflatables don't sell the cars. It's the salesmen who sell the cars."

My father shakes his head. The soft concern in his eyes has faded. The muscles in his face tighten and he looks frustrated.

"The duck has nothing to do with this," he says.

"The duck has everything to do with this!"

This is as close to the truth as I can come right now.

"Sarah, don't make this about something it's not."

"You never listen to me," I say.

"I'm listening to you right now."

"The duck mattered to me. It was a decision I helped make."

My father nods.

"I understand. But King Kong altered the equation. A duck would have been below par."

"But I picked the duck. I never pick anything. Don't you see that?"

"Sarah, I think you're trying to dodge the issue. Let's talk about the jar."

"The jar wasn't my decision."

"I knew it," my father says. His mouth cracks into a smile. "Who put you up to it?" He's stroking his fuzzed chin. His eyes look pleased, almost like he's won something.

"Nobody put me up to it," I say.

"But you just said that it wasn't your decision."

"I meant that the duck was my own cool idea. Stealing shit from a store is the oldest crime in the book."

"Shit?" my father asks, his eyebrows raised.

"Shit," I say. I uncross my arms and pound my fists on the table. "Shit! Excrement! Fecal matter!"

"Sarah, you don't need to be so emotional. I'm trying to understand what happened."

"I took the jar to be part of something," I say.

"Part of what? Do all your friends steal?"

"I don't have any friends anymore. I haven't had a friend in weeks."

"Sarah, don't get melodramatic. You'll make new friends. Everybody cycles through different peer groups in high school."

I'm so mad at him. I'm not being melodramatic. And he's being totally simplistic if he thinks that a high school senior can attach herself to any new social group she seeks out. Yeah. I'll just start hanging with the cheerleaders. No, I'll sit at the table with the drama kids. Maybe I'll try out for the part of Lady Macbeth in the upcoming play.

"I'm not like Liam. I don't walk into a room and make automatic friends."

"You don't have to be like Liam," he says. "Nobody is comparing you to Liam."

"But you'd love it if I were exactly like Liam, wouldn't you? Wouldn't that be great? I mean, Liam practically raised himself."

"Sarah, you're accountable for your actions, not us."

"Yeah. You and Mom are blameless. I forgot."

I stand up.

"We're not through."

"Yes, we are."

"Sarah, I'm trying to get to the bottom of something."

"I'm already there. I'm at the bottom of everything."

"Just because you're a teenager doesn't mean you have to freak out like this."

I turn and walk away. I'm not exactly blown away by his comforting words.

"Sarah, I'm still talking."

I don't look back.

"You're going to work with me tomorrow. No debate."

"Great, I'll plug in the fan that inflates Godzilla for you."

"This isn't about the duck, Sarah. This is about your circle of friends."

My brain is at war with itself. Part of it is convinced that the issue at hand is the duck and my father. But the other half of my brain, perhaps the one comprised of its more reasonable lobes, understands his concern and knows that he's just trying to uncover the truth. And not because he wants to punish me further. No, it's more awful than that. My father wants to understand why I did what I did.

And what is the truth about that? Where would I start? Fourth grade? Sarah A saving me from the bus? The lip gloss? The contest? How can I help him comprehend *anything*, when I'm so confused about *everything*?

"It's your friends who determine your course!" my father yells after me.

I don't know why he keeps referring to my friends. If anyone has ever been a ship alone at sea, it's me. Friends? They're gone. And I wish he could at least try to see the importance of the duck. My own father took Sarah A's suggestion over mine. It just proves how flimsy I am. My own father doesn't want to go along with my idea. How many things have I ever picked out? None. Never. Would it have been so hard? Would it have been that difficult?

*King Kong changed the equation.*

One side of my brain: I can't believe he said that.

Other side of my brain: Maybe I do need different friends.

# Chapter 19

I attach John Glenn to his newly established dog run outside. The line runs between two trees. He seems to like this. His tongue unfurls out of his mouth like a flag as he zooms back and forth. This was my father's idea. He doesn't think it's healthy for a dog to spend all day inside. He's probably right.

As we drive to the car lot, neither one of us speak. Last night, right as I was falling to sleep, I heard my mother come into my room. She didn't say anything. She walked to where I was pretending to sleep and raised the blankets to cover my shoulder. She also patted John Glenn on the head. She might be coming around.

We pull into my father's car lot and I catch my first long look at Godzilla. It's hideous. In addition to listing to the right, it's got these enormous yellow claws. I have no idea how such a monstrous beast is supposed to drive up sales. Maybe a passing driver might see it and, startled, careen off the road and strike a telephone pole, thus requiring the accident victim to purchase a new vehicle. But that seems like a risky way to drum up business.

"What should I do?" I ask.

My father lets out a long sigh.

"Stay out of trouble," he says.

"So I shouldn't do anything?" I ask.

"They could use your help in the detailing area," he says.

That means more cleaning. I'm sick of cleaning. I'm a teenager. We're used to a certain level of filth in our daily lives. In fact, we prefer it.

"I'll need to be home by four to feed John Glenn," I say.

"We'll be leaving at three."

Great. I'm going to spend the next three hours polishing cars. I hate wax. It's always been a substance that's difficult for me to appreciate.

"Your Godzilla is crooked," I say.

"No, it's not. You're just looking at it from an angle."

I shake my head. And walk off to the detail shop tucked at the back of the car lot.

"Lenny," I hear my father yell. "Is the lizard leaning?"

I don't turn back around. I hope Godzilla falls on its fire-breathing face. Big-time.

"Q-tips work well for cleaning crevice dirt," Johanna says.

Johanna Izzo is a plain-looking brunette. She's always

been kind to me. I think she had a crush on Liam. But I don't think Liam crushed back. She's worked at my father's car lot since she graduated from high school three years ago. Just like those woolly mammoths that wandered into the tar pits during prehistoric times, I think she's stuck. Why else would she be here? This place reeks of glass cleaner.

"You're great at polishing tires," Johanna says.

She knows I'm miserable. She's trying her best to cheer me. Really, all I'm doing is spraying a thick foam coat onto the tire's surface and watching the white fluff melt away.

"Are you excited for your senior year?" she asks.

"I guess," I say.

"I know what you mean. It's not the big deal that everybody makes it out to be. It's just another year."

I nod, but really, I think she's wrong. It's a HUGE deal. After senior year, you aren't in high school anymore. Unless you fail, you're booted out into the real world. Or if you're lucky, you land in college for a few years until you get booted out into the real world for real.

"So you like it here?" I ask.

I think it's a dumb question. But I don't realize this until after I ask it.

"It's okay. I'm saving up to move to Florida."

"Do you have family there?" I ask.

"My grandma lives there. I want to work at a resort."

"Doing what?"

"Anything. I want to live in a warm climate."

"You and alligators," I say.

She looks up and laughs. When she does this, she comes across as less average, almost cute.

"How much money does it take to move there?" I ask.

It seems like in three years that she should have been able to save up enough funds for the journey. How much is bus fare?

She shrugs and blushes.

"Well, I'm saving for me and my boyfriend."

"I didn't know you had a boyfriend."

Something about cleaning cars makes people confess everything. It's a little weird. I even feel on the verge of telling her a bit about my criminal past. But I know I won't.

"So how's Liam?" she asks. "Is he still in California?"

"Yeah, he's a sophomore now. At Stanford."

I always feel a little pretentious when I mention that he's at Stanford. But he is.

"He was a lot of fun to work with," she says.

Immediately, I feel tense and on guard. I sense in her comment an implicit comparison, like she's saying detailing cars with Liam was more fun than detailing cars with me. It always comes down to this.

"He was so smart," she says.

"He's not dead," I say.

"What?" she asks.

"You referred to him in the past tense. He's not dead."

"Oh, I didn't mean to," she says. "It's just my experience with him was in the past."

"Yeah."

"He's so smart," she says.

"Stanford thinks so too," I say.

"No, I'm being serious. I feel like I learned a lot working with him. He was always talking about interesting stuff."

I so wish Johanna would shut up immediately. I could be talking about interesting stuff too. If I wanted.

"Did he talk about books?" I ask. Because, really, that's not a true demonstration of intelligence. That's just a demonstration of his ability to read and regurgitate facts that he gleaned from reading. It merely proves that he's literate and has a memory.

"I learned a lot about the Potawatomi."

I feel my stomach tighten. I don't like to think of Johanna knowing more about my own heritage than I do.

"Before Liam I had no idea that the word Potawatomi meant keeper of the fire," she says.

"Yeah," I say. I guess I learned that too, at some point. But foreign words and phrases are pretty easy for me to forget. I struggle to retain vocabulary in Spanish class too.

"And he talked about the different bands. You're part of the Pokagon Band of Potawatomi, right?" she asks. "Or was it the Prairie Band Potawatomi? I mix those two up."

"Pokagon," I say. But I don't even know if that's right.

"We need more Q-tips."

I point to a large pile that I've accumulated while swiping dust from the corners of the dashboard and vent slats.

"You can use them more than once," she says.

"Oh."

I start reswiping them.

"Are you going to come in every day until school starts?" she asks.

She's rubbing the windshield with newspapers until the glass squeaks.

"I don't think so," I say. "I think it's just today."

I swipe too hard. A Q-tip breaks off and falls inside a heating vent. I can see the torn end of the white stick, but I can't reach it. I don't mention this to Johanna.

"So, are you like Liam? Do you take culture trips? Do you go look at historic markers?"

Nobody has ever asked me questions like these before. Culture trips? They sound like field trips, only nerdier. And I'd never really thought of visiting historic markers as a legitimate activity. It's something you do while scouting for rest areas when driving cross-country with your family.

"I live in a historic house," I say.

I flip the vent closed to further conceal the broken Q-tip.

"You don't drive out and look at Indian stuff?" she asks.

Besides Liam, I have never met anybody so hung up on American Indians. I almost don't know what to say to her. It seems culturally insensitive to harp on somebody else's culture like this. When I hung out with the Sarahs this never happened. We were too busy planning our crimes to consider any of our heritages.

"No, I don't drive around looking at historical markers for Indian stuff," I say.

"Liam took me to the monument of Chief White Pigeon at the 12 and 131 junction. It was neat," she says.

I have heard of Chief White Pigeon, but I have no idea what he did. I wonder if this outing with Liam was an official date. How cheap of him if it was.

"I'm not like Liam," I say. "I'm not hyper-curious about any of that. I'm busy with school. And I'm in the choir. And I have a dog now."

I feel Johanna's hand on my shoulder. It startles me. I hadn't realized she was standing right there.

"I think Native Americans are cool," she says. "I've read *Ceremony* by Leslie Marmon Silko. And I'm a huge fan of Sitting Bull and Geronimo and Sacagawea. It's terrible what our country did to you guys."

She's frowning down on me, her face filled with sympathy. This is so weird. I wish she'd stop talking. She's behaving like a public service announcement and it's creeping me out.

"I'm only one-quarter Potawatomi. None of my family grew up on reservations. We've been completely suburban for generations," I say. "I consider myself white."

Johanna's eyes widen. "Oh," she says.

She walks away and resumes cleaning the windows. Things feel so weird. I wonder what she's thinking? I'm not ashamed of being part Indian. It's just not that important to me. I feel like I should explain this to her. But she's practically a stranger. Why do I have to justify anything to her? I keep my hands moving. Sometimes a rote task can be a pleasant distraction.

"It's time for my lunch break," she says. "If you want, you can get started on the Subaru while I'm gone."

She points to a green car parked outside the detail shop.

"Okay," I say.

Johanna smiles at me before she goes. I almost smile back. She didn't mean to be a weirdo. She was just trying to connect. She is such a nice, stuck person. Actually, probably most stuck people are nice. Most likely, that's part of why they're stuck. I wave good-bye to her.

"Oh, shit," she says.

"What?" I ask.

"Godzilla," she says. "It's fallen on top of the Miata."

"It has?" I ask. I find this fantastic. Finally, something has happened to cheer me up.

"That thing had been a catastrophe since day one," she says.

I walk outside and watch Lenny and my father furiously pulling on the ropes, trying to lift his balloon body off of the shiny red car.

"A duck wouldn't have tipped like that," I say. "Ducks are sturdy."

"What?" Johanna asks.

A guy pulls up in a turd-brown Buick and honks.

"See you in an hour," she says. She climbs into the car and pecks the driver on the cheek. It seems automatic and unaffectionate.

I watch them drive off. The car looks old and heavy. Johanna's hair flies out of the window in long wisps. I wonder if she'll make it to Florida. Change is harder than it looks. "This is your fault!" I hear my father yell. "You slashed my line! You're a cutthroat maniac!"

I walk toward the shouting. My stomach flutters with excitement. This is the most interesting thing that's happened in a long, long time.

# Chapter 20

My father is holding a thick yellow rope. He's wagging it at a fat man in a gray suit.

"Sabotage!" my father yells. "Pure and simple."

"You're out of your mind, Trestle," the fat man responds.

I look back and forth between the two. Lenny has taken hold of my father by the arm. Is my dad really going to fight the man in the suit?

"Your lizard's too big and there's a breeze. That's your problem," the fat man says.

"Big Don's right," Lenny says. "I think it's the breeze."

My father stares into the end of the rope like it contains some sort of answer. His face wrinkles in a pained disappointment.

"My ape may be shorter, but it holds its balance better," Big Don says. "Lower center of gravity. It's why squirrels don't fall off roofs."

"It's the truth," Lenny says.

Lenny lets go of my father's arm and pats his shoulder.

Big Don twists his mouth into a smirk and turns on his heel to leave. "Only a dip would think a lizard would move cars," he says.

My father springs forward. Lenny tries to grab his arm but it's too late. This isn't as amusing as it was five seconds ago. I don't want to see my father assault the fat man. Big Don must be able to hear my father's approach, because he tries to run. His belly wobbles over his pants.

"Dad! Stop!" I yell. "It's not worth it."

Amazingly, my father pauses. He ends his pursuit of Big Don and turns to face me. Big Don slows his pace and flips around.

"Your lizard isn't the only unstable thing on your lot," he says.

My father looks at him and looks to me. I think he might lunge toward Big Don again. That guy is a totally bloated jerk. But my father doesn't. He shrugs his shoulders and shakes his head.

"Godzilla might be unstable, but he's a helluva lot more attractive than your big, ugly ape," he says.

Big Don takes a step back toward my father.

"All apes are ugly. They're supposed to be, chief," Big Don says.

My father looks away, like he didn't hear the word "chief." Normally, I might not have noticed it. But because of Johanna, because of my mother's recent breakdown over my grandmother and great-grandmother, my mind is tuned to a frequency where I hear the word "chief." And it stings. I turn back to look at my father. His chin is lifted. It sort of doesn't make sense that Big Don would call my dad "chief." He's not Indian. It's my mother who is half Potawatomi. I guess bigots shoot at the most available target. Even if it strains accuracy.

"My ape is a fine-looking specimen," Big Don says.

I can't take it. There's something about his smug face that makes me want to erupt. Suddenly, I hate this guy. I totally and completely hate him. And I want to show him that he's wrong. That he doesn't know anything.

"Well, when standing, my dad's lizard dwarfs your squatty ape," I say.

I take my hand and karate chop the air at my waist. Then I karate chop the air a foot over my head.

"Dwarfs that horizontally challenged monkey," I say.

I can feel everybody looking at me. Not glancing, but focusing all their attention on me. Big Don, Lenny, my father. It's almost as if their eyeballs, their stares, give off some sort of heat, because I feel very, very warm. I realize that my hand is still extended in the air. It's no longer making a chopping motion, but it's still up there. I lower it.

Big Don inhales so deeply that his nostrils cave in. I'm not quite sure what's going to happen next. Several cars whiz by us. Some of them brake so they can get a better look at the toppled Godzilla. From the right angle, it probably looks like it's attacking the Miata.

"Godzilla rules," a slow-going motorist yells. "Buy American cars!"

In Michigan, some people still believe that you should buy American-made and not foreign-made autos. This sentiment is dying out along with a ton of factory jobs. Every time I drive down West Main I get tailgated by either a Honda or Toyota.

Surprisingly, my father doesn't jump in. He stands back and lets me have my first official argument with a total idiot. Big Don's face continues to redden. It's sort of scary. I'm not used to looking at such a ketchup-hued face. It's unnatural.

"Everyone knows Kong is mightier than Godzilla," Big Don says. "Besides, Kong has the better movie."

"You're joking," I say. My mind replays the two versions of *Kong* that I watched along with *Godzilla 2000*, the worst movie that I've ever seen.

"I'm not joking. *Kong* does big box office. *Godzilla* is an import. Nobody loves that thing. It doesn't have a heart."

I walk toward Big Don and close the distance between us. The toe of my shoe nearly touches the toe of his.

"That movie requires a stupid boat to even be interesting," I say. "No boat, no Skull Island. No Skull Island, no movie. Your ape should be on a boat lot."

"That's not true," he says.

"Yes it is. Plus, Kong hits a woman. What kind of message does that send to future car buyers? Kong is a dangerous, tantrumming ape. He has to be tranquilized to even ride in a motor vehicle."

"Now you're taking him out of context. Kong isn't all bad."

"You've got to be kidding," I say.

I've never felt this way before. I've never wanted to stand up for anything until now. But this guy has attacked my mother, *my mother*.

Big Don takes a few breaths and lets his nostrils flare some more. I keep going.

"Godzilla can breathe fire," I say.

"Kong can climb buildings," Big Don says.

"But he also falls off of them," I say.

"Only when shot at by planes," Big Don says.

"They weren't very high-tech planes," I say.

"Guns are guns. Shoot anything in the chest and it'll bleed. Anything."

When Big Don shouts the word "anything," he sort of spits on me. Also, I don't really have a good comeback for his last observation. He has a good point. Anything mortal will bleed out from a chest wound. I wipe his spit from my cheek.

"Godzilla can stop a meteorite that's capable of destroying the earth," I say.

Big Don has had it. He takes his hand and points his finger at me like he's taking aim with a gun.

"Yeah, but he falls down on top of sports cars and scratches the paint," he says. "Enjoy your lizard."

He turns to leave. As he's doing this, I can suddenly think of a string of new Kong-related insults. But the opportunity to unleash them has passed. The argument is over. I'm not sure who officially won, but I feel good about my cinematic observations. Big Don wastes little time in bouncing away.

"We will absolutely enjoy our lizard. And any paint scratches were superficial and can easily be buffed out, chicken chest," my father says.

"Chicken chest?" I ask, turning to look at Lenny and my father.

"It was a comment on his man boobs," my father says.

"Dad!"

I don't want to hear my father say the word boobs, even in reference to a pompous, chesty ignoramus.

"You know a lot about monster movies," Lenny says.

"Movies aside, I like the cut of your jib," my father says.

He walks to me and pulls me to his side, kissing the top of my head.

"Can you really buff the scratches out?" I ask.

The Miata is barely visible beneath Godzilla's gargantuan, plated tail.

"Sure," he says.

My father puts his arm around me and walks me to his car. It's a new feeling for me. I feel almost electric and incredibly strong. I wonder how long it will last.

"Should we set our dinosaur back up?" Lenny asks.

"No. Shut off the fans," he says. "I think we can retire the big guy. It's the salesmen who sell the cars. Not the inflatables."

# Chapter 21

It's after dinner and the tingle of power is wearing thin. I should write my statement of purpose for college, especially while I still feel a sense of purpose. There's a lot of paper and envelopes and typing and collation involved with the college application process. It's probably a glimpse of what lies ahead. I wonder if the other Sarahs have started? Maybe the guy phase has delayed them. Let's face it, desensitized against their pheromones or not, boys can be so distracting.

Colleges want to know so much about me. A common theme seems to be *What can I do for them*. It reminds me of our Sarah freewrite. Except this time around, I'll omit any wildebeest references. The application for the University of Michigan has very specific questions that it wants me to answer. Here's one I have to respond to in 250 words or less:

*At the University of Michigan, we are committed to building a superb educational community of diverse talents, experiences, opinions, and cultural backgrounds. What would you as an individual bring to our campus community?*

That question is so deep. As an individual, what do I have to offer? This is something that I've spent a great deal of my life not thinking about. I'm used to being a part of something. A cog in the wheel. One note of the melody. The toasted marshmallow portion of the s'more. Liam got into every school he applied to, including Michigan. I bet he had an awesome answer. I bet he said he'd bring all the right things. Shouldn't he want to help me?

*Me:* I'm stuck. I have a question.
*Liam:* Why is it that you always call when you want something, but you never dial me up just to say hello?
*Me:* Because I know you're busy.
*Liam:* What's your question?
*Me:* What do I have to offer a university?

*Silence.*

*Me:* You think I don't have anything to offer?
*Liam:* I'm thinking.

*Me:* I'm that dull?

*Liam:* Oh, you're not dull. But you're not supposed to be able to answer these questions right away. You're supposed to really think about them.

*Me:* I have.

*Liam:* For days and days and days. Possibly weeks.

*Me:* Oh.

*Liam:* Is that all? Do you want to talk about anything else?

*Me:* I can tell that you're fishing. I don't know how much Mom and Dad have told you about my situation.

*Liam:* We're a pretty open family. I know you knocked off a convenience store.

*Me:* How come you didn't call me to make sure I was okay?

*Liam:* I wasn't exactly sure what to say.

*Me:* Oh.

*Liam:* Are you okay?

*Me:* I'm stuck.

*Liam:* Are we talking big picture or college essay?

*Me:* I don't know.

*Liam:* I'm never too busy to talk to you. You can always call.

*Me:* You don't have to worry about me. I'm not going to rob any more stores.

*Liam:* I'm not sure what to say to that. Should I congratulate you?

*Me:* I guess not.

*Liam:* Listen, when I'm stuck like this, I try to freewrite my way out of it.

*Me:* Freewrites can be dangerous.

*Liam:* I guess it depends on what you say.

*Me:* Liam, I'm not the only one who's stuck.

*Liam:* Are you pregnant?

*Me:* Holy crap! No! Where did that come from?

*Liam:* You sounded upset.

*Me:* I'm not that upset. I'm worried about Johanna Izzo.

*Liam:* She's pregnant?

*Me:* No, Liam. Nobody who I know is pregnant. She wants to move to Florida, but she's stuck at Dad's car lot. She works in the detail shop.

*Liam:* I know Johanna. She's a nice person.

*Me:* I think that's why she's stuck!

*Liam:* You should work on your college essays.

*Me:* I want to help Johanna.

*Liam:* Maybe she needs to help herself.

*Me:* Maybe she's too stuck to realize that.

*Liam:* Friends shouldn't be projects, Sarah.

*Me:* She's not my friend. I don't have friends.

*Liam:* I'm sure you've got someone.

*Me:* You're sounding parental. I think I'm through talking.

*Liam:* You sound depressed.

*Me:* I wasn't before I started this conversation.

*Liam:* Call me tomorrow and report on your progress.

*Me:* Okay.

*Click.*


I don't ask him about his Godzilla lunch box or action figure. It gives me something to talk to him about later. If I want to.

John Glenn sticks his wet nose against my leg. I'm wearing khaki shorts. He licks at a mustard stain on the cuff. I ate a ham sandwich for lunch.

"Do you want to go for a walk?" I ask.

John Glenn sits down at my feet and wags his tail. I lead him to the back door.

"We're not going for a big walk. Just a backyard walk," I say.

He lowers his head in disappointment. He understands, but he doesn't like it. Once outside, he runs back and forth across the yard, stopping to pee on the azalea bush. I watch him pad around the side of the house toward the front yard.

"Stay here," I say.

He doesn't.

"John Glenn!"

He won't come. I jog around the house after him. That's when she appears again. The phantom Sarah A.

"Aren't you going to say anything?" Sarah A asks.

"You're real?" I ask.

"Is that a serious question?" Sarah A asks.

"I think so," I say.

"We need you," Sarah A say.

My heart beats faster.

"You do?" I ask. "All three of you?"

"Mainly me. Meet up with us tonight at the Big Burrito," Sarah A says.

"What time?" I ask.

"Seven o'clock."

"I have a curfew," I say.

"Figure a way out of it," Sarah A says. "It's very important."

"I won't be able to stay long," I say.

"I'm not asking for your entire evening," Sarah A says.

John Glenn comes to my side.

"He looks fat," Sarah A says.

"He's growing," I say.

"In girth."

Standing here, listening to Sarah A insult my dog, doesn't

feel pleasant. I'm not sure that I want to go to the Big Burrito. I'm not sure that I'm ready to hang out with the Sarahs again. A lot of people are counting on me to stay reformed. They're certain I'm a good person. They believe in me.

"I don't want to steal anything," I say.

"What?" Sarah A asks.

"I don't feel like breaking any more laws," I say.

"The sisterhood is about more than being criminals."

I nod.

"Is that a mustard stain?" Sarah A asks. "It's huge."

"I had a ham sandwich for lunch," I say.

"That's not coming out," Sarah A says.

"You're probably right," I say. "Hey, have you guys started applying for college? Have you thought about what you have to offer them?"

"Sarah T, it's August. The guy phase is in full swing. We haven't had time to think about college. We're in the midst of man issues."

My mouth drops open.

"Is this why I'm coming to the Big Burrito?" I ask.

"Just make sure that you look good," Sarah A says. "And change those shorts. Seriously. You look way cuter in jeans."

# Chapter 22

It's awful. The timing couldn't be worse. I've regained my parents' trust. So if I lie to them and ask for permission to go out tonight and do something college-oriented and responsible, they're going to say yes. The only thing keeping me away from the Sarahs tonight is myself. And it's so tempting to meet up with them. I miss them. And I'm getting tired of sleeping with Roman Karbowski and his pheromones. I'm seventeen and ready for a real guy.

My parents and I are sitting outside on lawn chairs. We're watching John Glenn enthusiastically roll around on top of what we presume to be mole holes.

"He has so much energy," my mother says.

"Do you know if he's still a puppy?" my father asks.

"I think he's just immature," I say.

My parents are holding hands. Even though it's a couple of hours away, I think they're planning on watching the sunset together. They're both big fans of looking at the sky and commenting on its varying shades of purple.

"How are your applications coming?" my mother asks. "Your room looks like a file cabinet exploded."

"I hope attending college is more fun than applying for it," I say.

"Oh, it is," my father says. "Those were the days. Did you know that I belonged to the same fraternity as Frank Lloyd Wright? Phi Delta Theta."

"You joined a frat? No wonder you thought college was fun," I say.

"History is peppered with Phi Delts who've made lasting contributions: the twenty-third U.S. president, Benjamin Harrison, Neil Armstrong, and Lou Gehrig. Going Greek can be a responsible choice."

"Maybe I'll join a sorority," I say.

"Oh, Sarah, groups tend to swallow you up," my mother says. "You should go to college and stand on your own."

"I don't know. I met a lot of people in my fraternity," my father says.

"He means women," my mother says. She clears her throat. "College isn't just about having fun," she says.

"Right. Right," my father says. "It's a time of growth. A time of change."

John Glenn assumes a crouched position and takes an enormous dump on the lawn in front of us.

"I'll get a bag," I say.

When I come back my parents aren't holding hands anymore.

I think my mother has dragged her chair farther away from my father's.

"All I'm saying is that it has its drawbacks. Okay, Frank Lloyd Wright was an architect ahead of his time, but why did he build such small kitchens? I can't open the refrigerator and the dishwasher at the same time. It's impossible! It can't be done," my mother says. "And there's hardly any natural light. It's gloomy in there. That kitchen is far too restrictive for my culinary needs."

I walk between them, bypassing their argument, and scoop the poop.

"But the heart of the home is the hearth, honey," my father says.

"The wiring is substandard. The oven won't get above three hundred degrees. And the roof leaks," she says. "It's time to make some upgrades."

"I'm going to throw this away," I say. I lift the bag and its contents up so they know what I'm referring to.

"The roof has always leaked," my father says.

"But now it's leaking on the couch," my mother says.

"Let's move the couch," my father says.

"We have. Twice," my mother says.

I return from the garbage can. My father isn't saying much. I think he's hoping this will blow over.

"Is this why you've been cooking everything with the toaster?" I ask.

"The toaster is the only thing that works properly in there," my mother says.

So Sarah A was wrong. My mother wasn't on a Pop-Tart bender to satisfy a soul craving. She had staged a kitchen appliance protest in hopes of forcing an upgrade.

"But Frank Lloyd Wright is an architectural icon," my father says. "I like living in the house he designed."

"Oh, please. Frank Lloyd Wright was a real womanizer. He abandoned his first wife and family to run off to Europe with a married woman."

"He was ahead of his time—loyal only to his imagination," my father says. He shakes his head.

"Statements like that frighten me," my mother says. "Let's not forget that he violated the Mann Act twice."

"I don't even know what that is," I say.

"It's legislation passed by Congress that makes it a crime to take women across state lines for immoral purposes," my mother says.

"A pimp built this house?" I ask.

"Frank Lloyd Wright was not a pimp! He took a couple of mistresses across state lines," my father says. "It happens."

My mother leans so far back in her lawn chair that it groans. "I want to remodel the kitchen," she says.

"Wright is probably rolling over in his grave," my father says.

"Well, that's doubtful, as I remember reading that he was cremated," my mother says.

"This will be tough on Liam," my father says. "He looks up to Wright. Remember when we reglazed all the tubs in the house? Liam didn't speak to us for a month. He felt we'd violated Wright's original tub intent."

This seems like a good time for me to exit.

"I can't think in this atmosphere," I say. "I need to go to the library. Then, I want to sit and work on my college essays at Full City Cafe."

"I guess that sounds like an acceptable plan," my father says.

"Bread helps fuel the mind," my mother says.

"Good luck with your discussion," I say. "I'm sure you'll reach some middle ground."

I race into the house.

"Sarah!" my father yells.

Oh, no. Has he already changed his mind?

"Be back by ten," he says. "You're not completely out of the doghouse."

"Okay," I say. "Bowwow."

"And don't make this a social outing," my mother says. "Library. Cafe. Home."

"Okay," I lie.

"Change doesn't always mean destruction," my mother says.

"If we need to rent a commercial Dumpster to complete the project, I'm fairly certain there's a sizable amount of destruction involved," my father says.

I grab a book bag and look around my paper-cluttered room. In the last few weeks so much has changed for me. I am not the same person I was the night I returned the donation jar to Mr. King. And I am not the same person who stole that donation jar either. All that person wanted was to fit in at any cost. And that person was willing to take way too much abuse. If things were just a little different, if there wasn't any stealing or putting one another down or taking each other's life metaphors, the Sarahs could be an amazing group. Like a family. I wonder if any of the other Sarahs have changed? Without me, things had to have been different for them.

I turn to leave, but I notice the Godzilla lunch box. Next time I talk to Liam I'm going to ask him about this. I pick it up, but it feels empty. I shake it and it doesn't make a noise. When I unclasp the lid I see that the Godzilla action figure is missing. Sarah A must've taken it, even though I asked her not to. She must have ignored what I said and stuck it right in her stupid pocket and sold it on the action figure black market.

I'm not shocked about this, but it does suck. Sarah A doesn't respect anybody else's property. She never has and she never will. She's guided by her wants. That's why she's always taking things. Maybe she's trying to fill up some sort or emotional hole. Some people probably can't recover from the loss of a mother. That kind of absence must leave a huge empty space. I bet Sarah A tries to fill it with anything she can find. But it must not work. Because no matter how much Sarah A takes, she continues to want and want and want.

# Chapter 23

When I walk into the Big Burrito, I feel like I've stepped back into my old life. There they are: the Sarahs—bare-armed, smiling, and wearing skorts. Nothing has changed. Except Sarah B is wearing a Tigers cap. And she also has a stylish new purse strapped around her neck. I've seen that kind of purse in magazines. It has long black fringe flowing down one side. It looks like a horse's mane. Or tail. And the skorts are sort of a new thing. They must've been a recent purchase. I mean, I don't have one.

Sarah B tugs down on the bill of her cap, adjusting the hat low on her head. It does make her look a little boyish. I'm surprised Sarah A permitted Sarah B to resume cap-wearing.

"You look great," Sarah C says.

I look down at myself. I'm wearing jeans and a pink shirt. I look good but not spectacular.

"Hey, Sarah T," a male voice calls.

I look at the cash register. It's Bjorn Walters, our student-body vice president. He's talking to Roman Karbowski. It looks like Bjorn is ordering a torta.

"What's going on?" I ask.

"Doyle Rickerson is out," Sarah A says.

"Groin injury?" I ask.

"We think he might not like girls," Sarah B says.

"He's gay?" I ask.

"He's something," Sarah C says.

"What happened?" I ask.

"We don't have time to break it down for you," Sarah A says. "Your new guy is Bjorn."

"I'm still a Sarah?" I ask, pointing to myself.

"We can't successfully complete this leg of the guy phase without you," Sarah A says.

"You're using me?" I ask.

"Please," Sarah A says. "You're dying to be part of the guy phase."

It's hard for me to deny this. And there is a certain rebel quality that I've always liked about Bjorn. There's something about him that's just so attractive and tall and . . . Swedish.

"I'm going to go talk to Roman. You," Sarah A says, aiming her finger at Sarah C, "catch Sarah T up to speed. And you," she says, turning her finger on me, "don't drink anything. We don't want an accident."

"Wow," I say. "It's weird to be back."

"Does it feel good?" Sarah C asks.

"I think so," I say. "To be honest, I feel like I've been through a lot since I last saw you guys."

Sarah B and Sarah C look at each other and then back at me.

"We can relate," Sarah C says.

"What have you been up to?" I ask.

Sarah C scans the restaurant.

"It's a little too crowded in here to disclose that kind of information," Sarah C says. She leans forward over her half-eaten tacos to speak to me.

"Let's just say that the guy phase has had a few glitches," Sarah B says.

"Because of Doyle?" I ask.

"I wish that was our problem," Sarah C says. "Something like that is manageable."

"It sounds like you guys have faced some major obstacles," I say.

Sarah B and Sarah C look at each other again.

"Let's just say that Sarah A overlooked a few things," Sarah C says.

"Wow. I find that hard to believe," I say.

"Oh, you better believe it," Sarah C says.

Her comments feel loaded and almost spooky.

"Hey, I like your purse," I tell Sarah B.

Sarah B reaches over and pets it. "My mom gave it to me," she says.

"It's got a cute tassel," I say. I'm glad that she and her mother are speaking again.

My mouth feels dry. I reach for a glass of water to take a drink, but I stop when I see a panicked look break out on Sarah B's face.

"I'm not going to pee myself. Guys don't make me wet my pants," I say.

"So can I ask you a personal question?" Sarah C asks.

"I guess," I say.

"What does make you wet your pants?" Sarah C asks.

"Keep your voices down," Sarah B says. "This is so not something people want to hear about at the Big Burrito."

"What are you feeling before you wet yourself?" Sarah C asks.

"I feel like I need to use the bathroom." I say.

"No, where does it come from?" Sarah C asks.

"My bladder," I say.

"I'm being serious, Sarah T. The look on your face at Barnes & Noble scared me," Sarah C says.

"What did I look like?" I ask.

"Like a complete and total failure," Sarah C says.

"I guess that's what I feel like," I say.

"Is that what it feels like every time? At Circuit City? Sears? D&W?" Sarah C asks.

"She also peed herself in kindergarten," Sarah B says. "It happened on my row."

I shake my head.

"I don't want to think about this," I say.

"I just wanted to know where it came from," Sarah C says.

"Why do you even care?" I ask. Sarah C is so good at pretending like she's concerned about me. But I know the truth.

"You're one of my best friends," Sarah C says.

I look away.

"Maybe you need to talk to somebody," Sarah C says.

"Like a therapist?" I ask. "Only people our age who are total nuts see therapists."

"I see a therapist," Sarah B says.

"You do?" I ask.

My eyes must be huge. This is very shocking news. How can a Sarah be in therapy and this is the first that I'm hearing about it?

"When did this start?" I ask.

"After my mother left," Sarah B says. "Two years ago."

"Why didn't you tell us about this?" I ask.

"She told me about it," Sarah C says.

I feel a little hurt. Why did Sarah B tell Sarah C and not

me? Do they share some sort of close relationship that I'm not aware of?

"Hey Sarah T, come on over here," Sarah A says.

She's sitting at a table with Bjorn. He's with his younger brother, Sven, and Gerard Truax. All three of them have floppy hair that falls over their foreheads in long, curvy waves. Maybe they have the same barber. Bjorn and Sven are blond. Gerard has hair the color of a chocolate bar. I've never touched a guy's hair before. I wonder what if feels like. I sit down next to Bjorn. He smells much better than Doyle Rickerson's shirt. I smile. This is the first time I've talked with a guy since Sarah A called off the purity vow. I feel light. And happy.

"Did you know that Bjorn skis?" Sarah A asks.

"That's cool," I say.

"Maybe we could go sometime. After it snows," Bjorn says.

I watch Bjorn take an enormous bite of his torta. His teeth are huge, almost as big as horse teeth. They tear through the thick bread like a machine, and it frightens me.

"Well, we've got to get going," Sarah A says.

She smiles and waves good-bye by fluttering her fingers. I get up and follow her.

"Stop making that face," Sarah A whispers to me.

"What do you mean?" I ask.

"You've got that expression you get when you watch surgeries on television," Sarah A says.

"Oh," I say.

"Let's go," Sarah A says to Sarah B and Sarah C.

"But you haven't told Sarah T what we need her for," Sarah C says.

"You haven't gotten there yet?" Sarah A asks. "What have you been talking about?"

"Other issues," Sarah C says.

We walk outside and congregate around Sarah C's car. She parked on the dark side of the building. My white sneakers look like they're glowing. I'm relieved that I'll be making it home well within my curfew. I rub my arms. It's cold. It's still August, but Kalamazoo already feels like fall.

"I need something from you," Sarah A says.

"What?" I ask. I want to be able to help her out, but in a noncriminal kind of way.

"I need John Glenn," Sarah A says.

Sarah C opens her car door. I follow Sarah A around to the passenger's side.

"But he's my dog now," I say. "We've bonded."

"I know. I don't want him forever. Just the weekend," Sarah A says.

"But why?" I ask.

"It's not like I'm asking you for both of your kidneys," Sarah A says. "We need him up at Yankee Springs."

"The designated wilderness area?" I ask.

"No. It's a recreation area," Sarah C says.

"I'll be staying at a cabin up there," Sarah A says.

"You will? Like camping?" I ask.

"I did my 'alone' time in the hotel until Vance got shipped off. But he's coming back tomorrow. I can't stay at the house with him," Sarah A says. "My parents rented the cabin for a week for a summer vacation, but now that Vance is scheduled to re-arrive, they've abandoned those plans. I'll be staying there by myself for three days."

"So your parents are sending you to live in a cabin in a recreation area?" I ask.

"Just for three days," Sarah A says.

"Did Vance go super-crazy?" I ask.

"No, he'll be getting released from his first wilderness class and needs to attend another wilderness class to reinforce the lessons. But he'll be home for three days. The point is, I'm going to need a guard dog. The cabin where I'll be staying gives me the creeps. I stay there with my family every year, but never alone."

"But you don't want a Sarah to stay with you?" I ask.

"Sarah B will be there. And a special friend," Sarah A says.

"Do you mean your period?" I ask.

"No, not my period. Roman Karbowski," Sarah A says.

"Roman Karbowski?" I ask, pointing back to the Big Burrito.

Sarah A breaks into a wide grin. "I need a dog tomorrow night. Bring him in the afternoon," she says.

"My parents won't let me," I say.

"God, Sarah, can't you think about somebody besides yourself? What if I get killed by an ax murderer?" Sarah A asks.

Sarah B opens up her back door.

"An ax murderer?" I ask. "Are you serious?"

"It could happen," Sarah A says. "I'm young, female, attractive, and will be staying overnight in a wooded area."

"I'm missing more than the first three innings," Sarah B says. "Don't you get how huge this is? The Tigers have a shot at making it to the World Series."

"Whatever," Sarah A says. "There's no way they can beat the Yankees."

"John Glenn sleeps a lot. Maybe you should borrow a more alert dog," I say.

"Are you saying no?" Sarah A asks.

"She's not saying no," Sarah C says. "Are you?"

"When will I get him back?" I ask.

"I'm not going to steal your dog," Sarah A says.

"I know," I say. "I just don't know what I'll tell my parents."

"Say that he ran away," she says.

"But then they'll be worried and go look for him," I say.

"I'll bring him back. Does my life mean nothing to you?"

"Please, Sarah T," Sarah B says.

"It's not a big deal," Sarah C says. "I'll drive up with you."

"What's your answer?" Sarah A asks.

"I guess I'll bring him up tomorrow," I say.

I'm looking at Sarah A. She winks at me. Then I hear the sound of a horse neighing.

"Don't do that!" Sarah B yells.

I look over Sarah A's shoulder and see a boy dressed in a gray sweatshirt and jeans pulling at the fringe on Sarah B's purse. Another boy laughs. There're three boys, just standing around laughing at Sarah B. They look like elementary school kids. Where did they even come from? Why are they here?

"We're just playing," the first boy says. "Your purse looks like a mare." He releases several high-pitched whinnies and laughs.

"You hurt my neck," Sarah B says, rubbing the area around her collar, where her purse strap rests.

"Are you gonna go cry to your mother about it?" the boy asks. He balls his hands up into fists and rubs them against his eyes. "Whah, whah, whah," he whines.

This kid is so annoying. He needs to grow up.

"You piece of shit!" Sarah A yells. She lunges forward and pushes the boy against Sarah C's car. His body knocks against her trunk with a thud. Sarah A kicks him in the leg, and then punches him in the chest.

"Who's crying now?" Sarah A asks.

"You're crazy," the boy says.

Sarah A kicks him hard between the legs. He doubles over and moans.

"That's enough," Sarah B says, standing between Sarah A and the boy. I don't move. I'm too shocked. Sarah A is attacking schoolchildren outside the Big Burrito.

"It's okay," Sarah B says. "What he said didn't bother me."

"What the blonde girl just did is assault," the second boy says. "We're only ten-year-olds. My friend could sue her."

Sarah A doesn't say anything back to him. She just glares. Sarah C circles around the car to stand next to us. Sarah A is shaking. I don't know if it's from anger or adrenaline or a combination of the two. The boys walk off. The one Sarah A hit lumbers away, bent over, while his friends stand on either side of him, leading him toward the apartments behind the restaurant parking lot.

"What an asshole," Sarah A says. "I can't believe he said that to you."

"It's just a saying," Sarah B says. "And he was a kid. It didn't bother me that much." She moves closer to us and opens her car door.

"Well, kids can't go around mouthing off about people's mothers. It's not right. The word 'mother,' that means something," Sarah A says.

"Yeah, but they're not evil or anything. They're just stupid. I was mostly worried that they were trying to steal my purse," Sarah B says.

"He shouldn't have said what he said," Sarah A says.

"I think Sarah B's right. They were just being stupid," I say.

"Yeah, ragging on somebody's mother is completely unoriginal. It's too cliché to pack any emotional punch," Sarah C says.

I'm nodding when I see a sudden movement. It's Sarah A's fist. She aims it at Sarah C and socks her in the chest. Sarah C stumbles backward.

"Ouch," Sarah C says, putting her hands up. "What are you doing?"

"Don't tell me how to feel," Sarah A says.

"I didn't mean it that way," Sarah C says. "I was trying to make you feel better."

"Going away. Going to Yankee Springs and spending some time with Roman, that will make me feel better," Sarah A says.

"And I'll bring John Glenn," I say, trying to make things feel less weird.

"Yeah, I know," Sarah A says.

"Maybe Sarah T should drive you home," Sarah C says. She's rubbing her chest with her hand.

"That's probably a good idea," Sarah A says.

I get the feeling that this isn't the first spat these two have had since I've been gone. Sarah C gets in her car, flips on her lights, and backs out.

"What just happened?" I ask.

"We had a fight," Sarah A says. "It happens. We're girls."

"You just punched Sarah C," I say. "You used your fist."

"Not hard," Sarah A says.

Sarah A grabs my arm and links herself to me. We walk to my car and I don't say anything else about the incident.

At the stop sign, I turn to go left and take Sarah A home.

"No," Sarah A says. "Let's go for a drive."

"I've got a ten o'clock curfew," I say.

"We've got an hour," Sarah A says.

"Where do you want to go?" I ask.

"I just want to stay in motion. Let's drive out of town," Sarah A says. "Do you need gas? I'll pay for it."

"I've got a full tank," I say.

"That's great," Sarah A says. "Let's head out toward the lake. Let's blow down the road."

# Chapter 24

"The guy phase is so complicated," Sarah A says.

"Are you sure it's the guys that are making it complicated?" I ask.

"I hope we can weather all this," Sarah A says.

"Guys or not, you shouldn't have hit Sarah C," I say.

"I pushed her," she says.

"No, it was a hit," I say.

"Can we go all the way to the lake?" Sarah A asks.

"I'm turning around at Paw Paw," I say.

Sarah A reclines her seat back all the way.

"Do you have any scars?" Sarah A asks.

"Like from wounds?" I ask.

"What other kind of scars are there?"

I can hear her sliding off her shoes.

"I guess I was thinking about emotional scars," I say, starting my own mental list of them.

"No, I mean real scars. An actual place on your body where your flesh has been injured."

"Why?" I ask.

"I'm curious," Sarah A says.

"Are you asking me if I'm a cutter, because I'm not," I say.

Sarah A turns her head to look at me.

"I know that. I'm asking because I have a scar. It's shaped like a small bell. It's right here," she says, pulling down her skorts and pointing to her hip. "I must've fallen on something. As a kid. I bet I slipped going down the stairs."

"Maybe," I say.

"If my mom were around, my real mom, I could ask her how I got my bell scar."

"Yeah," I say.

"It might be a funny story. I might've been running away from a pigeon or something."

"You don't consider Mrs. Aberdeen to be your real mom?" I ask.

"She's okay."

"You call her Mom," I say.

"I'm glad I have her. I love her. But it's not the same thing."

"Are you mad at her and your dad because you've got to go stay in a cabin?" I ask.

"It's not their fault that Vance is crazy. I guess this is an okay solution."

"Do you ever think that you'll go look for her?" I ask.

"My real mom?" Sarah A asks.

I nod.

"Probably not," Sarah A says.

"Mr. and Mrs. Aberdeen are nice," I say. "And Vance is so screwed up. You're like a total gift."

Sarah A doesn't say anything. She turns and looks out the windshield.

"Sarah A?" I ask.

"That makes sense," she says. "Because a gift is something that you give away."

I turn the radio on real soft. We drive for a long time and when we reach the Paw Paw turnoff, I make a U-turn and head back toward Kalamazoo.

"Can we pull over and get a drink?" Sarah A asks.

"Where?" I ask.

"That 7-Eleven up ahead."

That's the 7-Eleven where I stole the donation jar. I don't take my foot off the accelerator.

"I'm really thirsty," Sarah A says. "Come on." She bumps me on my arm.

"Don't hit the driver," I say.

"I'm not hitting you. I barely touched you."

I take a deep breath and turn on my blinker. I pull into the parking lot and watch Sarah A walk into the store. The clerk working is not the clerk I robbed. It's a woman. Her hair is pulled back behind her ears. It relieves me that I have no idea who she is. When Sarah A comes out of the store, she's carrying two bottles of water.

"For you," she says, climbing into my car.

I twist off the top and take a big drink. Her face looks tired and sad.

"Let's sit and talk," Sarah A says.

"I've got to get home," I say. "I'm almost late."

"For five minutes," Sarah A says.

"Why? What are you thinking about?" I ask.

"Deep stuff," Sarah A says.

"Deep how?" I ask.

I'm wondering if this has anything to do with the guy phase and its multiple glitches.

"I wish I knew my family history," Sarah A says.

"You just said that you didn't want to find your mother," I say.

"I don't. I wish there was a way to learn everything else, and not have to figure that piece out," Sarah A says.

"What are you most curious about?" I ask.

"I wonder about my dad. I wonder if he's funny. Not just a little funny, but the kind of person who can make anybody laugh," Sarah A says. "Maybe he's a stand-up comedian. Remember when I told you that I'd found a body in your backyard. That was so hilarious. I've heard that comedic timing is learned, but I bet there's something hereditary about it too."

I didn't think Sarah A telling me there was a body in my backyard was all that funny. But I don't challenge her memory of the event.

"Do you wonder whether or not you have brothers and sisters?" I ask.

"Oh, I know I do," Sarah A says, turning to face me. "I get these feelings all the time, for no reason at all, I'll feel excited or sad and I know it's because something good or bad is happening to one of my siblings somewhere."

"Vance must be a huge disappointment," I say.

"Yeah," she says. "For everyone."

She slips off her shoes again and closes her eyes.

"I might come from a big family," she says. "I might be related to famous people: scientists, movie stars, writers, billionaires."

I find it doubtful that she's related to billionaires.

"Some of my relatives might live in Europe. They might own their own planes."

"That's one possibility."

"One day, I bet I learn my story."

"But what if it's sad?"

"I don't care," she says. "I want to know."

"What if it's really sad?" I say.

"How sad could it be? Like they're all dead?" she asks.

"Or worse," I say.

"What's worse than being all dead?"

"I don't know. What if your entire family and their family and everybody's family who they knew died in the Holocaust?"

"That couldn't have happened. I'm sixteen," she says.

"Maybe all your distant relatives were killed. Just rounded up and taken to camps and exterminated," I say.

"Then how would I even be here?" she asks.

"I don't know. Maybe, like, one person made it out and escaped to the suburbs," I say.

"I'd want to know," Sarah A says. "I'd want to know the whole story."

"You're only saying that because you know that's not your story," I say.

"Maybe. But what you gave me was an impossible scenario. That could never happen. I don't think anything *that* dramatic has ever happened," Sarah A says.

I don't disagree with her.

"Hey, do you want any chips?" Sarah A asks.

"No."

"I'm going to get some for the drive back," she says.

"Hurry," I say.

As I watch her go inside, I'm trying to figure out how I

feel. This morning, I thought I was on the brink of becoming an individual, but now I'm right back where I started. Mostly. This time Sarah A doesn't wait in line. She walks in and she walks out.

"They're corn chips," Sarah A says climbing into the car. "These are my favorite." She pulls the bag from her jacket pocket.

"Did you buy them or steal them?" I ask.

"You don't want to know," she says.

It's official. I'm back on the roller coaster. I barely like that ride. The rattling of bolts. The feeling that the whole crazy thing could give way. I prefer the flume ride. It's just one plunge and you can see it coming. Plus, you're not connected to a string of fast-flying cars. It's just your flume. Being on that ride gives you the illusion that you're drifting at your own pace. It's almost like you're in control of it.

# Chapter 25

When I call Liam I don't tell him about the planned renovations of our home. That's a body blow that should be delivered by a parent.

"Liam, I found something buried in the backyard and I want to talk to you about it," I say.

"Was it a body?" he asks. I can hear him laughing. I don't know why everybody thinks that's a funny joke. People really do find bodies buried in backyards. And I'm sure they don't stand around and laugh about it when it happens.

"No, I found a Godzilla lunch box," I say.

"Wow, that was a long time ago," Liam says. "Was my Godzilla action figure still inside? I loved that thing."

"Yes," I say. But I don't mention that Sarah A swiped it.

"Hey, Sarah, what were you doing digging around in the backyard?"

"Seasonal work," I say.

"What does that even mean?" he asks.

"Listen, I'm just calling to figure out why you did that. I'm curious."

And that's the truth.

"Well, let's see. How to sum it up for you? I guess I buried the Godzilla stuff because I grew disillusioned with the way pop culture had commandeered the image of Godzilla for commercial purposes."

"How old were you?"

"Twelve."

"And you cared about that?"

"Sarah, that sort of stuff, for me, is about who I am and why I'm here."

"Godzilla?"

"Listen, Godzilla is a Japanese creation that represents that culture's fear and anxiety over being the only country to have atomic warfare used against it. The whole idea of Godzilla is about a dormant sea beast being disturbed and altered by nuclear testing. Radioactive bombs created it, and nobody even thinks about that. Most people look at it as just another monster. Capitalism has divorced it from its real meaning."

"People don't enjoy thinking about atomic bombs."

"Sarah, I know you don't like talking politics, so I'll spare you my position on nuclear weapons. So that's it?"

"Yeah," I say.

"You're not going to ask me about the book?"

I know I should want to ask him about the book, but I don't. "No," I say. "That's it."

"You should take a look at it. It will bother you too."

"I don't know if that's true," I say.

"Sarah, I don't know who you think you're kidding, but deep down you care about who you are. We all do. It's part of being human."

"But I'm not like you. I'm not political. Hot topics don't stir me. At all."

"Dad told me about what you said to Big Don. That seemed to stir you," Liam says.

"That guy attacked Mom," I say. "That's different."

"Not really. You care about your family. Some people care about their relatives *and* other issues."

I want Liam to understand me. I don't think anyone really understands me. He's my brother, shouldn't he get me?

"When I was at the car lot cleaning cars with Johanna, she kept going on and on about the Potawatomi, and do you know what I told her?"

"I don't want to guess."

"I told her that I thought of myself as white. And I believe that. I'm not an Indian, Liam. I wasn't raised to be one."

"I don't even know what the last part of your statement is supposed to mean," Liam says. "But this isn't just about you."

"Sure it is," I say.

"When you come out to visit, I'm going to take you to Alcatraz."

"I'm not interested in looking at a prison. My criminal days are behind me."

"In 1969, a group of Indians took it over. They held the island for months," Liam says.

"Why?"

"There was a loophole in a treaty that allowed for land to revert back to Indians, so a group seized Alcatraz."

"Why are you telling me this?"

"Our great-grandmother went there. She didn't go over in the beginning on the Thanksgiving takeover. She went later and brought supplies."

"Nobody has ever told me this," I say.

"It's a sad story."

I don't say anything.

"It was such a weird situation. I mean, one day to have Anthony Quinn and Jonathan Winters parading around the island, then next to have so much turmoil. And then a little girl died."

"Were we related to her?" I ask. I'm trying to figure out what makes this story so sad.

"No, it was Richard Oakes's little girl. He was one of the leaders. She fell three stories down a stairwell. She suffered a lot of head injuries. She died the following week."

"That is sad," I say.

"Well, our great-grandma was one of the people who found her. And after she came back, she was never the same. Seeing that changed her—"

I interrupt him. "Liam," I say, "I don't want to hear anymore."

"It's important to think about who came before you and what their lives were like. And as long as you're on this planet, you should try to make it a better place. It's not just about you."

"I know that," I say.

I think about my hallway metaphor. Maybe I got it backward. Maybe it's not about the doors before me that remain unopened. Maybe it's about the doors that are behind me, the ones people have already passed through for me. Maybe I need to open them, and look inside and see what has happened.

"I don't expect this conversation to change your life," he says.

"Okay," I say.

"Call me later if you've got more questions. About college. Or Godzilla. Or anything."

He hangs up and I walk over to my desk and pick up the Potawatomi book. I flip to the first page.

"These stories are written for third-grade children to use in Social Studies. They present background information on the Potawatomi Indians in Kalamazoo."

That seems innocent enough. I turn several pages. At the end of the chapters there are questions to think about.

"What are many of the ways we keep healthy and strong that the Indians did not know about?"

That's a lame question. It sort of implies that Indians weren't smart enough to stay in shape. I turn until I reach a section titled "When The White People Came." It sounds like it's going to be an awful read. I go there anyway.

*"But the white men were more progressive and better educated than the Indians. They could see how this country could be made into good farmland and how great towns could be built. They wanted this land for their homes. The things which happened were not surprising. The stronger men drove away the weaker men."*

No wonder Liam buried this thing in the earth. It's flat and misleading and egotistical and boring and totally wrong. I close the book and let it fall to the floor. Here's the truth: I have a story and I don't like my story. Not because it's sad, which it is, but because I don't know what I'm supposed to do with it.

# Chapter 26

My parents ordered the commercial Dumpster and it will arrive next week. Apparently, my mother knows a designer who restores old homes, so our house will be enhanced but not altered. My father seems okay about this.

While I still consider myself reformed, I've decided not to tell my parents about lending John Glenn to Sarah A. I won't be informing them of his day absence either. Why worry them? And as long as I don't break any laws, what's the hurt? I'm going to pretend that John Glenn is still here. I'll make it look like he's eating his food. I'll claim to take him out for walks. I'll talk to him as if everything is normal. I might even put a dog turd in the driveway just to throw everybody off.

I grab my newly reinstated and fully charged cell phone and kiss John Glenn on his blond snout.

"We're going for a ride," I say.

I open the front door, but instead of trotting obediently

to my car, my dog has other plans. He races down the trail toward the lake.

"Come back!" I yell.

He doesn't.

As I run after him, tree branches thwack me in the face. I watch John Glenn plunge into the lake and paddle around its shallow edge.

"We don't have time for this," I tell him.

He treads water and pursues a pair of ducks.

"Leave it!" I yell.

I feel powerless.

"Please, John Glenn," I say.

My parents are getting coffee a few blocks away at Water Street. I need to get out of here. John Glenn finally pads up the shore toward me.

"You're going to smell like wet dog," I warn.

He walks toward me and pauses to shake loose the water.

"Get over here," I tell him. I am not using my special dog voice with him. I'm pissed. He follows me back up the hill and I stick him, dripping wet, in my backseat.

"I'm very disappointed in you," I say.

He pants excitedly. He loves car rides.

Sarah C is politely waiting outside her house. She's wearing a deep green tank top and denim shorts. She looks fantastic. Redheads always look good in green.

"John Glenn is wet and I think he has gas," I say.

"Good. He'll keep any interlopers at Yankee Springs to a serious distance."

Sarah C is so funny. I forgot what a great sense of humor she has. Too bad she isn't loyal.

"By the way, when we pick up Sarah B, she's going to be in a bad mood."

"Why? Did the Tigers lose?" I ask.

"No. They're winning. But she's going to spend the night with Sarah A at the cabin and will miss tomorrow's game."

"Can't she listen to it on a radio?" I ask.

"Sarah A doesn't want a sports distraction when Roman Karbowski is there."

"Is it just Roman and Sarah A and Sarah B?" I ask. "That seems like a weird way to kick off the guy phase."

"As I already mentioned, the guy phase isn't going according to plan," Sarah C says.

I'm dying to know the full extent of these complications. But I'd rather hear about them from Sarah B. She's the only Sarah who's never totally turned on me.

When I drive up to her house, Sarah B isn't waiting outside.

"Do you want me to get her?" Sarah C asks.

"Here she comes," I say.

She's barefoot, her sneakers flung over her shoulder. She's

pulled her Tigers cap low over her forehead. I think she's frowning, but it's hard to tell.

"What's that smell?" Sarah B asks. "Is there a dead animal in your trunk?"

"No. There's a wet and gassy animal in her backseat," Sarah C says.

John Glenn sits calmly in the center of the backseat.

"Can he move over?" Sarah B asks.

"Try not to sit downwind of him," Sarah C says.

"Nice idea, but I'm in a compact car," Sarah B says. "What do you feed your dog anyway?"

"Breeder's Choice," I say.

John Glenn finally moves over so that he's directly behind Sarah C. I flip on the radio to a pop station and we proceed for a long part of the drive in silence.

"Vance is bipolar," Sarah C says. "He's been officially diagnosed."

"That's too bad," I say.

"I don't think Vance is the only Aberdeen with mental problems," Sarah C says.

"Is this because Sarah A hit you?" I ask. "That was totally uncalled for."

"I'm not even talking about that. Since you left, things haven't exactly been normal," Sarah C says.

"What do you mean?" I ask.

"I don't know if we should go there," Sarah B says.

I glance in the rearview mirror, but Sarah B avoids looking at me.

"Sarah A has been acting sort of erratic," Sarah C says.

"She's been hanging out with Roman a lot," Sarah B says.

"But that's good, right? It means the guy phase is off to a great start," I say.

"Emotionally speaking, spending time with Roman hasn't exactly leveled her off," Sarah C says.

"We really shouldn't talk about this," Sarah B says. "Meena Cooper's family plans to prosecute the culprits to the fullest extent of the law when and if they find out who's responsible for their property damage. FYI, it was us."

"Sarah T isn't going to rat on us, are you?" Sarah C asks.

"No. I would never rat on you guys."

"Well, Roman's girlfriend, Meena, has been experiencing a certain amount of property damage," Sarah C says.

"He still has a girlfriend, but he's also seeing Sarah A?" I ask.

"He's a classic two-timer," Sarah B says.

"So was Frank Lloyd Wright," I say.

"Okay. Well, Sarah A has been framing Roman's ex-girlfriend for the crimes," Sarah C says.

"His ex-girlfriend?" I ask.

"Maryann Lehman," Sarah C says.

"But Maryann Lehman would never do anything wrong," I say. "She's virtuous."

"I know," Sarah C says. "We've been framing her. Or, more accurately, Sarah A has been framing her."

"What are you guys doing, vandalizing Meena's car?" I ask.

"No," Sarah C says.

"Her house?" I ask.

"Not exactly," Sarah B says.

"What?" I ask.

"We're girdling their trees," Sarah C says.

I gasp. That sounds horrible. Wait. What are they doing?

"What does that even mean?" I ask.

"We each take a pocketknife and scratch the bark all the way around their trees, so that the xylem, phloem, and cambium system breaks down, rupturing their nutrition cycle, and the trees die."

"Sounds slow-going and not all that serious," I say. "Lawfully speaking, is that really considered vandalism?"

"When you take out an apple orchard, trust me, it's serious," Sarah C says.

"You destroyed Meena Cooper's apple orchard?" I ask.

"It's the other trees we took out too," Sarah C says.

"The other trees?" I ask.

"Yeah, we've been celebrating the antithesis of Arbor Day for weeks," Sarah C says.

"Why?" I ask.

"In order to frame Maryann Lehman, we've been destroying a lot of trees in and around her neighborhood," Sarah C says.

"How many trees?" I ask. Their tree-girdling spree strikes me as weird, destructive, and environmentally unsound.

"Well, I can't speak to the numbers, but I have been keeping a list of the varieties," Sarah C says.

"What have you killed?" I ask.

"Let's see. We've snuffed out birch, juniper, boxwood, crabapple, pine, sycamore, spruce, purple leaf sand cherry, willow, elm, quaking aspen, hackberry, sassafras, sourwood, magnolia, maple, and American beech," Sarah C says.

"That's a lot of pulp," I say.

"I know," Sarah B says.

"Will they grow back?" I ask.

"Never," Sarah C says.

"That's awful. And oddly assaultive," I say.

"I know. It's really starting to get to me. I don't think I can commit another hit."

"That's pretty violent crap," I say. "You're running around with knives at night slashing up trees?"

"Don't act too innocent. You did rob a convenience store," Sarah C says.

I bite my bottom lip. I don't like thinking about that. But my situation was so different. I just flew into that store and distracted the clerk and grabbed the donation jar and didn't hurt anyone. Except maybe the horse.

"So whatever happened to Buttons?" I ask.

"Who?" Sarah B asks.

"Buttons. That impaled draft horse," I say.

"He was put down," Sarah C says.

"Right away?" I ask.

"No, they gave him a few weeks, but he was pretty much lame," Sarah C says.

"Was he an old horse?" I ask.

"No," Sarah C says. "He was, like, two."

"Shit," I say. "That stinks."

Death by impalement is always a tragedy.

"Aren't you just sick with guilt about those trees?" I ask.

"A little bit," Sarah B says.

"I try not to think about it," Sarah C says. "Also, I make a habit of leaving a small patch of bark uncut. It gives the tree a fighting chance."

"I didn't know you did that," Sarah B says. "I do that too."

"It's the only humane thing to do," Sarah C says. "I totally dig trees."

"Do you think trees can feel?" I ask.

We're approaching the turnoff to Yankee Springs.

"I do," Sarah C says. "Not the kind of intelligent feeling that we're capable of, but they sense stuff."

"Yeah. They totally sense stuff," Sarah B says.

The station's reception crackles, so I click off the radio.

"I've missed you," Sarah C says.

"You say that like you mean it," I say.

"Of course I mean it," Sarah C says.

There it is. I can't hold it inside of me anymore. I know Sarah C stole my analogy. And I know when she did this that she jeopardized my fate. Did she care about me then? I doubt it. She's part phony. She hides it well, but it's there, like a mole near your bra strap that nobody ever sees.

"What are you trying to say?" Sarah C asks.

Sarah C needs to know that I know about this phoniness so that she can own up to it right now, to the side of my head, and give me the chance to forgive her so we can possibly move on.

"I know what you did," I say.

"I just told you what we did," Sarah C says.

"No. During the freewrite, I know what you put down," I say.

"Oh, that. I don't do well under pressure. I get good grades and am smart enough, but when given timed essays or exams I always choke. We'd just been talking about your analogy, so that's what popped into my head," Sarah C says.

I'm shocked. She doesn't sound apologetic at all.

"Well, you can't *steal* other people's ideas," I say.

"I didn't steal it," Sarah C says. "I footnoted you."

"You what?" I ask.

"I wrote at the bottom of my freewrite that this was your idea and I was borrowing it to build my argument," Sarah C says.

I'm sort of flattered that I was footnoted. To my knowledge, it's the first time that it's ever happened.

"How did you know what I wrote on my freewrite?" Sarah C asks.

"Sarah A told me," I say.

"But she didn't tell you about the footnote?" Sarah C asks.

"No," I say.

"Typical," Sarah C says with a snort.

"You shouldn't sound so indignant," Sarah B says. "Considering what you said about me."

"I never said anything bad about you," I say. Did I say something bad about Sarah B? I might have.

"Your nickname for me is Teflon face. Sarah A told me," Sarah B says.

"It was so not a nickname," I say. "And it was Teflon complexion." That probably doesn't sound like a great defense, but I only said that phrase a couple of times. "And I didn't mean it maliciously."

"Right," Sarah B says. "Because every high school girl is secretly hoping to have her friends compare her skin texture to cookware coating."

"You're right," I say. "I'm sorry. It was thoughtless and I never should have said it. I'll never say anything snarky like that again. I promise."

"I promise too," Sarah C says.

"I never said snarky stuff to begin with," Sarah B says. "So I'll stay that course."

I listen to the tires turn against the road. Why are we heading to Yankee Springs? Out of loyalty to Sarah A? Out of devotion to the Sarahs? Out of a desire to press forward with the guy phase? Out of an urge to remain popular? Out of fear that Sarah A might get hacked to pieces by an ax murderer? Why?

"I'd just like to say that our group hasn't been the same without you. Four white chicks is a lot more fun than three," Sarah B says.

"I think I could stand hanging out with three white chicks and a dog," Sarah C says. "It just has to be the right three white chicks and the right dog."

Sarah B laughs. I don't. For some reason being lumped into a group referred to as "white chicks" feels a little wrong. A month ago it probably wouldn't have, but today it does. If I'm one-quarter Potawatomi, is that the right word for me?

"Hey, I need to tell you something," I say.

"Shoot," Sarah C says.

"It's a confession," I say.

I've silenced everyone.

"What is it?" Sarah C asks.

"I'm not white."

"What do you mean?" Sarah B says.

"Are you a descendant of slaves?" Sarah C asks. "Are you a quadroon?"

"A what?" I ask.

"A quadroon. It's a person who has one-quarter black ancestry," Sarah C says.

"No. I'm one-quarter Potawatomi. I'm part Native American. I think my great-grandmother grew up on a reservation. But she left it. Afterward, she lived alone and had a ton of cats. I don't know if those events are related."

"My grandma has a ton of cats and she's just plain white," Sarah B says.

"I think that's neat," Sarah C says.

"About my grandma's cats?" Sarah B says. "I don't. I think she needs to have them spayed and neutered. Her house smells like ammonia."

"I'm talking about Sarah T being part Potawatomi. I think stuff like that is cool," Sarah C says. "I think it's good to be connected to things bigger than yourself."

I'd never thought of it that way.

"I'm not going to start acting like Liam," I say. "I won't be driving out to visit the monument of Chief White Pigeon on the weekends or anything."

"Okay," Sarah C says.

"I'll probably read a book or two," I say. "You know, about my ancestry."

"Yeah," Sarah B says.

"Change takes time," I say.

"Haven't you always known you were one-quarter Potawatomi? How is this change?" Sarah C asks.

"The way I see myself. It's different now," I say.

We drive along the 131 until the Yankee Springs exit. I merge onto the off ramp. A small animal scurries across the road in front of me and I brake hard.

"Look," Sarah B says. "It's a cat."

"That's a fox," Sarah C says.

"I've never seen a fox before," Sarah B says.

"How would you know?" I ask. "You probably thought it was a cat."

We laugh. We're almost to Yankee Springs.

"Why do you think women collect cats?" Sarah C asks.

"It's not really a gender thing," I say.

"Sure it is," Sarah C says.

Nobody answers right away. I think we're really mulling it over.

"I think it's all about your own helplessness," Sarah B says.

"First, a cat is smaller than you and so you see it as vulnerable. Plus, it depends on you for food and stuff. By saving the cats maybe you think you're somehow saving yourself. Also, cats are covered in fur and most people like the way that feels."

"Okay," I say. "So why do some people not like cats, especially in packs? I mean, my mom can't stand them."

I'm surprised when Sarah B has such a quick response.

"First off, and most obvious, is the odor. Nobody likes that kind of stink. But the bigger reason is probably related to that same sense of helplessness. Visiting a place stuffed with cats would make a person feel vulnerable but also responsible. I mean, all those cats have needs. And then you've got the broken person who hordes the cats and she has needs too, but she doesn't even recognize that. It's like the cats are her Band-Aids so she doesn't have to see her own wound," Sarah B says.

"That's so deep," I say.

"Totally inner core," Sarah C says.

"Imagine how it must feel to visit a massive cat dwelling, to be able to recognize this. There's somebody you love. And there's this pool of cats. It's like you'd feel more helpless than the animals," Sarah B says.

"You've thought a lot about this," I say.

"I think it's because my mom's not around. I think about being helpless a lot. I also think about women a lot and why they do what they do. It's something I talk about in counseling."

I glance in the rearview mirror at Sarah B. Tears are slipping down her cheeks, rolling off her jawbone onto her shirt.

"Plus, volunteering at the shelter has helped me see that our pet population is completely out of control," Sarah B says.

"That's an understatement," I say.

I open the moonroof and let a cool breeze flow through the car.

"Do you two feel like singing?" I ask.

"Sure, what song?" Sarah C says.

"I don't feel like singing anything," I say. "I think I might quit choir. And do something else. Something I really want to do."

"Like what?" Sarah C asks.

"Maybe join Activists for Action," I say.

"The campus environmental group? Don't they just recycle stuff after school?" Sarah B asks.

"Yeah," I say.

"Maybe I'll join Forensics. Or Mock Trial. Or maybe take a class in zoology," I say.

"I didn't know Central offered classes in zoology," Sarah B says.

"I didn't know you hated choir," Sarah C says.

"I don't hate it," I say. "But I don't love it either. After all these years of it, I think I'm choired out."

"Hey, I've got a confession, too," Sarah C says.

I don't know if our car can handle more confessions.

"What is it?" I ask.

"My name isn't Sarah," she says.

"That's impossible," Sarah B says.

"No, it's not. I never officially changed it. I lied. Legally, I'm still Lisa Sarah Cody."

"Did you forge those documents?" I ask.

"Just for Sarah A's benefit. I didn't break any laws."

"You were always a little different," Sarah B says.

All this talking has made me feel much less burdened. Literally, I feel lighter.

"I haven't made a confession," Sarah B says.

"Do you have one?" I ask.

"Yeah," I say.

"Then shoot," Sarah C says.

"I don't chew gum anymore," Sarah B says.

That doesn't seem like a confession that's at the same level as mine and Sarah C's.

"Don't you want to know why?" Sarah B asks.

"Did your dentist tell you to stop?" I ask.

"No, it's because I've decided to forgive my mother," Sarah B says.

"Really?" I ask. "I don't know if I could forgive my mother if she ran off with the meter reader and moved to North Dakota."

"So how does gum chewing play into that?" Sarah C asks.

"My mother has TMJ. She can't chew gum, so I was chewing it all the time to spite her," Sarah B says.

"But your mom was never around to see you chewing it," Sarah C says.

"The point wasn't that she had to see me; the point was that I could do it and she couldn't," Sarah B says. "But I don't anymore. I'm over it. I forgave her."

"Why?" I ask.

"Because staying mad at her every day was a huge energy suck. She is what she is. Sometimes people screw up," Sarah B says. "And sometimes they don't stop screwing up."

"That's so big of you," I say.

And as we all seem poised to experience a major epiphany, we don't quite get there. I pull into the parking lot, and Sarah A bursts out of her cabin and races to the car, slapping my window with her hands. Her fingers leave greasy marks on the glass.

"There's a problem!" Sarah A yells. "It's a situation!"

I pull on my parking brake and turn off the car. We all climb out.

"You look awful," Sarah C says.

"I am. I am awful," Sarah A answers. "We need to get back inside the car."

We hurry back inside my little Jetta, Sarah A in the passenger seat, and Sarah B and Sarah C in the backseat, with John Glenn riding on Sarah B's lap. Then we slam all the doors. Sarah A's face is red. She's sweating. Her blonde hair sticks to her cheeks in clumps. She reaches over and grabs my arm. "Thank God you're here," she says. "Thank God, thank God, thank God."

# Chapter 27

I pull out of the parking lot and attempt to turn right.

"Go left! Go left!" Sarah A yells.

I do.

"What's going on?" Sarah C asks. "You act like you're being attacked."

"You guys," Sarah A says, flipping around to look into the backseat. "You'll never guess what's going on at Yankee Springs."

"Does it involve an ax murderer?" Sarah C asks.

Sarah A shakes her head.

"Why are you sweating?" Sarah B asks.

"It's, like, a hundred degrees in those cabins. And I don't have a fan. Or a cooler," Sarah A says. "Turn left here."

I do.

"Are we going to the Shell station?" I ask.

"Yeah," Sarah A says. "I totally need ice."

"Is that your emergency?" I ask.

"What emergency? I never said there was an emergency," Sarah A says. "I said I had a problem."

"You were freaking out," Sarah C says.

"I need some lip balm," Sarah A says.

"You said something was going on at Yankee Springs," Sarah B adds.

"Something is totally going on at Yankee Springs," Sarah A says.

I pull the car to a stop in front of a metal cage where people can refill small propane tanks.

"Oh, it smells awful," Sarah A says.

"It smells like propane," I say.

"No, it smells like poor people camping," Sarah A says. "Do you want anything?"

Because I don't know if she's going to be buying what I want or stealing it, I say no. I watch Sarah A practically leap out of the car.

"She looks like she's going mad," Sarah C says. "Is it safe to leave Sarah B with her for the night?"

I look in the rearview mirror.

"Sarah B is scrappy," I say.

"I don't want to have to fight anybody," Sarah B says.

"I think we're jumping to conclusions. I'm sure there's a logical explanation to everything," I say.

"Wow, and I thought I was the group Pollyanna," Sarah C says.

"Can we listen to the radio?" Sarah B asks. "There's some pregame commentary I'd like to catch."

"Pick your station," I tell her.

I tune out what the commentators are saying. Baseball doesn't hold much interest for me. Sarah A rushes out of the gas station with a large fountain drink. She gets back in the car and presses the cup to her forehead.

"Besides the heat," I say, "what's going on?"

"I can hardly hear you," Sarah A says, turning off the radio.

"Sarah B was listening to that," I say.

"What is it with you and the Tigers?" Sarah A says. "Everybody knows Detroit sucks. As a team. As a city. As an idea. It's basically a fact that Detroit is our nation's anus."

"I wouldn't call that a fact," Sarah C says. "And I definitely wouldn't call it an anus."

"Yeah," Sarah B says.

"I've only been there a few times, but it never struck me as an anus," I say. "The mall in Novi is cool."

"If our country has an anus, it's probably in Cleveland," Sarah C says.

"I like Cleveland," Sarah B says.

"I don't even want to think of our country as having an anus," I say.

"Everything has an asshole," Sarah A says, taking a big suck of her drink. "Everything."

"Especially you," Sarah C says. But she murmurs it so quietly that I think I'm the only one who hears her.

I'm tempted to turn the radio back on, but I don't. It seems like a better idea to let the whole Detroit/anus debate blow over.

"Whatever," Sarah C says. "So what's going on at Yankee Springs?"

"You're not going to believe this," Sarah A says. "Last week, they held a retreat there for University of Michigan professors."

"That's shocking," Sarah C says, her voice tinged with sarcasm.

"This could be our ticket to college. To Michigan!" Sarah A says.

"I thought our tickets into college were our SAT scores, GPA's, application essays, and all that free money from the Kalamazoo Promise," I say.

"The woman staying in the cabin next to me is Gail Boatwright," Sarah A says. "She's a straggler. She stayed after the retreat wrapped up. She's on the entrance committee. She screens the applications. She reads the essays."

"So you think we should suck up to her?" Sarah C asks. "I'm down with that."

"We don't even need to suck up to her," Sarah A says. "I have a better plan."

I'm almost back to Yankee Springs, but Sarah A seems impatient.

"Can't you drive faster?" Sarah A asks.

"I'm going the speed limit," I say.

"Break the speed limit," Sarah A says. "We've got to get back while she's still out on the lake. She kayaks every day for two hours. She's old. And totally addicted to her routine. We have about an hour."

"To do what?" Sarah B asks. "Are we going to kayak with her? I'll need to change into my bathing suit."

"I didn't even bring a bathing suit," Sarah C says.

"I don't really feel like swimming, but John Glenn can join you," I say.

"There's not going to be any swimming," Sarah A says. "I want to look at her laptop."

"You want to steal her computer?" Sarah C asks.

"No, I just want to look at it," Sarah A says.

"What do you think you'll find?" Sarah C asks. "Helpful secret information?"

"What's wrong with you? We could find anything. Maybe fantastic essays from last year. Maybe internal memos from Michigan about what they're looking for. Maybe scandalous personal information that we can use to blackmail Gail."

Sarah A continues to suck on the straw. She has her window rolled down and her blonde hair flies around her face in choppy sections. Her ends look split. Her nails are chipped. Maybe it's the fact that she's living in a cabin, but she seems to have really let herself go.

"This doesn't sound like the best idea," Sarah C says as I pull back into the campground.

"She can't stay on the lake forever. We've got to do it now," Sarah A says.

She climbs out of the car and sets her drink on the roof. We all get out too. Sarah A walks over to me and threads her arm through mine.

"Are you with me or not?" Sarah A asks.

I look at Sarah B and Sarah C. They both shrug.

"You and John Glenn watch the lake. Sarah B, stand outside the cabin. Sarah C, help me download the files," Sarah A says.

John Glenn runs to a pine tree and relieves himself.

"This idea sounds weird," Sarah C says. "We might not find anything useful. And we'd be committing breaking and entering. That's a felony." Sarah C smooths her tank top over her stomach. "We could get caught. Maybe even prosecuted."

Sarah A lets go of my arm and charges Sarah C.

"Are you saying you won't do it?" Sarah A asks. She glares

at her and licks her lips. "It's stupid to say that. We won't get caught and we could get an upper hand on all the other jerks applying to Michigan. What if we don't get in? Imagine how that rejection would feel."

Sarah C removes the elastic band from her ponytail and lets her red hair fall around her shoulders.

"It seems unlikely that she'd have old essays on her computer," Sarah C says.

"I agree," I say, displaying a thumbs-up sign. "Very unlikely."

Sarah A pivots to face me. "You're agreeing with Sarah C?"

I keep making the thumbs-up sign.

"Stop doing that. You've got freakishly stubby thumbs," Sarah A says. "What about you, Sarah B? Are you with me?"

Sarah B pulls off her cap and situates it backward on her head. Her brown eyes look unfazed by the drama and somewhat distracted.

"It seems a little random," Sarah B says.

"Yeah," I say. "This is *so* random. Let's bag it."

"So you're all saying 'no'? After all we've been through, you're just going to abandon me?" Sarah A asks.

"I wouldn't exactly call this abandonment," Sarah C says.

"That's what it feels like. You're all just turning your backs on me. And you," Sarah A says, stabbing her finger at me, "apparently, pinky-swears mean nothing to you."

"That's not true," I say, lifting up my pinky, wriggling it in the air. "I'm totally here for you. You're the one who wants to run off and commit another crime. It's more like *you* are abandoning *me*."

Sarah A shakes her head at me and groans.

"What's happened to you? It's like you've become a totally different person," Sarah A says. "A sucky one."

"Let's not start calling each other names," Sarah C says.

"What I want us to do isn't even a real crime," Sarah A says. "Real crimes have victims. In this situation, nobody will get hurt."

"It feels like a crime," Sarah C says. "And I'm not in the mood to feel like a criminal."

"Yeah, I've already contributed to the demise of a horse," I say.

"And I've got a ton of tree carcasses weighing on my conscience," Sarah B says.

Sarah A reaches down and grabs a handful of gravel from the parking lot. She looks at all of us and then spins around, throwing the small rocks at our legs.

"I'll do it without you. And don't expect any help from me. Now or ever. As for the guy phase, you're on your own. Good luck securing relationships. I can't believe this."

"Calm down," I say.

"Don't tell me how to feel!" Sarah A screams.

Her quaking voice bounces off the trees.

"You three do whatever it is you're going to do. But I'm going to make something of myself," Sarah A says.

"We all want to make something of ourselves," Sarah C says. "We just don't want to break into that woman's cabin."

Sarah A tosses her hair over her shoulder and then folds her arms across her chest.

"You don't get it," Sarah A says. "I'm going to be somebody important. And my parents, my real and awful parents, they will look at me and wish they'd made a different choice. They'll look at everything I've done and they'll know, they'll have to know, that what they did was a mistake."

I watch Sarah A breathe. Her chest is heaving, her shoulders rise and fall.

"Sometimes, that's how I feel about my mom," Sarah B says. She pulls her cap off and holds it at her side.

"That's so different," Sarah A says. "You choose not to talk to your mom. You're pissed off about her affair. It's not the same thing. This wasn't my choice. Somebody made me and then didn't want me. Somebody grew me inside of her and she gave me away."

"Maybe she thought it was the better choice," Sarah C says.

Sarah A can't hold back her tears. They stream down her cheeks like a flood.

"Better for who?" Sarah A asks. She takes a step backward and then another. "I don't need you guys. I don't need anybody."

Sarah C, Sarah B, and I watch Sarah A stomp off toward a small cabin near the lake.

"I think she's wrong. I think she totally needs us," I say.

"She's so upset," Sarah B says.

"Her new level of violence is completely disturbing," Sarah C says. "It's like she's going to have to be physically restrained."

Sarah A turns onto the path that leads up to the cabin.

"Can't the woman in the kayak see Sarah A entering her porch?" Sarah C asks.

"I think so," I say.

"We should do something," Sarah B says. "Sarah A has gone off the deep end."

I don't think that any of us know what to do to help Sarah A. She's acting way more unpredictable and crazy than she ever has before.

"I think Sarah A is our friend and we shouldn't let her self-destruct," I say. "If we don't want to commit a crime, maybe we should talk her out of it."

"That isn't going to happen," Sarah C says. "Didn't you see her? She's lost it."

We watch Sarah A partially disappear behind a clump of pines.

"This is so stupid," Sarah C says. "All I ever wanted was Benny Stowe. Is that so wrong?"

"You might still get Benny Stowe," I say.

"The guy phase is a disaster. And now Sarah A is acting way too reckless. The only way I'll get Benny Stowe is the old-fashioned method."

"Sex?" I ask.

"I wish," Sarah C says. "I'll befriend him and see if he's interested in me."

"We have to do something," Sarah B says. "Now!"

"I'm tired of being a thief," Sarah C says. "I'd rather just knock Sarah A out and drag her back to the car."

"Okay," I say. I'm surprised by my quick and affirmative response to Sarah C's violent strategy. "But don't hurt her in a permanent way."

"I won't really knock her out. I'll just hold her back," Sarah C says.

"Right," I say. "I'll help carry her legs."

"She's very strong and knows quite a few jujitsu moves," Sarah B says. "So watch out for those."

"What are you going to do?" I ask Sarah B.

"I'll open the car door for you," Sarah B says. "Also, I'll warn you if I see her making any sudden or powerful thrusts."

"Jesus," Sarah C says. "I can't believe I'm doing this."

"Wait up!" I yell after Sarah A.

We all take off running after her, even John Glenn. All we have to do is prevent her from committing a crime. How hard can that be? Three against one? Even with a few of her jujitsu moves thrown in, aren't the odds completely in our favor?

# Chapter 28

Sarah B serves as our lookout, while Sarah C and I enter the cabin. Sarah A stands at Gail's desk, frantically pecking at her laptop.

"There's all kinds of stuff on here," Sarah A says. "It's the mother lode."

"Sarah A, we need to talk," Sarah C says.

"When I'm finished," Sarah A says. "And Sarah T, you need to get out to the lake. We don't need three people in here."

I watch Sarah C walk up behind Sarah A and grab her by the shoulders. She pulls her to the ground.

"Stop it!" Sarah A screams. "You're ruining everything."

They roll on the wood floor. Sarah A tries to push Sarah C off her, but Sarah C has wrapped her long legs around Sarah A's waist. Sarah A can't pull herself to a standing position.

"Do you need help?" I ask Sarah C.

"I've got her," Sarah C says.

"What's wrong with you two?" Sarah A asks. "Let go of me."

Sarah A flips onto her back and begins crawling like a crab toward me. She swings her arm and grabs my ankle. I fall on the floor too.

"It's for your own good," I say, trying to shake off Sarah A's hand.

"Ouch!" Sarah C screams. "She's using her teeth."

I roll over onto my stomach and crawl away from Sarah A and her snapping jaws. When I look back, I see that Sarah A has Sarah C in a headlock. How did that happen?

"Listen, I don't know why you two want to wrestle, but you're both on the verge of wrecking our lives. I found the file that I want. I'm going to print it. Sarah T, go out to the lake and watch for Gail. Sarah C, stay here with me and help me. This is important. Plus, it's the last wrong thing I'll ever do. I promise."

Sarah C is turning such an intense shade of red that she's beginning to look purple.

"Does she need air?" I ask, pointing to Sarah C.

"Probably," Sarah A says. "But I'm not releasing anybody until you guys promise to help me. It's the last time. Can't you be a friend to me in this?"

I feel cornered. I feel like maybe I should help Sarah A. I mean, our plans to haul her out to the car certainly didn't work. Maybe this one last act of friendship is all she needs.

"I'll help you," I say. "I'll stand by the lake."

"What about you?" Sarah A asks Sarah C.

"Okay," Sarah C says. "I'll stay here with you. But I'm not touching her computer."

Sarah A releases Sarah C and she stumbles forward, gasping for breath.

"By the way, you two are terrible at restraining people. You should take a self-defense class," Sarah A says. "Or buy some mace."

So there it is. Sarah A won. We assume our positions. Sarah A and Sarah C remain inside the cabin. Sarah B stands approximately ten feet away from the cabin. And I stand, John Glenn at my side, almost thirty feet away from Sarah B. And the woman in the kayak is about fifty yards away from the lake's edge. It's somewhat of a relief to know that I'm taking part in the Sarahs' last crime ever. No handcuffs. No lineups. No prison jumpsuits. John Glenn lowers his head and laps up several drinks of water.

"Nice day!" I yell to the woman in the kayak.

"Don't try to talk to her," Sarah B says to me. "That's suspicious."

"We live in the Midwest. Polite conversation is expected of us," I say.

"Are you almost done?" Sarah B asks.

"We found essays!" Sarah A yells.

"We don't even know if they're entrance essays," Sarah C says.

Did she find another file? I thought she found the one she wanted already. There Sarah A goes again. Wanting more and more and more.

"Keep it down," I say. "I can totally hear you. Your voices probably carry across the water."

I watch the woman dip her oars in the calm lake. She pulls through the water, aiming her small boat toward the shore. I watch the kayak's tip grow closer. Every time she digs into the water with her oar, she stirs the lake into fragile shivers.

"You're really good at that," I yell. "I mean, you've got so much speed."

The woman in the kayak tosses back her head and laughs. She seems nice. I look over at Sarah B. She pulls her baseball cap off and wipes her forehead.

"Hurry up," I hear her say.

Sarah A bolts out of the cabin and races toward me. She kicks off her sneakers and peels out of her socks. "She needs more time. She's printing stuff out," she says.

"We're using the woman's printer?" I ask.

"Of course," Sarah A says. "And we need to stall Gail."

"How will you stall her?" I ask.

"Tip her boat and dump her in the water," Sarah A says. "I'll make it look like an accident."

"That's stupid," I say.

I reach out and grab Sarah A by the wrist.

"Tell Sarah C to stop printing stuff. Let's end this. We've got time," I say.

"No. It's useful information," Sarah A says. "We're dumping Gail."

"She looks like a strong swimmer. That might not slow her down," I say.

"So I'll whack her with the paddle," Sarah A says.

I tighten my hold on her wrist and stare right into her eyes. I want her to be kidding.

"You can't attack her with her own oar," I say.

"Why not?" Sarah A asks.

"That's assault," I say.

"I'll hit her in the head. I'll knock her out. She won't remember anything. Head injuries usually lead to memory loss," Sarah A says.

Why have multiple Sarahs begun to want to knock other people out? It must be stress.

"That's crazy," I say.

"Don't call me that."

She rips her arm away from me and runs down the long, narrow dock. Her feet sound like drums. I panic. I need to stop her.

"Get her, John Glenn!" I yell.

I slap him on his rump to encourage an enthusiastic pursuit, but he sits down. Sarah A dives off the dock and takes long strokes toward the kayak. I can't believe she's going to do this.

"She's done!" Sarah B yells.

I look back to the cabin. Sarah B is racing down the steps toward my car. She's holding a stack of papers. Our last crime is finished. There's no need for further drama.

"Come back!" I call, flashing the peace sign over and over.

But Sarah A doesn't stop. She's traveling through the lake on a course that's going to intercept Gail's kayak. Before I know what I'm doing, I feel wet. I'm in the water, swimming after my awful, crazy friend. At first, John Glenn is at my side, dog paddling with me, but he's not used to being in deep water. After several feet, I watch him turn back to shore. I don't have that option. I need to correct this disaster.

It's surprising to me that I'm able to overtake Sarah A. Maybe she's only the strongest Sarah on land. Because here I am, within striking distance. I grab on to her foot, so that she knows that I'm here. This must really freak her out, because she kicks her heel free and slips onto her back. At first I think she's going to float on her back. Instead, she splashes the water uncontrollably with her arms.

"Stop it," I say. "Go back with me."

But Sarah A seems to be on a whole other planet. She's slapping at the water, fighting to keep her head up. It's like she's forgotten how to swim or float or anything.

"Relax," I say.

I try to reach around her to grab her waist, but she pushes away from me. I reach for her again, but she struggles against me. I'm trying not to swallow water. But it's hard. We're both whipping the lake into a white foam and things feel very out of control. I don't want to give up. But I don't know what to do. The kayak isn't that far away from us either.

"You'll flip me!" I hear a voice yell. "Are you drowning?"

I can't tell if Sarah A is in trouble, or if she's purposely trying to tip the kayak. She looks like she's drowning, or at least she looks like how I imagine a person who's drowning would look. But I don't want to capsize anybody. And I can't keep wrestling with Sarah A in this deep water. My muscles are tired and I can't seem to take in enough air. I don't try a third time. I let go of her. And I let go of the idea that I can neatly save everything by pulling this unwilling person back to shore.

"Sarah A?" I yell. "I'm going back."

She continues to flail as the kayak approaches. But she's not trying to tip the boat. She's in trouble. She keeps slipping under the water. Then it happens. She goes under and she stays under. I watch the top of her blonde head disappear. It doesn't resurface.

"She's drowning!" I yell.

Gail is wearing a life jacket. She rolls the kayak on its side and slips into the lake.

"I've got her," she says.

I watch Gail lift a very pale Sarah above the waterline.

"Can you make it back to shore?" she asks me.

I nod. And then roll over onto my back, kicking hard to make it to the dock. I don't bother asking her about the welfare of the kayak. I figure in matters of life and death, boats don't figure into the equation.

I make it back before Sarah A and Gail. Sarah C and Sarah B are waiting for me. They each grab one of my arms and haul me onto the dock. John Glenn nervously runs back and forth.

"Are you okay?" Sarah B asks. "Did you swallow water?"

I cough and roll onto my side.

"Hit her back," Sarah B says. "She's filled with water."

"I don't think that's what you do," Sarah C says. "It's not like she's choking on a grape."

They each sit beside me. Sarah C brushes my wet hair away from my face, and Sarah B holds my hand. John Glenn protectively sniffs my soggy sneakers.

"You don't look blue," Sarah B says. "That's a good sign."

I close my eyes and concentrate on my breathing. I didn't save Sarah A. I *couldn't* save Sarah A. I left her in the middle of a lake to die.

"She wouldn't let me help her," I say.

"She's fine," Sarah C says. "She was acting crazy. She could have drowned you both."

"Maybe if I could have gotten a better grip on her heel," I say. "Or if I could have reached her calf."

"People who are drowning are totally dangerous, because they're so panicky," Sarah B says. "I think that's part of the reason life preservers have such long ropes."

"If I was on land, I bet it would've been different," I say.

"She's fine," Sarah C says.

"She is so *not* fine," I say.

I open my eyes and turn to look at Sarah B and Sarah C. Their faces look so kind and concerned. Do they always look this way? I close my eyes again. The warm dock feels solid and pleasant beneath me.

"We're going to check on Sarah A," Sarah C says. "Don't go anywhere."

John Glenn curls up next to me. It feels so nice to have a dog. I can hear Sarah A being lifted onto the dock by the other Sarahs.

"Let's set her on the dock," Gail says.

All three of them haul Sarah A out of the water.

"I'm okay," Sarah A says. "I got in over my head."

"We know," Sarah C says.

"She'll be okay," Gail says. Her voice is low and strong.

"Thanks so much," Sarah C says.

"It's what any decent person would have done," Gail says.

"I'm just thankful you're a decent person," Sarah B says.

"Your friend is staying in that cabin there, right?" Gail asks, pointing to Sarah A's weekend cabin.

"Yeah, for a couple of nights," Sarah B says. "I'm staying with her tonight."

"That's good. Do you need help getting her to her cabin?" Gail asks.

"We've got her," Sarah C says.

"I'm fine," Sarah A says. "I don't need any more help."

"Well, it was nice to meet you. Even if the circumstances were fairly dramatic," Gail says. "Stop by later if you want. I've got to fetch my kayak before she makes it to Lake Superior." Gail waves good-bye.

"Wow, you have huge biceps, do you work out?" Sarah B asks.

"At my age, lifting weights is highly recommended," Gail says.

"What's your age?" Sarah B asks.

"If you must know, I'm a spry sixty-five."

Gail does not look like an elderly person to me. She looks like the kind of person who hikes.

At the mention of the word "kayak," John Glenn leaps to his feet and commences barking.

"John Glenn, no," I say.

"You named your dog John Glenn?" she asks.

"Yes." I'm tempted to ask Gail her professional opinion

about this. She'd know whether or not I'd score brownie points for writing a college essay about my shelter rescue dog. But it seems a bit inappropriate to bring up now, after this near-death experience.

"That's too bad about John Glenn," Gail says.

"Did he die?" Sarah B asks.

"No, not too long ago he caused a serious car wreck in Ohio. He failed to yield and put himself, his wife, and the driver of the car he hit in the hospital."

"That's awful," Sarah C says.

"Well, accidents happen," Gail says. "You girls really should stick closer to shore. This is a pretty wide lake."

She smiles and waves and jumps into the lake.

"Thanks!" I call again.

All four of us wave, even the somewhat stunned Sarah A.

"What now?" I ask.

"I think you should rename John Glenn before you write that essay," Sarah C says.

"Really?" I ask.

"What about Neil Armstrong?" Sarah C asks.

"What about Lou Gehrig?" Sarah B asks.

"That's so weird," I say. "Did you know that they were all members of the same fraternity, Phi Delta Theta? So was the twenty-third U.S. president, Benjamin Harrison, and the architect Frank Lloyd Wright."

"That seems like a lot of useless information," Sarah A says.

"What?" I ask.

I'm a bit surprised and saddened that after her near-death experience she's so eager to spew negativity.

"Nobody but a nerd would know that Benjamin Harrison was a U.S. president," Sarah A says.

"I knew that," Sarah C says.

Sarah A sits up and coughs. Then she rolls her eyes.

"It doesn't matter," Sarah A says. "You don't need to re-name your dog. He looks like a John Glenn, and just because an ex-astronaut failed to yield, it doesn't make him a bad guy."

I like this idea.

"You're right," I say. "His name stays."

"So now what?" Sarah B asks.

"Do you really have to spend the night here?" I ask. "Couldn't you spend it with one of us?"

"My dad totally wouldn't mind," Sarah B says.

Sarah A blinks several times.

"Roman is going to come up to visit," Sarah A says.

"Forget Roman," Sarah C says.

"But I like Roman," Sarah A says.

"What about his pheromones?" I ask.

"I like those too," Sarah A says.

"But you haven't smelled his pillow in weeks," I say.

"I've been smelling the real thing," Sarah A says.

"You could call him on my cell phone," I say.

"What would I say?" Sarah A asks.

"That you're staying at my house," Sarah B says.

Sarah A gathers her wet hair between her hands and twists it hard, wringing the lake's water from her ponytail.

"Let's get your stuff and get out of here," I say.

Sarah A nods.

"It'll be a snug fit," I say.

Sarah A grabs her drink from the roof and offers to let Sarah C ride shotgun, because of her long legs. This is the first time Sarah A has ever made that considerate gesture.

"Do you have enough room back there?" Sarah C asks.

"No," Sarah A says. "And I've got a wet dog on my lap."

"It's only an hour and a half home," I say.

We all laugh.

"Hey, I've got some bad news," Sarah C says.

"What?" I ask.

"Those papers I printed out. They're not what we thought they were," Sarah C says.

"What are they?" Sarah A asks.

"They're the freshmen entrance requirements for Western Michigan University. Actually, I think it's stuff you can download off their website."

"No way," Sarah A says.

"Yes way," Sarah C says. "Did Gail tell you that she worked for Michigan?"

"I thought she said Michigan," Sarah A says.

I turn on the radio. This is sort of disappointing news. None of us want to go to Western. We want to get away from home and have a real college experience.

"What should we do with that stuff?" Sarah B asks.

"I've got a huge Dumpster at my house. I say we throw it out and all turn over a new leaf." This feels like the absolute right thing to say. To take our old selves and huck them right into the trash. That's what I'll do with all my stolen stuff, too. I won't bury it. I'll toss it. If I'm really at a new place in my life, I need to start acting like it.

At first, nobody says anything.

"I'm finished with crime. It's behind me," I say, jerking my thumb over my shoulder.

"Me too," Sarah B says.

"Me three. I fail to see the upside anymore," Sarah C says. "Also, you guys can start calling me Lisa again."

"What?" Sarah A asks. "Are you kidding?"

"No," Sarah C says.

Sarah A lets out a big breath.

"But being part of the Sarahs is so much fun," Sarah A says.

"It was so much fun," I say. "But also stressful."

"Wait! Wait!" Sarah A yells. "Stop driving!"

I pull off to the side of the road and stop the car. Sarah A unlocks her door and pushes it open.

"We're in a moving vehicle," Sarah B says. "Don't do that."

"I don't want to be in this car," Sarah A says.

"I know it's a tight fit," I say.

"No. I'm not finished. If you want out, that's fine. But I'm not done. I'm still a Sarah. I don't care if I'm the last one."

"You can't mean that," I say.

"But I do," Sarah A says. "I'm not done. I've still got the guy phase to look forward to."

"We don't need to call it that anymore. We could just start dating," Sarah C says. "It'd be more fun than thrashing innocent trees at night to try to manipulate people into breaking up so that we can forge relationships with them."

"Roman is coming up tonight," Sarah A says. "I'm not ready to quit."

"Doesn't Roman have a girlfriend?" I ask.

"It's rocky," Sarah A says. "They won't last another week."

"You don't know that," Sarah C says. "Personally, I've lost all respect for Roman Karbowski. He's stringing you along, Sarah A."

"Maybe I want to be strung," Sarah A says.

"Don't you want a boyfriend who you don't have to share?" I ask.

"I like Roman. I've always liked Roman. We're, like, destined," Sarah A says.

"Listen. Roman Karbowski is the kind of guy who will rip your heart out of your chest and throw it down an elevator shaft just to watch it go boom," I say.

Sarah A bites her lower lip. "But before the ripping and the part where my heart goes boom, I bet things will feel really great."

Sarah A starts to climb out of the car.

"Don't do it," Sarah B says.

"Have some self-respect," Sarah C says.

"We're a half mile away from your cabin," I say.

"Walking will dry me off," Sarah A says. She slams the door. Sarah C rolls her window down all the way.

"I thought you were ready for a change," Sarah C says.

"I like my life. And now I have a chance at Roman. All right, I can understand no more destroying trees and stuff. And I get that we don't want to commit any more crimes. But I am who I am. I like being a Sarah. And I don't ever want to stop."

"But if you're the only one, then you're not a Sarah anymore," I say.

Sarah A looks down. I think she's crying, but when she glances at me I can see that her eyes are dry.

"I guess you're right," Sarah A says.

We watch her turn around and walk along the road's shoulder toward her campsite at Yankee Springs. She is so strong. In all the wrong ways.

"Do I keep going?" I ask.

"I guess so," Sarah B says.

I don't feel like there's a good option here.

"Should we try to wrestle her into the car again?" I ask. "She'll probably have much less energy."

"That's not our job," Sarah C says. "People have to make their own decisions."

I know she's right. I know I can't dedicate my future to physically restraining Sarah A every time she's on the verge of doing something stupid. As I drive past the Shell gas station I slow down.

"Last pit stop for a while. Anyone need to go?" I ask.

"I'm fine," Sarah B says. "But don't you need to go? You haven't gone in a long time."

"I'm good," I say. "Sarah C, remember when you asked me what I think about before I pee myself?"

"Yeah," Sarah C says.

"I'm usually stressed-out about a crime I'm about to commit. And then somebody looks at me. Not a glance, but a real hard stare. I guess I think they're seeing parts of myself that I don't want anyone to see. I feel exposed. I feel vulnerable. Then I feel this tingling sensation and I have to pee."

"I think that's called 'anxiety,'" Sarah C says.

"Then why did it happen in kindergarten? What crime were you committing then?" Sarah B asks.

"I'd accidentally taken Madeline Murphy's pencil box instead of my own. I was trying to put it back on her desk without anybody seeing. But Mr. Larsen looked right at me while I was doing it, and I wet myself."

"I imagine that was hard to live down," Sarah C says.

"You have no idea," I say. "Being unpopular in grade school is like enduring trench warfare before mustard gas was banned."

John Glenn barks. It sounds like he wants something.

"What do you think Sarah A is doing?" I ask.

"She's probably still walking," Sarah B says.

"We shouldn't have left her," I say.

"I bet a piece of her is wishing that she'd just stayed in the car with us," Sarah C says. "She's all alone."

"It would suck to have your family ship you off to a hotel and then a cabin," Sarah B says. "Sarah A so doesn't belong in a cabin."

I try to picture what she's doing. Maybe she's wrapped up in a towel. Maybe she's curled up on her bed and attempting to take a nap. I guess I thought, in the end, that standing up to Sarah A would make me feel a lot like how I felt when I stood up to Big Don. But it's not the same thing at all.

Because Big Don is a jerk. And Sarah A, while she may act like a jerk, is a wounded person who has real issues. And I care about her.

"It's rotten to think of Sarah A up there totally wet and cabin-bound. Does she even have a towel?" Sarah B asks.

"This isn't how it's supposed to end," I say. "Endings are supposed to be happy. We're supposed to wind up entirely transformed and on a positive course. This feels so, so . . . unpleasant."

"This is real life," Sarah C says. "Endings aren't scripted. They just happen."

John Glenn presses his body between the front seats and sets his snout down on my wet pants.

"How do you know this is the end?" Sarah B asks.

"Because things couldn't go on the way they were," I say.

The scenery flies by. Tree. Tree. Fence posts. Car. Mailbox. Pasture. Dead raccoon.

"I can't do this," I say.

I tap on the brakes.

"Are you turning around?" Sarah C asks.

"Maybe we should," Sarah B says.

I flip on my blinker and prepare to make a three-point turn.

"It's the right thing to do," I say.

"She might not come," Sarah C says.

"That's true," I say. "But at least we can say we tried."

"The more I think about your analogy, the more I think you're right," Sarah C says.

"About life being like a moving sidewalk?" I ask.

"Not that one."

"About life being like a path?" I ask.

"No, the hallway metaphor," Sarah C says. "It's as if Sarah A thinks she knows what's behind the Roman Karbowski door, but she doesn't really know. She has no idea what she'll get. And she's passing by all these other doors."

I imagine my metaphor. I picture door after door. They spread out before me and behind me. They go on and on. I don't know why I've made them so mysterious. They're not magical. They're just doors. Open it or don't open it. And then move on. You shouldn't spend your life wondering what's on the other side. Just look. Just open it. Open as many as you want. Go ahead and see what's there.

"She still has time to figure it out," I say.

We drive and drive. Then I pull into the Yankee Springs parking lot for a third time. Sarah A is sitting at a park bench by herself. The shade of a pine tree casts a dark shadow over her. She looks at us and turns away.

"I'll go," I say.

I get out of the car and slowly walk to where Sarah A sits. A breeze stirs leaves across my path and I crunch over them.

Sarah A turns to face me. Her bottom lip trembles. I don't say anything. I just move toward her. I can sense the other Sarahs watching me. I feel new and certain. Maybe change doesn't take as long as I thought. I don't know how this will end. All I know is that I'm not doing this out of guilt or obligation or pity. I am Sarah A's friend. And I go to her because this is what I want to do.

LIKE WHAT YOU JUST READ?

Here's a peek at another novel by Kristen Tracy:

lost it

I DIDN'T START OUT MY JUNIOR YEAR OF HIGH SCHOOL planning to lose my virginity to Benjamin Easter—a senior—at his parents' cabin in Island Park underneath a sloppily patched, unseaworthy, upside-down canoe. Up to that point in my life, I'd been somewhat of a prude who'd avoided the outdoors, especially the wilderness, for the sole purpose that I didn't want to be eaten alive.

I'm from Idaho. The true West. And if there's a beast indigenous to North America that can kill you, it probably lives here. My whole life, well-meaning people have tried to alleviate my fear of unpredictable, toothy carnivores.

But I was never fooled by the pamphlets handed to me by tan-capped park rangers during the seven-day camping trip that my parents forced upon me every summer. The tourist literature wanted you to believe that you were safe as long as you hung your food in a tree and didn't try to snap pictures of the buffalo within goring distance. Seriously, when in the presence of a buffalo, isn't *any* distance within goring distance?

And they expect intelligent people to believe that a bear can't smell menstrual blood? A bear's nose is more sensitive than a dog's. Every Westerner knows that. In my opinion, if you're having your period and you're stupid enough to pitch a tent in Yellowstone Park, you're either crazy or suicidal. Maybe both.

It's clear why losing my virginity outdoors, in the wilderness, with Benjamin Easter should be taken as an enormous shock. I could have been eaten by a mountain lion, mauled by a grizzly bear, or (thanks to some people my father refers to as "troublemaking tree huggers") torn to pieces by a pack of recently relocated gray wolves.

Of course, I wasn't. To be completely honest, I may be overstating the actual risk that was involved. It happened in December. The bears were all hibernating. And the event didn't end up taking that long. Plus, like I already said, we were hidden underneath a canoe.

But the fact that I lost it in a waterproof sleeping bag on top of a patch of frozen dirt with Benjamin

Easter is something that I'm still coming to terms with.

I can't believe it. Even though I've had several days to process the event. I let a boy see me completely naked, and by this I mean braless and without my underpants. I let a boy I'd known for less than four months bear witness to the fact that my right breast was slightly smaller than my left one. And would I do it again?

We did do it again. After the canoe, in the days that followed, we did it two more times. I remember them well. Honestly, I remember them *very* well. Each moment is etched into my mind like a petroglyph. After the third and final time, I watched as he rolled his body away from mine. With my ring finger, I tussled his curly brown hair. Then, I fell asleep. When I woke up, Ben was dressed again, kissing me good-bye. I find myself returning to this moment often. Like it's frozen in time. Sadly, you can't actually freeze time.

Last night, Ben told me, "You're acting outrageous." He said this while inserting a wooden spoon into the elbow-end of my plaster cast. He was trying to rescue the hamster. The hamster had been my idea. I'd just bought it for him. I wanted him to take it to college and always think of me, his broken-armed first love.

But the rodent had weaseled its way into my cast. I hadn't realized that hamsters were equipt with burrowing instincts. I also had no idea how to make a boy stay in love with me. Hence, the pet hamster.

It's been hours since I've talked to Ben. Since the hamster episode. And the argument that followed the hamster episode. That night Ben told me to stop calling him. He was serious. I told him to have a happy New Year. And he hung up on me. The boy I'd lost it with in a sleeping bag in the frozen dirt had left me with nothing but a dial tone.

I swear, the day I woke up and started my junior year of high school, Benjamin Easter wasn't even on my radar. I didn't know a thing about leukemia. And because I was raised by deeply conservative people, who wouldn't let me wear mascara or attend sex education classes at Rocky Mountain High School, I wasn't even aware that I had a hymen or that having sex would break it.

Actually, in the spirit of full disclosure and total honesty, I should mention that my parents only became born again rather recently, at about the time I hit puberty, following a serious grease fire in the kitchen. Before that, they only ventured to church on major holidays. Hence, my life became much more restricted and we gave up eating deep-fried foods.

The day I started my junior year, I woke up worrying about the size of my feet. Once dressed, looking at myself in my full-length bedroom mirror, they struck me as incredibly long and boatlike. I squished them into a pair of shoes I'd worn in eighth grade, brown suede loafers. They pinched, but gave my feet the illusion of looking regular-size instead of Cadillac-size. Then I noticed a newly risen zit. Of course, under the cover of darkness, it had cowardly erupted in the center of my forehead. I held back my brown bangs and popped it. Then I dabbed the surrounding area with a glob of beige-colored Zit-Be-Gone cream.

I started the first day of my junior year of high school zitless and basically happy. I was sixteen and feeling good. I didn't have any major issues. Okay, that's not entirely true. For weeks I'd been growing increasingly concerned about Zena Crow, my overly dramatic best friend. She'd been going through a rocky stretch and had been talking incessantly about building a bomb. Not a big bomb. Just one that was big enough to blow up a poodle.

**Kristen Tracy** grew up in Idaho and has lived in many other places since, including Kalamazoo, Michigan. (She never committed any crimes while she was there.) She now lives in San Francisco, where she is busy writing and also not committing crimes. Her poems have received three Pushcart Prize nominations and have appeared in numerous literary journals. She coedited *A Chorus for Peace: A Global Anthology of Poetry by Women* (University of Iowa Press). She has a PhD in English from Western Michigan University.